By LINDSEY BLACK

Fishy Riot

Published by DREAMSPINNER PRESS
www.dreamspinnerpress.com

LINDSEY BLACK

fishy
RIOT

DREAMSPINNER
PRESS

Published by
DREAMSPINNER PRESS

5032 Capital Circle SW, Suite 2, PMB# 279, Tallahassee, FL 32305-7886 USA
www.dreamspinnerpress.com

Fishy Riot
© 2017 Lindsey Black.

Cover Art
© 2017 AngstyG.
www.angstyg.com
Cover content is for illustrative purposes only and any person depicted on the cover is a model.

ISBN: 978-1-63533-448-7
Digital ISBN: 978-1-63533-449-4
Library of Congress Control Number: 2016917544
Published April 2017
v. 1.0

Printed in the United States of America

∞

This paper meets the requirements of
ANSI/NISO Z39.48-1992 (Permanence of Paper).

1
ROCKET LAUNCHER

"Is THAT an RPG?" Clay squinted through the dirt haze engulfing them. "No, seriously... I think that's an RPG!"

Annoyed, Taylor finished reloading and traded places, giving Clay the time he needed to do the same while he took a look for himself. It was hard. They were perched midway up the wall on a crate shelf beneath a mezzanine, trying to get a better vantage of the enormous shipping warehouse. Manoeuvring around one another and the crates without giving away their position was proving difficult. Sure enough, one of the morons was hefting a rocket launcher onto another's back while he sighted. A small, decrepit-looking piece of machinery that had no doubt seen better days, before it had endured several wars and a rebuild in the back of a Cambodian arms house.

"What the fuck." He took aim and got rid of the shooter in the top right end of the warehouse, not far from where they were huddled. It was hard when you weren't allowed to fire without risking severe disciplinary action. Needing to be able to prove every bullet that left your weapon was necessary to subdue a deadly threat was almost impossible. Once people started shooting at you, decisions weren't being made rationally. You were just reacting, and there was always the chance you were going to have the wrong reaction, but Taylor would rather lose his badge than his life.

"I told you. Rocket launcher." Clay grinned at him, finishing his reload and pushing in hard against his side.

"I'm not sure you can call that a rocket launcher. That's like calling a slingshot a gun," Taylor argued, mostly because he could. He shifted uncomfortably around the next crate to get a better line of sight, pleased with the clear view he then had of the main floor.

"Can you see Jones and Hale?"

Taylor shook his head. He'd lost them in the initial fire, somewhere off near the front of the warehouse, when he and Clay had made a run for the stash they had come to find. No matter what else happened, Taylor wasn't letting them get away with the guns. A whole lot of guns, as it turned out, and that was weird, considering gun laws made it damn hard to get arms into Australia, let alone this many. Or this kind.

"Seriously, who even needs an assault rifle?"

"Some dude with a really small dick." Clay laughed at him, spotting movement on the mezzanine and firing. They watched the man jerk and wail, and then he fell, hitting the floor hard, knocked out cold from the impact. They stared at the still body, following the strange wire attached to him back to the gun in Clay's hand.

"That's a Taser," Taylor pointed out, biting his lip to keep from laughing because these things were not supposed to be funny. Clay's Glock was still in his right hand, but for whatever reason, he'd pulled his Taser and shot with his left, his gun still pointed down at the warehouse floor.

"I did not mean to do that," Clay mumbled, shoving his Taser back in his belt and slipping off the shelf, landing hard on the cement floor. Taylor leapt down beside him, the impact jarring his knees.

Movement by the doors caught Taylor's attention, and he swore under his breath as he grabbed Clay and hauled him down behind more armoured crates just as the roller doors smashed inward, ripping off the roller and sailing through the air. The doors hit two of the gunrunners in the chest, downing them permanently. The sound was deafening and bullets ricocheted around the warehouse as whoever was left tried a last-ditch effort at the riot squad armoured vehicle.

Taylor waited, because, really, the vehicle was effectively a tank.

The rocket launcher fired, but missed the squad truck and the warehouse was effectively a titanic-sized tin can. The rocket punched a hole through the wall and disappeared, a loud explosion echoing from outside a moment later. The explosion sent the crates inching back toward the wall, pinning Clay and Taylor momentarily.

"That sounded bad," Clay hissed. "Right?" He was rubbing his knee where a crate had collided with him, but otherwise seemed fine.

"Well, it hit something," Taylor sarcastically rumbled. "So, yeah. Probably bad." He checked the mezzanine but couldn't see any movement through the smoky haze filling the warehouse from the rocket.

"Reckon it was a ship?" Clay was crawling to the edge of the crates and peeking around the edge, trying to see what was going on.

"Seriously?" Taylor focussed on trying to shove the crates back to free them from where they were pinned so they could get back out. "Just, coz the ship might sink then, right? Can you imagine what the boss is gonna say if we sink a ship?" Clay's hands were moving, indicating where there was still movement happening in the warehouse.

"Can we finish the gunfight?" Taylor interrupted. "Then we can go see if there's a ship sinking, okay?"

"Of course we're gonna finish the gunfight...." Clay scowled and nodded his head in the direction he intended to go, still able to find cover behind the crates if it was needed but otherwise ready to push forward. Taylor agreed with the course of action.

Guns up, they forced their way into the fray, aware of the other officers doing the same, the flash of gunfire the only thing they heard for several minutes, until as quickly as it had all erupted, an eerie silence fell over everything.

Dust wafted through the air in lazy spirals.

Amazingly, the dead were limited. Bodies lay scattered throughout the warehouse, mostly foe, blood pooling around riddled forms, men clutching burned limbs and bleeding wounds. A few were loudly demanding help, screaming about their rights at the top of their lungs. The guns sat innocently in their crates against one wall. Taylor glared at the mess all around them while Clay spun in a slow circle, taking it all in.

"Fuck," Clay swore. "This is gonna be so much freakin' paperwork."

THEY STILL sat in the office after midnight, empty paper coffee cups littered the open-plan area, as if it were a requirement of getting work done that they be able to see one another. Taylor added a cup to the pile, wondering if anyone was actually going to bother to pick them all up, or if even the cleaner would be stuck with overtime tonight. He finished the last few lines on his own report and checked it over before printing it off and swapping with Clay.

It was an old habit, developed as children. As twins they'd shared a room, until they graduated university with twin criminology degrees, and even at the academy, they'd requested rooms side by side. The request had been granted. Now they shared an apartment in Crows Nest. As teenagers, when the work had gotten harder at school, they'd gotten into the habit of handing off assignments to each other to read through and check for errors. Taylor refused to submit anything his brother hadn't checked first, and Clay did the same.

"Typo on page three," Clay noted wearily, and Taylor looked it up, fixing it in the computer document. Clay's was fine, and they both hit Send ten minutes later before collapsing back in their chairs.

"Ready?"

"Seriously?" Clay rolled his eyes and got up, stretching. Taylor followed suit, grabbing his keys and heading for the door.

"Don't forget, the harbour at six tonight," Mendel grumbled from where he was still writing his report. He was always last to finish. Taylor blamed his size. It was hard to hit one key when your finger was the size of four. Taylor grunted in response because while he wasn't pleased they were working that evening, it did mean they had the day off, and he intended to sleep like the dead.

"Jameson and Jameson." The security guard grinned at them on their way out. Clay bothered to say something, but Taylor just kept walking. He didn't care if the guard liked him. Clay did, so Clay talked and he walked. Simple as that.

"You're an asshole." Clay laughed at him when he finally climbed in the passenger side of the Hilux.

"It's nearly one in the morning," Taylor pointed out. "No one should be expected to do small talk at one in the morning, especially when they're leaving work… at one in the morning."

"No one expects you to do anything. They all know you're an asshole. But you could surprise them every now and then."

"To what end?"

"My own personal entertainment." And that really would have been enough of a reason, if Taylor could be bothered, but they both knew he couldn't.

Technically, the Hilux was Clay's car. Taylor had his own, but his was black while Clay's was silver. He drove because he was an asshole and refused to be the passenger even in someone else's car. Clay was used to it and didn't say anything. He fished the gate remote out of his pocket and hit the button when they approached the entrance for the underground parking of their apartment complex.

"I'm so fucking hungry," Clay complained, and Taylor grunted in agreement. Each of them was six foot six with a good hundred and ten kilograms of pure muscle to haul around every day. It took a lot to feed them, and while they'd eaten enough through the day, they hadn't had anything since dinner, and that had been literally hours ago. It felt like his stomach was going to start trying to eat itself.

The apartment sat on the fourth floor, and there was no lift. Most old complexes like theirs didn't have one, but it kept body corporate fees down and they didn't mind the stairs, so it hadn't been a consideration when they were looking to buy. They jogged up the stairs and were careful not to slam the door behind them, not wanting to wake their neighbours. As soon as they were inside, boots were kicked off by the door, and they were hauling off their overalls, stumbling past one another as they tossed filthy clothes in the hamper and headed for the showers.

Taylor had the larger bedroom with the en suite mostly because he was an asshole and refused to let Clay have it, but Clay liked having the bigger main bathroom anyway. Besides, Taylor brought home one-night stands occasionally, and Clay had a steady boyfriend, so it wasn't like he needed to impress anyone. Not that Taylor felt the need to attempt to impress the twinks he brought home anyway. He walked into a bar; they were impressed. Done deal.

He washed his hair and scrubbed himself until his skin felt raw, but he could still smell gunpowder, so he scrubbed again. When he was satisfied he was clean, he wrapped a towel around his hips and wandered out to find two plates on the bench and Clay already heating up some leftover pizza from the fridge, watching it go round and round in the microwave while he waited.

"Where's Joel?"

"He had papers to mark so stayed at his," Clay scowled. Taylor snickered because his brother was clearly not okay with his boyfriend's decision to not be waiting in bed for him.

"It is one in the morning," he pointed out. The man could not be expected to keep riot squad hours when he had to teach all day at a university.

"Oh, I know." Clay waved him off, the microwave dinging. He reached in to pull out the heated slices and tossed them on the plates.

Silence reigned but for the sounds of food being blown on and hurriedly devoured.

Taylor finished first. He dumped his plate in the sink to deal with in the morning and headed to bed.

"Night, Tay!"

"Night, Clay," he called through his door, but he was already naked, towel left by the door as he stumbled to the bed, landing face-first and descending immediately into the embrace of sleep.

"NO, SERIOUSLY! They had a fuckin' rocket launcher!"

Taylor groaned at his brother's raised voice through the bedroom door and pulled his pillow over his head. But it was too late; he was awake. Grumpily, he stumbled to the en suite and took another shower, letting the water run cold to wake him up a little more.

He dressed in comfortable jeans and a T-shirt, and wandered out, not surprised to find his brother on the phone.

"Oh, hey, Tay's awake, you wanna say hi?" He didn't actually wait for a response, just shoved the phone into Taylor's hands and went to finish making his breakfast. Lunch. Whatever. "Tell him there really was a rocket launcher!"

"There really was a rocket launcher," Taylor agreed wearily, and he heard their older brother laughing hard on the other end of the phone.

"What the hell does anyone need a rocket launcher for?" Brayden was having trouble getting the words out.

"Apparently they're good for firing on the riot squad," Taylor grunted in response, and Clay snickered as he made up a second bowl of muesli for him.

"No, but seriously, what would you do with it? Go 'roo hunting? It's not exactly compact…." Brayden took these things far too seriously, but what could one expect of an ex-military doctor. He had a point, though: if you went hunting with it, there wouldn't be enough of the kangaroo left to eat. How Brayden's mind went to that, he had no idea, and he couldn't muster the energy to think about it himself, so Taylor grunted in the right places and let him ramble until the silence on the other end of the phone told him it was his turn to speak.

"How's Kel?"

"Huh? Oh, she's fine. She's got the kids going to Sunday School or some nonsense, I don't even know, really. Said I was driving her mad, and they'd be back after the barbeque."

"They feed you at church?" He looked up at Clay and knew the stumped expression on his face matched his own. That didn't happen at Catholic Church!

"You can't go to church just to get a free feed at the end," Brayden lectured loudly through the phone.

"Not every week," Taylor agreed. "But you could drop in once a month…."

"You are not going to join a church so you can get free food whenever you pull an all-nighter on a Saturday!" Brayden was screaming at them.

"Sounds legit to me." Clay grinned, handing over a bowl and sitting down on one of the single-seater couches to eat his breakfast with a happy sigh. "Do you think you have to go to the sermon, or could you just turn up for the last like fifteen minutes and say work held you up?"

"I don't know, maybe if we wore our uniforms, we could act like we just dropped by on our lunch break or something." Clay nodded in agreement, and Brayden continued to lecture through the phone. Another call came in.

"Got another call, gotta go," Taylor said to Brayden, not even sure if his brother heard him before he hung up. "Hello?" He answered the new call.

"Was there seriously a rocket launcher? It's on the news and everything!"

"If it's on the news, then obviously there was a rocket launcher," Taylor explained to the oldest of their younger sisters, Hayley, rolling his eyes.

"Oh, as if. Not everything they tell you on television is true, you know!"

"Of course not," Taylor agreed, handing the phone off to Clay because it was far too early in the morning to be dealing with her antagonizing voice as it lectured them on the evils of mass media.

Clay laughed in all the right places and was grinning when he hung up the phone thirteen minutes later, leaving Taylor with an empty bowl and nothing to do but stare at him.

"That was oddly… quick?"

"She was at work."

"And yet she called to discuss a rocket launcher in our raid."

"Well, she wasn't doing anything when she called, but then they got a call out so…."

It was a drill they all knew well. He wondered, sometimes, if his family felt they needed to compensate for something, being that they contributed to the public service as spectacularly as they did. Brayden, the doctor; twin Public Order and Riot Squad officers, one of whom dated a teacher; an ambulance driver for a sister; and a baby brother in training with the Firies. His parents had blue collar down to a fine art. The government should put them to good use brainwashing the next generation about duty to one's country. Hell, Brayden had even served four years in the military when he had first left school before deciding to be a doctor.

The Jamesons had public service mastered.

"So, I was thinking of going to the harbour early, having a wander, maybe stop in at Starbucks and people watch until the cruise tonight?" Clay mused.

The cruise. Taylor wanted to groan on principle. There was some kind of youth rally-cum-fundraising event for animal rights being held by the Salisbury Foundation for the youth of Sydney's elite. And since lately those events had been growing increasingly out of hand, a few of the more politically minded parents of the youths involved—who needed their names kept out of the mass media for various reasons—had asked for some help from the police.

The police, wanting nothing to do with it themselves and being drastically understaffed, had put the request through to the Public Order and Riot Squad. Joy!

"Sounds good" was what he eventually said to Clay, because at least if he had several hot green tea lattes warming his belly, when he caught socialites popping pills or having unprotected group sex by the bow, he might feel less inclined to toss obnoxious twenty-somethings overboard. These things just never went well, and each one made him resent the requests for their protection more. How about kids just stop doing dumb shit so he could focus his attention on actual real-world problems instead of how you couldn't save Fluffy the bunny because you were too busy getting high to remember to go break into his lab and liberate him?

He went and grabbed his uniform and shoved it into his work bag, putting in some muesli bars and a few juice packs as well because he wasn't going to last the night shift without snacks. He wasn't surprised when Clay put in a box of pizza shapes. And salt and vinegar chips. And a stick of salami.

"Really?" Taylor stared at the salami.

"What? I get hungry."

THE "FERRY" was huge. Taylor grunted at it while Clay gaped. A long line of young rich brats with beautifully engraved invitations waited to have their ID scanned and walk through the security checkpoint. The riot squad van was parked farther down by the warehouse and security checkpoint for the port, but they could all see what they were heading toward as they strapped weapons to their belts and checked their gear. A team of eight officers in all, and not one of them looked happy. That said it all.

"That's not a ferry, it's a fuckin' cruise liner," Mendel whined softly, checking the clip on his holster and then looking over his partner, Harris. They were an odd pair. Mendel was the largest man on their team. A seven-foot brute with scruffy brown hair, an even scruffier beard, and enough muscle to bench press any other member of the team and then some. Harris by comparison looked like the Milkybar Kid, all blond surfer and straight white teeth. Innocent and usually relegated to driving the van because no one trusted him not to get shot if they weren't watching. Not that he was incompetent, far from it, he was just… little.

"There's gotta be at least three hundred kids getting on that thing," Clay muttered darkly. "We shoulda brought everyone!"

"Everyone else had to go to that music festival up by Newcastle," Jones grumbled. "We got put on this coz we finished late last night." Jones was the oldest member of their team, a third-generation Greek Australian who looked like he'd just stepped off the boat. It had taken Taylor six months to remember his name was Jones and stop calling him Mario. Jones complained about every job they went on, mostly because he wanted to get home to his seven kids so his poor wife didn't hang herself, but he got the job done.

"Great," Harris grunted. "Bring in a rocket launcher. Get rewarded with babysitting duty! Next time I'll remember to let 'em keep it."

"Why is everyone so fuckin' worked up about the rocket launcher?" Taylor asked, exasperated.

They were all staring at him. He didn't get it. What did it matter if it was a pistol, a rifle, a rocket launcher, or a damn tank? Their job was to track it, find it, and confiscate it, plain and simple.

"It shoots rockets?" Mendel eventually dared to suggest, and Taylor scowled darkly enough that they all turned away from him and finished checking their gear, slamming the doors shut before heading toward ferry hell.

"Even Joel asked about the rocket launcher," Clay reasoned with him softly. Taylor grunted, really not seeing what the deal was. Everyone had lost their minds, plain and simple.

"What time does this shit finish again?" Jones hissed, but then they were being pulled aside for security screenings of their own, signing in everything they had on them and following the security guard through a back entrance to the ferry so they could be shown around and get the layout of the ship.

It really wasn't a ferry. It was far too large to be a ferry. Thankfully, the guests were mostly kept in two areas; the massive deck out front and a huge ballroom type space beside it in case the cold air got the best of everyone and they felt the need to go inside. There was an upper deck, but it had been reserved for media and crew. That didn't mean there weren't other spaces, there were. It was just that guests were supposed to stay in those two areas. The VIPs were permitted below deck, but for the most part, everyone was supposed to stay up top.

Like that ever happened.

There was an aquatic theme to the whole affair. They were raising awareness and funds for marine reefs, and the event was being sponsored by the Salisbury Foundation who were lobbying to have mining banned in and around all Australian reefs and wanted to restrict commercial fishing around the continent. All good in theory, until people lost their jobs, the price of seafood went up…. But politicians rarely seemed to think of the impact their decisions were going to have on others; they just cared about getting re-elected. Still, Taylor had to admit that if you were trying to get the young person's vote, starting a marine conservation policy that had your face in the paper trying to save the whales was a good way to go about it. And Johnathan Salisbury needed positive media coverage. He was on the Project only a few nights ago, trying to justify yet another education budget cut. It was hard to argue why school Parents and Friends committees were having to raise additional funds just to pay the power bill in schools, but he'd somehow managed to put the blame on working-class parents who weren't willing to pay their voluntary school contributions. He'd even gone so far as to suggest if parents wanted their children to have luxuries in their schools, they should be willing to pay for private schooling. Luxuries being things like air con and the lights turned on.

Minister Salisbury was in dire need of a positive headline in the papers, and was using his environmental foundation to do it. Ironic, since as the Minister for Environment, he'd blocked every piece of legislature designed to move Australia toward a clean-energy economy. The Foundation was an obvious media stunt. Something the Minister could point to whenever he was questioned about his commitment to saving the environment while he continued to assist oil and gas companies instead of promoting environmentally friendly options. And he almost always managed to come out of a press conference looking like a good guy, because he was so reasonable in his arguments and people were shallow enough to think a bright smile and an attractive face meant a person was trustworthy.

There was no denying the Salisburys knew how to throw a party. The ferry looked like it came from a fairy tale. They were even towing a giant, inflatable iceberg. It was hilarious.

"Extravagant, much?" Jones grumbled. Clay snickered at his displeasure, pointing to Hale at the food buffet, pinching samosas. Taylor liked Hale best. He was quiet, kept his head on straight in every situation, and was by far the best shot on the team. It paid to be nice to the guy most likely to kill you.

"Dammit." And Jones was gone. Taylor was tempted to join Hale because he was hungry, but he had a few muesli bars shoved in his back pocket if he got desperate.

The ferry launched without hassle, and it felt like no time at all before all they could see was a distant smudge of lights on the horizon where Sydney slept. All the rest was dark water.

"Hi, Officer!"

Taylor glared down at the petite thing smiling up at him, and grunted. She was beautiful, if you went for small women with skinny legs in sparkly dresses and ridiculously high heels, but he liked a different set of plumbing with far less feminine appeal. Still he forced a smile as she held up a can of Coke to him.

"Caffeine hit?"

"Thanks."

"You're very welcome. It's so great to have you guys here, thank you so much for taking care of us!"

Technically, it wasn't their job to take care of the people on the ferry. It was their job to ensure no one did anything stupid that would require protecting the masses. As part of the Major Events and Incidents Group of the New South Wales police force, they were mandated to perform a variety of duties including riot control, search warrants, bomb searches, major incident responses, and unfortunately, in the case of the evening's fundraiser, crowd control.

"Oh, please." Clay came up behind him, reaching over his shoulder to snatch the can of Coke and drink it all down in several long swallows, leaving Taylor's hand pathetically empty.

"Now who's the asshole?" Taylor grumbled. Clay just shrugged, and the girl looked from one of them to the other and back, repeatedly, eyes wide and mouth in a small oval of amazement.

"Oh my God, there are two of you! There are, right? I'm not just really drunk already? Or seasick? I mean, you're twins? You're twins, holy crap! How are there two of you?"

"That's generally what twins mean," Clay pointed out, and she just nodded in complete agreement.

"I know, but how did two of you come out at the same time? I mean... you're... you...."

"Huge," Mendel laughed from behind her. "Twin tanks," he elaborated, and she spun to look at him, nodding hard, no doubt stunned to find him even bigger. Taylor worried her large head was going to fall off her tiny shoulders.

"They're also very gay," Mendel whispered too loudly not to be overheard by anyone with half-decent hearing.

Her face changed immediately, all silliness disappearing. She eyed them dubiously.

"Well, damn!" And then she was gone, Clay and Taylor staring after her, stunned.

"I will never understand women," Clay said.

"You stole my Coke," Taylor grumbled and went off to get another.

"Oh, please, you wanted an excuse to go hide in the corner anyway." He heard Clay laughing over his shoulder, and since he had to agree, he didn't bother to reply, just kept walking down into the galley.

There was a small fridge there stocked with cold drinks for them to have throughout the night. He grabbed a lemonade and drank it quickly before grabbing a second and deciding to do a check below decks. He wasn't quite ready to dare returning to the main area.

A few of the staff were wandering below decks, but he saw nothing suspicious. They'd been given a copy of a headshot of every staff member on board, and he was good at memorising faces. They were supposed to look for suspicious activity, and a large part of that was recognising when someone wasn't where they should have been.

A young teenager lay on one of the beds in the captain's quarters, headphones in his ears, but they'd been warned the Salisburys would have their family on board for the speeches, and Taylor recognised the kid as Micah Salisbury, the politician's youngest son. Even if he hadn't seen the picture, you couldn't miss that he was a Salisbury.

They all had jet black hair and rich blue eyes, with a faint caramel colour to their skin. Clay often joked that the only reason Minister Johnathan Salisbury got elected was women had been given the vote, and he was a ridiculously pretty man. Taylor could almost be convinced to vote…. Well, in a manner that didn't ensure his vote was as useless as everyone else's. There were way too many options on those slips, and they were adamant something go in every box! If they expected a serious vote, they needed to dumb that shit down! Still, Salisbury was hot, and if one was inclined to vote as if it was Hottest Man Alive instead of Australian political parties, then sure he'd have Taylor's vote.

But Salisbury Senior and Junior were not half as pretty as the man Taylor found sitting alone in one of the side rooms off the captain's quarters. When Micah didn't stir, Taylor checked the adjoining rooms, and sitting there, bent over a textbook, was another Salisbury; one there had certainly not been a photo of on the security list, because he would have remembered.

The same dark hair and blue eyes, but his hair had grown long, hanging down past his shoulders, cut in a classy series of faint layers that framed his face artfully. He had thick-framed Gucci glasses that matched his face shape, and high cheekbones that cast long shadows on all the right places on his face. He was dressed in tight trousers, a designer long-sleeved shirt, a vest with a brand name Taylor didn't recognise. He looked up and gaped at Taylor, a flash of fear in his eyes before he recognised Taylor's uniform.

"They convinced the riot squad to babysit?" Amusement was clear under the weary tone of his voice. He spoke softly, a little husky, and the sound went straight to Taylor's groin. He was far too polished for Taylor; not what he went for at all. Too rich, too spoilt, too educated. But right then Taylor wanted to lift the man off the chair, push him up against the door, and taste him, some primal instinct waking in the back of his mind demanding he lay claim before anyone else could.

He didn't because he was at work, and he knew how to behave. Mostly. Also… the paperwork!

"They convinced someone," Taylor agreed wryly, staring at the man. There was definitely something to be said for good breeding. Whatever else could be said about them, the Salisburys had won the genetic lottery. The man had geeky sex mastered. "Studying?" Was he a student? He looked the right age, but where and what and how, and please could someone tell him more about the man?

"Yeah…." He leaned back in his chair, spotting Micah, and visibly relaxed a little once he knew where his brother was. "He didn't give you any trouble?"

"Doesn't know I'm here, I think."

"No, he knows," the man mumbled, gaze narrowing as he stole another glance at Micah, then shrugged as if the doings of teenagers were mysterious. They weren't. Taylor could pick what teenager was doing drugs in a heartbeat, and which wouldn't know what a drug was. Teenagers were horribly predictable and boring as sin.

"So you were… doing the rounds?"

"Just looking for any trouble." Taylor knew he had intruded on private quarters, but no one had said they couldn't check what was going on, only that the Salisburys would be there if they did.

"Did you find any?" The man arched a lean perfectly manicured brow at him, and the smile on his lips was wicked. Taylor imagined what else those lips could do and barely restrained a groan.

"Perhaps a little."

"But not more than you can handle?"

"Never." Though if Taylor spent enough time looking behind those geek glasses, he might find himself in uncharted water.

"Is the whole riot squad here?" He was looking Taylor up and down, his lips slightly parted as if he wasn't sure what to make of what he was seeing, but the light blush on his cheeks told Taylor that Salisbury liked what he was looking at. He deliberately put his shoulders back and stood a little taller, making himself larger.

"Not all of us, no."

"Just those of you who drew the short straw?" That soft chuckle was doing strange things to his insides. Very good, strange things.

"Something like that." Taylor let the man's gaze wander, enjoying the attention. But when those eyes settled on his face once more, it was like the man was reading a book, as if everything and anything he had ever been or could ever be was written there on his face, and Salisbury hadn't decided if he liked it or not.

"How exactly do you draw a short straw that lands you on a ferry full of rich brats who think they're being political activists by wasting a bunch of money on a sea jaunt and waving a bunch of banners?" Clearly he was not impressed by his own predicament, any more than Taylor.

"Oh, you successfully intercept the biggest gun haul in Australian history, arrest thirty-two people, put a whole bunch of holes in a warehouse, and blow the tyres on your squad truck. And then take too long to do the paperwork so your next shift gets pushed back and happens to coincide with… this." He indicated the cabin they were standing in.

"Oh. Do you mean that thing on the news this morning? The one with the rocket launcher?"

For real? People needed to stop watching the news!

"Yes." Really, what else could he say? Salisbury's eyes went wide, and then he chuckled at the unimpressed look he was being cast.

"Sorry, I bet you've had a lot of that."

"You have no idea," Taylor muttered, but his lips were twitching, wanting to smile. The man was cute and sexy and smart, and really… those glasses were killing him.

"No, I don't suppose I do," Salisbury mumbled, but there was sadness behind the sarcasm that made Taylor frown and feel as though he'd punched a kitten.

"And what about you? How did you end up here? Friends on board? Hanging with the family? Stalking someone?"

"Stalking… what?" He laughed, that same dark, throaty sound Taylor was getting far too used to, far too quickly. "Uh, no. Family thing, I suppose. One of those 'you will come and represent the family or else' kind of things." There were some dark undertones to that statement that made Taylor frown. It wasn't the words, but the way they were spoken and the expression on his face, the way it changed as he spoke. He didn't want to be there. Family things were like that, but this seemed different somehow.

A bell chimed and the man sighed, waving a hand at the door. "I have to go… give a speech, apparently."

"Apparently?"

"Well." His smile changed then, a wry but troubled turn of lips that never reached his eyes. "It's been a while. Since I was in public." He stood slowly. So much so it seemed odd to Taylor, as if he were trying out standing for the first time, or wasn't sure his feet would hold him up. He looked pale, maybe even a little green.

"Seasick?"

The man stood there staring at him, confused for a moment before he chuckled. Again the sound did strange things to Taylor's insides.

"Uh, sure. Seasick." Taylor didn't like being lied to, but he didn't know what else to say. Drunk? That sounded insulting. Incapacitated? The guy did look sick, but no one ever liked to be told so.

"I'll take you topside," he offered quietly, mostly because he didn't want to go up either, but also because he wanted to stare at him some more. He was so exceedingly well put together, like something out of a magazine. There was something wrong about it all. He was almost too flawless. Like politics, something off that he couldn't quite figure out.

"Thank you" was all he got in response. "Micah!"

The foot stopped tapping and Micah looked up from the bunk. Taylor chuckled as the kid's eyes went wide, and he hurriedly pulled the headphones from his ears.

"Holy shi… you're huge!" He gaped at Taylor, and it only made him laugh more, going over to haul the kid onto his feet and get him moving with his brother, since it seemed like they were supposed to go together.

"I'll take that as a compliment."

"Oh do." Micah was still staring at him, his eyes like two huge blue pools. "What did your parents feed you? You look like a Viking! Have you seen that show? I love that show! You could totally be off the promo poster or something!"

And he'd heard that a lot too. Their blond hair and grey eyes, with square jaws and muscles bulging out every which way made people expect him to start spouting Swedish. Who knew, maybe there was some back in the bloodlines somewhere.

"All Australian, kiddo."

"No, but really, was there a secret ingredient I can tell the chef to get?" *The chef? What the—?*

"Milk." He was proud of himself for keeping a straight face and not walking into the low bulkhead as they headed to the deck, but Micah only rolled his eyes and grumbled about a growth spurt he'd apparently been waiting on for a while. Taylor didn't like his chances; his brother barely reached Taylor's shoulder.

Noise by the door caught Taylor's attention, and Clay shouldered his way through, holding it open so they could pass into the main room where everyone was gathering for a presentation.

"Tay, where... oh heeeey." Clay smirked at the Salisburys.

"There are two of you? Really?" Micah threw up his hands in disgust, and Clay reached out to ruffle his hair.

"Our mother throws her hands up in disgust too," he promised. "Don't worry, we're used to it."

Micah took his brother's hand and let him pull him up to the stage where Johnathan and Louisa Salisbury were getting ready to give their speeches. The Minister for Environment and Energy, Education, and Health looked just as stylish as ever in beige linen pants and a white linen shirt with the sleeves rolled up. He even had boat shoes on. Louisa was in a conservative white cap-sleeved dress with a whale embroidered on the hem that looked like it had come from 'Stereotypes R Us.'

"Damn, he's pretty," Clay hissed as they shouldered their way to the back of the masses. "Were you doing horrible things to him downstairs?"

"Please, I'm on duty."

"But you thought about it."

"Look at him!" Taylor gestured in the direction of the stage. "Of course I thought about it."

The crowd hushed as soon as they were on stage, and then the whispers began. Shock rippled through the crowd and uneasiness ran through Taylor as he looked around.

"What's going on?" He looked at Clay, but Clay was taking a second look at the stage, and then his eyes went a little wider. Recognition?

"Ah, the guy you were downstairs with. I thought it was Anders, but he's way older...." Clay was frowning at the Salisburys gathered around the podium. "I think that's Sietta Salisbury. I'd just assumed he wouldn't be here."

"So?" What did it matter which one it was?

"So I don't think anyone has seen Sietta Salisbury in months. It's like the guy's a ghost." Clay mumbled, squinting at the stage as if trying to confirm it was who he thought it was. He wasn't the only one doing it. You would think Gandhi had risen from the grave with how the audience was reacting.

Johnathan Salisbury introduced himself and his wife and started talking about their campaign and what everyone was there to donate toward. Taylor tuned out, looking instead at the crowd and trying to ascertain if they were in for any trouble, but everyone was staring at the stage with rapt attention.

"So what, he's at school or something?"

"Supposedly at the Conservatorium of Music."

"Supposedly?"

"Again, no one has seen him there." Clay frowned then, his expression changing to dubious concern. "Ever."

Taylor grunted. How did no one think that was weird? But when Sietta Salisbury was introduced, the crowd roared as if he were their best friend, and he waved like it were true, and his smile was so bright it hurt to look at. He looked thrilled to be there, a completely different entity to the one Taylor had met downstairs. He supposed you learnt to fake it pretty early in political circles. Sietta Salisbury was already a master.

Louisa took Micah back offstage, and they had a photo taken with a photographer there, but as soon as Micah was released, he disappeared into the crowd while Johnathan came down for photos with his wife.

"I can't thank you all enough for coming…." That husky voice came over the loudspeakers, and Taylor felt himself getting hard in his pants.

"Really?" Clay was chuckling at him, but then two guys started arguing off to the left, and Jones was there from one side and Clay rushed in from the other. Taylor checked that they had it under control, but really it was two drunk rich kids in an argument. They were silent as soon as they looked up at Clay. And up. And up….

Something pulled on his arm, and Taylor frowned down at Micah's serious face. The kid pushed a USB into his hand and bolted back into the bowels of the ferry, fumbling his earphones back into his ears. That was weird.

Taylor was still staring at the small device, when his brother clamped his hand down on his shoulder and stared at it too.

"What's that?"

"No clue." He shoved it in his pocket. He would look at it later. Probably a playlist for Vikings to gym to, or something equally oddball.

Sietta Salisbury hesitated before leaving the stage and his adoring fans, who were chanting his name and calling for him to come and party with them. But he was staring at his parents and the photographer waiting to put his face in the papers. Something flickered in his expression, but it was gone before Taylor could make heads or tails of the hesitation. And then he stepped down between his parents and let the photographer take the perfect family portrait.

There was another argument toward the middle of the crowd, and Mendel was charging in from one side, Hale the other. Which left Taylor to part the sea toward the argument getting ugly somewhere up front. It wasn't hard, he simply tapped the kids on the shoulder and they literally fell out of the way in shock. By the time he got to the front, the kids had already seen him, made up, and faced him united with a heartfelt apology and a request to please not arrest them. Taylor grunted and turned away, meeting Clay's amused face over the sea of heads. It was going to be a long night. There better not be any paperwork needed at the end of it.

2
HOT TUB STONERS

"DUCK!"

Mendel was too slow to react and got hit in the head with a life jacket. He scowled at Clay, picked it up, and tossed it overboard, checking that one of the people bobbing in the water swam over to fetch it, holding on to it rather than trying to put it on. Probably a good thing, considering how high they all were.

At some point in the massive fist fight that erupted on deck, a poor girl had been pushed overboard, barely managing to swim away from the ferry before the undertow would have taken her down into the slowing propellers. The captain had the sense to stop the ferry as soon as the fight broke out, but the water was still churning as the propellers struggled to obey and stop.

Some of the kids were so off their face on whatever they'd taken, they mistook the churning water for a hot tub and leapt overboard to join the poor girl, who was trying not to drown in the swell coming off the slowing boat.

Seeing people jump overboard, others had thought it was a good idea and followed. The team was trying to get enough safety devices into the water while Hale ran to the captain to get the coastguard and some backup called in. Lots of backup; the kids were out of control! The fight was ongoing, and Mendel charged into the mass again, leaving Clay and Taylor at the railing to watch those in the water.

"Where are the damn lifesavers?" Clay searched the deck, running toward the rear, and they spotted them piled down the back on the starboard side, like a pack of the popular candy, surrounded by security guards.

"What the hell are you doing? Toss them in!" Clay screeched, charging over, Taylor on his heels. The men moved toward the buoys, but still didn't toss them overboard.

"Those kids could drown," Taylor snapped, picking up the first buoy and going to toss it in. He was tackled by one of the guards, who bellowed at him to stop, and they fell to the deck in a tangle of limbs, each struggling to get a hold of the device.

Taylor struggled to kick the man off, managing to get his legs free and then snapping a cuff around his wrist with one hand and hauling him to the railing with the other. He picked up the lifesaver and realised it was heavier than it should be and didn't feel like it would float. When he shook it, it didn't feel like he expected so he grabbed his knife from his tactical belt, stabbing the floatation device.

White powder spilled out across the deck, and Clay grabbed another guard, cuffing him beside his friend while Taylor lunged at another.

"What the hell? Toss in the buoys!" Harris yelled as he emerged from the fight, grabbing another guard and staring at Clay for help as to what was going on.

"They're full of drugs. They won't float!" Taylor snapped.

"You've got to be shitting me!" Harris gaped at the pile of floats and the men trying to protect them. Their uniforms weren't quite right. More like exterminator uniforms with security badges sewn on.

"Arrest them all!" Taylor ground out, grabbing another man, wishing he'd brought more cuffs, using the zip ties they habitually carried to cuff them to the railing instead. They subdued all seven easily and then turned to stare at the ongoing fist fights.

"The boss is gonna kill us." Clay tackled a guard as he tried to run.

"I wish we had that RPG from last night," Harris bemoaned, and they stared at him with nothing to say.

"How the hell did the drugs get here? There's gotta be millions of dollars' worth of it…." Clay was holding the buoy Taylor had cut open, rubbing his fingers in the white powder, incredulous.

"Someone here's gotta be the dealer," Taylor rumbled. "But it's gonna be impossible to figure out who."

"Not our job." Harris shrugged. "We just have to stop the fight and save the stupid kids in the water."

"Oh, is that all?" Clay gestured to the chaos around them.

"Yeah. Right."

THERE WAS paperwork. Paperwork sucked. Hale, the paperwork wizard, finished first, and had no qualms about leaving them all there staring at the screens, wondering what the hell had gone wrong.

A fight had broken out. No one knew why, or even how really, but someone threw a punch that hit the wrong person, and then fists flew in every direction. Eight riot squad guys could do a lot, but eight guys were never going to be enough against hundreds. They'd managed to get everyone mostly contained before someone had the fantastic idea of throwing someone else overboard.

There had been coastguards called and police boats and extra personnel were heli-lifted to the ferry, and all the while, every second drunk rich kid was threatening to sue them for daring to touch them, or touch someone else, or whatever they thought they could sue someone for, none of which was actually true at that point.

Harris stole Hale's report and practically copied it to get out. Jones and Mendel finished an hour later, and Mendel bailed. Jones came over to sit with them, spinning lazily in his chair while he watched them.

"It doesn't have to be perfect, you know. Just write what happened and hand it in. Between all our reports, the boss will figure it out."

"It has to be perfect," Clay corrected him as he went through and fixed the various typos and discrepancies Taylor had highlighted when he proofread it. Taylor was doing the same on his own screen.

Clay's phone rang, and he stumbled out of his chair to answer, wandering the length of the shared open-plan office space to stretch his legs as he talked in soft tones.

"Joel?"

"You ever hear him talk like that to anyone else?" Taylor snickered. But it was cute, in a weird way, how Clay melted into sugary crap the moment Joel was in a room. It had been like that from the start. They'd walked into a bar. Joel had been sitting there, drowning his miseries in a bottle of red wine. Taylor had made some sort of unsavoury comment about it and Clay had nearly decked him before hurrying to assure the man that wine was just fine and could they possibly please share and would he consider going home with him?

But Clay had always been a good guy. He was always 'the nice one' who had time for others' crap. Taylor expected everyone to be reasonable human beings. Unfortunately he suspected people in general were far from reasonable, and his expectations for life were something of an oxymoron.

When Clay returned he checked his screen one last time and hit Send. "I'm gonna go stay at Joel's tonight."

"You mean this morning?"

"Whatever." Clay reached out to squeeze Taylor's shoulder and rushed away before Taylor had time to realise that left him with Jones to do the final check on the mountain of arrests that had been made.

"Fuck."

They stared down at the pile.

Jones slumped down into Clay's chair and poked the pile of folders, scowling darkly. "I thought you were supposed to be the asshole."

"Why, because I don't smile nice and pretend to like you?" Taylor arched one brow and Jones sighed heavily. They could all be dicks when they wanted to be; they were guys. It was what they did.

Fortunately, Jones actually liked arrest reports, and he checked through them twice as fast as Taylor, so they were done in a little under an hour. Taylor was packing up and checked his keys were in his pocket so he would be able to get into the apartment. He pulled the USB out with them and scowled, because it reminded him of everything that had gone wrong on the ferry, and the fact he hadn't gotten to speak to Sietta Salisbury again. He tossed it on his desk wryly, wondering how Micah Salisbury had enjoyed the disaster the evening had become.

Bright eyes and a quiet smile came to mind, but they weren't Micah's, and a shiver of heat ran through Taylor before he shook it off and headed out the door.

"Boss wants us in by midday," Jones said after checking his phone, and Taylor wearily waved, and headed for the taxi rank. Clay had taken the car.

HE WOKE to his phone ringing and blearily fumbled around the bedside table until he found it and pulled it to his ear as he accepted the call.

"'Lo?" His voice sounded rough.

"They threw a girl off the ferry? Seriously?"

He groaned at Hayley's voice as she bellowed across time and space. Phones were not quite the marvellous inventions they were made out to be, in Taylor's opinion.

He pulled his pillow over his head. "Why are you calling me?"

"Clay's not picking up, so I'm assuming he's at Joel's, having gay monkey sex."

"He's at Joel's," he agreed haltingly. That still, in his opinion, didn't explain why she felt the need to call him. "It's the middle of the night!"

"No, the sun is up, stupid. It's morning."

Was it? He groaned and pulled the pillow tighter against his face, wishing he couldn't breathe through it because suffocation had to be easier than listening to her.

"If you haven't talked to Clay, how do you know they threw the girl off the ferry?"

"Are you kidding me? Have you seen the paper? Like half the *Herald* is about that party! So it's true? They threw her overboard?"

"And then the stoners thought it was a hot tub and jumped in too," he agreed, reliving it all in his head. It had been a disaster, plain and simple, and he fully expected to end up behind a desk for days when his boss finished wading through their reports and realised exactly how crap had gone down.

"You. Are. Not. Serious!"

"I am always serious," Taylor countered, and she swore colourfully over the line.

"What about the drug bust?"

"Hay—"

"Oh, fine, fine! I just wanted the goss that goes with your picture in the paper. And seriously, Tay, you should be way more excited about getting to meet Sietta Salisbury, you know no one ever gets to do that! I thought he died, or something! Is he as hot in real life?"

"What?" He was immediately awake, sitting up in bed and crawling out of his dark cocoon to get the pile of papers from downstairs.

"Salisbury? The uber-hot geek next to you in the socialite pages of the paper?"

"I'm in the paper?"

"Well, duh, that's why I'm—"

He hung up and stormed back upstairs, papers in his fist. He hadn't even opened the paper before the phone was ringing again, and he saw Clay's name on the screen.

"I'm in the paper?" Taylor demanded immediately. He was going to owe the office a carton. Suckage.

"It's you," Clay agreed, waiting while Taylor flicked through to the social section and found a picture of the ferry surrounded by police boats, helicopters, coastguard, and every other strange thing that had come to get a gander last night. But when he turned the page, it had a spread on the actual fundraiser, what had happened, the picture of Micah and his mother, and then lower, the evening descending into chaos, and there, frozen in black and white, was his face. He was lunging forward, he remembered, reaching to intervene between two girls who'd at that moment smashed their champagne glasses and were waving the broken remains at one another as if ready to duel. What he hadn't known was Sietta was being bodily dragged past him, his father's hand clenched so tight around Sietta's upper arm you could see the knuckles were white. But Sietta was looking straight at Taylor, for all the world like Taylor had wronged him and the headline was something about the riot squad endangering the Salisbury heir.

"He's not the heir!"

"I don't think they care, and I don't think the boss will care either," Clay remarked dryly. "Fuck that guy's hot, though! Shit, sorry, babe!"

"I agree," Taylor heard Joel reply, and Taylor shook his head and stared at the picture. He hadn't seen Sietta at all, had been fixed entirely on his job, which had not been protecting the Salisburys, who had their own family and security to manage them.

"What did you say to him? He looks pissed."

"Nothing, I don't think he's looking at me so much as looking away from his father," Taylor observed as he looked at the picture and realised that was exactly what it was. The photographer caught them both at awkward moments, neither even aware of the other. But it did look like they were having a tiff of some sort, and that was all kinds of weird, most of all because Taylor realised he didn't want to have a tiff with Sietta Salisbury. He wanted to drag the pretty man into bed and do a lot more than have a tiff, though he suspected the make-up sex would be legendary.

"Huh. I think you're right. Shit, look at how he's holding him!"

And Taylor was, because the more he looked, the less he liked what he saw. There was no way that wasn't going to leave a bruise, and the look on Johnathan Salisbury's face was pure fury. The aftermath probably hadn't been good for either of them, whatever it had been. And suddenly he wanted to know.

"Hey, Clay? Wanna take a drive?"

"Yeah...." Clay agreed, and Taylor knew they were on the same page. The picture didn't sit right with either of them, and it was one of the reasons Taylor loved having a twin because they were so alike and were always on the same wavelength when things looked fishy.

He didn't bother dressing up, but he didn't dress down either, putting on some jeans with no holes in them, his steel-cap boots, a shirt with the sleeves rolled up, and brushing his spikey blond hair into some semblance of tidiness. It didn't work too well, but he doubted Clay's would look any better. He had some growth along his jaw but didn't bother to shave. He didn't mind looking rougher right then, and work hadn't been on a rampage about appearances in over a year.

His phone buzzed, but he didn't bother checking. He walked downstairs and found Clay waiting in his Hilux on the street. Taylor glared at him.

"Get over it. I'm driving this time."

So Taylor got in, picked up the paper again where Clay had tossed his copy on his seat, and glared at his picture. Some of the other guys had been filmed on raids, or photographed and ended up on YouTube, or the news or in the paper, but it had never happened to him before. He was quietly grateful that he wasn't doing anything other than his job, but otherwise the whole thing sucked.

Clay's phone rang, and he put it through to speaker phone. Announcements were audible in the background, so they knew it was Brayden before he even started speaking.

"The stoners jumped in after the girl because they thought it was a hot tub? Seriously?"

Taylor shared a look with Clay. What was with their family? They needed to emancipate or something.

"Well, there were bubbles," Clay reasoned.

"From the propellers!" Brayden clarified, completely unnecessarily. "That's absurd!"

"Well, they were stoners," Taylor grumbled, and Brayden laughed at them both through the phone.

"So what are you doing today? Still good for Mum's barbeque lunch this arvo?"

"Uh… sure…." Taylor looked over at Clay, who mouthed "crap" while Taylor winced and rummaged for his own phone to shoot Joel a reminder message for Clay.

"You forgot? That's, like, the fifth time in a row!" Brayden lectured.

"Come on, man, we don't even know what day it is. How are we supposed to know when it's Saturday, and if it's the Saturday Mum's decided to throw a garden party coz she bought a new gnome she wants to show off?"

"You have a phone. It's smarter than you. Use the damn calendar and set reminders! Also, never mention garden gnomes in her presence. We don't need to deal with that sort of crap. I don't think she knows they exist." Brayden lived on his phone; Taylor couldn't remember the last time he saw his brother without the accessory practically glued to his hand.

"My phone is not smarter than me!" Clay was spluttering.

"It knew it was Saturday," Taylor drawled.

"So did I, coz Taylor's in the socials section of the *Herald*, and that only comes out on Saturdays, so ner! Bet my phone didn't know that!"

"Your phone can get a newspaper subscription," Brayden corrected. "Wait…. Tay's in the paper?"

"Yeah, didn't you know? I thought you knew coz you were asking about the stoners."

"Nah, the girl that got tossed in was brought into my hospital. Everyone was talking about it when I got in this morning."

"Huh." *Small world*, Taylor thought.

"Tay's in the paper! Holy shit!"

Taylor groaned, finishing off the message to Joel and scowling at Clay. If he'd only kept his mouth shut, Brayden at least wouldn't have known anything until he saw Hayley that afternoon. Or maybe it was better he didn't hear it from her….

"Wow, you met Sietta Salisbury? I thought he died…."

"Very much alive," Clay corrected. "And very smoking hot."

"Clay!" Brayden and Taylor scolded at the same time.

"What? Joel agrees with me!" he defended himself, and the conversation met a quick death when Taylor reached out to end the call.

"How does no one think it's strange that everybody thinks this Salisbury guy is dead? You're serious that he's enrolled at the Conservatorium, but he's never so much as shown up for a class? What about friends? He doesn't hang out with anyone? He's not living overseas if he's enrolled at university here, right? So what's the deal?" Taylor studied the world sliding past through the window.

"It's fishy," Clay agreed. "I was thinking about it all night, even asked Joel about it, and he thought it was all super suspect, so when you called I wanted to check it out some more."

"You called me," Taylor pointed out.

"I was thinking more like 'maiden calling for help, wanna take a ride' calling me, not... you know what I meant!"

Taylor agreed but was still frowning because Joel worked at a university, and *he* thought it was weird. That usually meant it was. Joel was frighteningly smart, and he actually had a good sense of humour, for a scientist. Taylor trusted him with his brother, which translated to trusting him with anything.

"How was Joel?"

"He's fine. Ranted about some kid not knowing what a quark was."

Taylor stared at him until Clay cast him a confused look.

"What?"

"What is a quark?"

"How would I know? Joel's the nerd, not me." Clay snorted, shaking his head and looking back on the road, checking the GPS and following the directions through to Point Piper.

"Man, I hate having to go over the bridge." Clay took the next exit to avoid the infamous piece of architecture, and the six-lane traffic hazard it represented.

"So take the tunnel."

"I don't like tunnels!"

Taylor didn't bother replying. He checked on the GPS that he knew the route, since they didn't often go into the harbourside eastern suburbs of Sydney. Not rich enough, with no friends who lived there.

The whole landscape seemed to change as they drew nearer their destination, until it didn't seem they were in Sydney at all. Small terraces packed into one-lane streets had at some point given way to houses and then into mansions and then into something else entirely. Estates? Taylor didn't know what to call them, each taking up a city block, several stories high and sprawling with pools and tennis courts and driveways larger than his whole apartment building. It was a crazy waste of money.

The Salisburys had a large iron gate belted in by two large sandstone pillars, pale gold in the late morning light. Beyond, the driveway curled up toward a house that more closely resembled a palace, passing a tennis court on the way. The pool was visible off to one side of the house as they approached and parked in one of the bays set aside for guests.

"Christ... how do people live like this?" Clay stared at the imposing entryway. Taylor shook his head and got out of the car, aware of a man coming down the stairs to meet them. They weren't even going to make it to the front door.

"Good morning. I'm afraid we were not expecting any guests today?" A polite way of asking who the hell they were and what they were doing there.

"I'm sorry, we are Officers Jameson and Jameson. We were at the fundraiser last night and accidentally ended up in the paper with Sietta. We were hoping to apologise."

"Oh, I'm sure that won't be necessary at all."

They all stood there, staring at one another, and after a minute, it started to get awkward. Well, Taylor got the impression Clay thought it was awkward because he was fidgeting with his watch, but Taylor wasn't punching anyone, so he didn't think it was that awkward. Yet.

"Well, we would still like the chance to apologise," Clay ventured, and Taylor could hear the hint of something other than cordiality in his tone. He was getting antsy, and that was never a good thing. Though, honestly, he didn't mind it that much when Clay did the punching. Then Clay got the lecture from their mother. That was always a good thing.

"I'm terribly sorry, but Mister Salisbury isn't home right now."

"Ah. Will he be long? We don't mind waiting," Clay suggested, and Taylor knew he was fishing, trying to see what the man would say. What was acceptable and what was not. Before he punched him? There was always hope. Taylor really wanted to punch the guy.

"I'm afraid I don't know when the young master will return."

Young master? What country were they in, again? Clay and Taylor both blinked at the man, and Taylor scanned the windows of the estate, looking for anything out of place, but it was just another rich politician's home. Worse, the Salisburys had money long before they got into politics. Several generations of mining and investments had ensured the Salisburys would never want for anything, and their home reflected that wealth.

It was so far removed from their own upbringing—not that they were poor. They would be considered wealthy by most standards, but they didn't throw it around. Not like this.

"I see," Clay was muttering, as if trying hard to think of a solution to their dilemma. Other than punching the butler in the face, of course.

"Would it be possible for us to leave a card? He could call us at his convenience and we could apologise?" Taylor asked.

"I'm sure that would be quite satisfactory," the man agreed immediately, seeming relieved, and that relief made Taylor narrow his gaze at the man. Taylor reached into his pocket for his wallet, but Clay beat him to it and handed over his card, watching the man read the name and match it to his face. Or both their faces, really.

"Thank you, Mister Jameson. I will be sure to pass your card on to the young master when he returns."

"That's very kind of you," Taylor agreed, but his voice was cold, making it apparent he would be following up to ensure the man did indeed pass the card on. He expected to hear from the "young master," and if he didn't, he would simply come back and wait in person until he could apologise to his face like he wanted to.

"How come you have my card?" Taylor muttered as they turned away.

"I only ever hand out your card. Like I want people calling me for work?"

They got back in the Hilux, and Taylor fidgeted with the window buttons while Clay headed back down the drive. They didn't speak until they'd left Point Piper and were well on their way back to Crows Nest.

"Something's not right at that house," Clay scowled.

"Nothing looks awry," Taylor countered, and Clay snorted. They'd both gotten the same gut reaction from the place. The butler, or whoever he'd been, hadn't wanted to let them in, and had politely sent them from the property. The question was why? Well, that was the main question. The question Taylor really wanted to ask was why they hadn't punched the guy out and stormed the castle. But he knew the answer: paperwork.

"WHAT MAKES you so convinced something's wrong at this house?" Hale grumbled, picking up another buoy from the dumbwaiter and carrying it into the cage open at the end of the dark corridor.

The basement of the Public Order and Riot Squad headquarters was a boring space, accessible only by one stairwell with a locked gate and a security guard, and the dumbwaiter, which again was guarded and locked. The room itself was simple, bare stone and cement with a series of large cages for storing confiscated goods while the paperwork went through to have them destroyed.

Unfortunately, no one liked paperwork, and things tended to sit for a long time. There was several billion dollars' worth of drugs and illegal firearms in the basement, including a pile of ice that would fetch 1.6 billion on the market, the biggest in Australia's history. That had been a fun raid.

"They have a butler," Taylor grunted, still disturbed by the man with his immaculate suit. Who wore a full suit at home in the lead up to summer? That was crazy!

"Lots of rich people have butlers, or housekeepers or whatever. That doesn't make them criminals." Hale was deliberately playing devil's advocate to piss Taylor off.

"They're politicians," Taylor argued, grabbing another buoy and tossing it on the large pile inside the cage. "And it was the way he spoke to us. He clearly didn't want us stepping foot inside the house, like there was something to hide. Everything about it made me uneasy."

"Well, there's probably something going on, then. Private poker games or something. It doesn't have to be illegal for them to not want you to know about it."

"No, it's weirder than that! I'm telling you, there's something not right at that house!"

"Then go back and find out!" Hale threw his hands up in exasperation. "We've unloaded thirty buoys of cocaine, and you have not stopped complaining about that house and its creepy butler the entire time! You're obsessed!"

Maybe he was, but it was annoying him, and usually Clay would be with him and they would talk it through together, but Clay got caught up on a phone call and Hale had come down to help unload instead. He'd have to get Clay to talk about it at lunch, or something. If they got to go to lunch. He still couldn't believe they'd been called in on their day off for no better reason than to help unload stuff, but apparently Harris was sick and Mendel got called out on a job with Jones.

"Do you have helmet footage of that guy Clay Tasered at the gun retrieval raid?" Taylor changed the subject.

"The one who fell from the rafter?" Hale put the last buoy in the cage and locked up. "Yeah, I think so."

"Can you get me a copy?"

"Of course. That's what friends are for."

Not for listening to you talk about your problems, apparently. You learnt something new every day.

"So, WHAT? They just picked this chick up and tossed her overboard?" Ashley looked from one of them to the other like there was something they weren't telling him. He still had his Firies uniform on, and Taylor had to admit he looked good. He'd been working out, and while he wasn't as tall as his older brothers, he was wider in the shoulders and he'd bulked up. Taylor knew Ashley had always felt intimidated by his older brothers, but he was growing up, fast.

"What were they even doing with drugs at that party?" Their mother sipped her spritzer on the back patio. Chloe Jameson was dressed in her weekend finery: a beautiful summer dress with a floral pattern in orange and yellows that accentuated the gold streaks in her blonde hair. She had minimal make-up on, but it was used to accentuate the almond shape of her eyes and the touch of colour brightened her eyes and highlighted her strong cheekbones. She was tall, six foot one, and it was all in her legs. The dress was a halter neck, so she'd pinned her hair up in a ballet bun that made her neck look longer. She was stunning, and she knew it.

"Chloe, sweetheart, you know how kids are these days." Daniel Jameson, their father, stood at the barbeque, turning the meat, in dress shorts, a T-shirt, and no shoes. He gestured with the tongs whenever he spoke and had a lazy, relaxed grin firmly plastered on his face, and a beer in his other hand, which he sipped liberally. He was a large, fit man, but not quite as tall as Taylor and Clay, with a head of wild sandy blond hair and green eyes surrounded by heavy laugh lines.

"Well, I'm not letting Leila go to any parties if that's how kids are these days!"

Leila, the youngest of their six siblings, lay sprawled at the edge of the garden path, also in a sundress, but barefoot like their father, soaking up the heat from the cement. At only fifteen she wasn't as tall as everyone else yet, but Taylor thought she'd gotten the best of all the genes on offer. Her blonde hair was loose and wild, waist-length and sprayed around her head like a pale gold ocean. She was classically beautiful, and Taylor dreaded the day she decided she was interested in boys. He was still hoping she was gay, though the odds were not in their favour.

"Mum! I don't do drugs!" Leila protested.

"Only because you can't." Brayden snorted at her, shaking his head as he looked at Taylor's picture in the paper for the hundredth time. "Can you imagine what would happen if you were at a party and these idiots turned up?"

"What the hell kind of parties do you think I'm going to, that the riot squad would rock up?" Leila squawked, and Brayden snickered, reaching out to grab his son Jay's arm as he tried to run past.

"Where are you going? Where's Emma?"

Jay squirmed, but he was only seven and Brayden wasn't letting him get loose, so he sighed and gestured back toward the house, rolling his eyes. "She's in the fridge," he confessed as if this were completely normal. Brayden paused and looked stumped for a minute before Jay was lifted over one broad shoulder, screaming for Brayden to put him down while he strode into the house, bellowing threats of punishment.

"How the hell did he fit Emma in the fridge?"

"I cleaned out the vegetable crisper this morning and haven't put the shelves back in yet," Chloe mumbled, sipping her wine as if she too thought her granddaughter being in her refrigerator was completely normal.

"Mum, Emma is in the fridge! And you're just sipping wine!" Hayley gaped at them all, finally looking up from where she was ensconced in the corner on a beanbag with a beer in one hand and *Woman's Day* in the other.

"Oh, please, Taylor and Clay put Ashley in the chimney once and then tried to convince your father to light a fire. Besides, Emma is my granddaughter, not my child. Brayden is perfectly capable of disciplining his own children."

"Whatever. You know he'll just tell Kelly and she'll have to lay down the law." Clay snorted, and they all laughed because Brayden was the biggest softie on the planet and it always fell on his wife, Kelly, to discipline the kids.

"Wait, you put me in the chimney?" Ashley was gaping at Clay and Taylor who shrugged, not seeing how that came as any surprise. They'd all been there.

"You were being a brat. Wanted us to play with you, so we did."

"Excuse me?" Ashley's mouth fell farther open.

"Besides, maybe that's where your love of fires came from," Clay mused.

"Mum!" Ashley protested.

"I don't see what you're so worked up about. You laughed like it was the best day of your life and told your father you were going to be Santa when you grew up." Chloe waved Ashley's concerns away and took another sip of her spritzer.

"Really, son, you look quite good in this picture," Daniel said, holding the paper Brayden had discarded. "Though the Salisbury lad seems quite displeased with his father."

Even Daniel, who was not known for being the best judge of character, thought there was something wrong about that picture.

"I don't like that man," Chloe said softly, and a little overly succinctly, trying to compensate for her tipsiness by speaking overly well. "There's just something not quite right about him. Everything they do in public is so staged. No one is that perfect. It makes me wonder what they're trying to hide, that they think they need to be that perfect."

"Says the woman dressed as if the prime minister could walk through the door at any moment." Hayley waved a hand at Chloe's outfit.

"Oh, dream on, as if I'd bother to even put my pyjamas on if that prick turned up at the door."

"Amen," they all said at once, toasting the air.

"But seriously." Leila squinted at them from under the shade of the arm she had slung over her face. "What did those guys need a rocket launcher for?"

TAYLOR GROANED as he lowered himself onto the bed that night, towelling his hair dry and flopping back onto the pillows. He loved his family, but an afternoon was all he could take. They were loud, and the conversations made no sense and went around in circles until his head ached. There was never enough food for the amount he drank, and then he had to stay longer to sober up before they could drive home, which led to more crazy conversations and somehow tonight had ended with him having to change Emma's undies three times. Gross. She was supposedly toilet trained, at five years old, but had gotten tired and overexcited, according to Kelly. He never wanted kids.

He was dozing off when his phone rang and "blocked" came up on the screen. Sitting up quickly, he unplugged it from the wall and answered on the third ring. "'Lo?"

"Uh… is this Officer Jameson?" That voice. He'd recognise it anywhere, and yet again it went straight to his groin. Taylor sat on the edge of his bed and strained to listen.

"Yeah. This is Taylor."

"Hi. Sorry it's so late. I should have called earlier…." Sietta sounded tired. His breathing was heavy.

"No, its fine. Thanks for calling me."

"Sure." Sietta exhaled heavily, and there was a hitch to the word. Taylor thought it sounded like pain.

"Are you okay?"

"Huh? Yeah, no… I'm fine." But he sounded confused. Taylor cupped the phone as if he could cup the voice and protect it from harm.

"I just wanted to apologise," he explained softly. "I didn't know I had been photographed. I hope it hasn't caused you any trouble."

"Uh… no, no you didn't." The hesitation was odd. Taylor replayed the reply in his head. No he hadn't caused him trouble, but that didn't mean Sietta wasn't in trouble, for something.

"That's good. I'd still like to apologise properly in person. Could you meet me for coffee sometime?" Taylor asked, trying to coax responses that might indicate what was awry.

"No" was the immediate response. It was too immediate. Taylor doubted Sietta had even heard the request. Saying no was a reflex. It made him blink as he listened avidly to the call.

"What, never?" He chuckled, trying to make sure Sietta knew he was playing. Sort of. Something was off, and he wanted to know what. That he was interested at all was off, but he was trying not to think about that.

"Never," Sietta agreed, and again it was so immediate that it was stunning. Taylor's mouth went dry and he struggled to think of something to say, but Sietta beat him to it.

"I'm very busy, Officer Jameson. I don't have time to meet you, and it's completely unnecessary to apologise for something that was neither your fault nor caused me any hassle, I assure you. Thank you for your concern. Have a good night."

And just like that he was gone, the line dead. Taylor immediately called the office and asked for a trace on the last number. His boss wanted to know why, and Taylor explained. His boss promised to look into it, and that was all Taylor was told.

There was a light knock on his door. Taylor hauled the sheet over his groin as Clay opened the door.

"He called?"

"Yeah." Taylor huffed, feeling hot and bothered for no real discernible reason.

"It's fishy?"

"It's so fishy," Taylor agreed. "Boss is tracing the number."

Clay dubiously studied Taylor a little too closely, but then the door was closed and Taylor exhaled loudly, flopping back on the bed and staring at his phone screen. He willed it to ring again. It didn't.

Never. He'd never been turned down so abruptly.

3
REINFORCED STEEL

"So, LET me get this straight," Clay said again as Taylor drove them in to the office. "You hadn't even finished asking and he turned you down?"

"Yes."

"Just flat-out refused. You?"

"Yes." Like it hadn't been embarrassing enough the first thousand times he'd explained it.

"He actually said never?" Did his twin brother really need to spell it out, repeatedly?

"Yes!"

"That's so harsh, man."

"You don't say," Taylor muttered darkly. He'd spent most of the night waking up from dreams he couldn't quite recall, to lie in the dark and ponder his strange late-night phone call. The more he thought about it, the more he'd been convinced something was wrong with Sietta Salisbury. But he also felt increasingly depressed because he never dealt well with rejection, probably because he was almost never rejected. Like, ever, really. But Sietta probably wasn't gay, and he had no reason to go to coffee with him, so really Taylor had no reason to be upset. But he was and it was taking a great deal of effort not to show it.

So he was pleased. So extremely over-the-moon pleased when they drove into the carpark to find the van being loaded up, everyone already in their gear, waving them over to suit up because there was a time limit on the warrant they needed to execute.

"Oh hell yes," Taylor huffed as he locked the car and went to get his body armour. Clay was still laughing as he checked him over.

"Jamesons!" Mendel called, and they looked over to see him standing with their favourite toy.

"You guys get the ram."

"Look at that." Clay slammed a hand on his chest. "You get to raid someone's house, and you even get the honour of kicking in the front door."

"The only way was up," Taylor grumbled, but he was feeling better already.

"WHAT DO you mean the door was reinforced steel?" Brayden's voice snapped nearby, and Taylor groaned, not sure why his brother was screaming in his ear. Taylor was flat on his back with no idea how he got that way, and wherever he was reeked of disinfectant. He guessed he was at the hospital. That couldn't be a good thing.

"I mean the slimy bastard had reinforced the door from inside with fucking steel!" Clay snapped back from somewhere by the bed to Taylor's left. They both sounded pissed, and Taylor tried to move, but his head spun and ached and he wanted to vomit. So he whimpered and prayed they noticed and would stop screaming over his head.

"And so what? Taylor ran at it head first?"

"No, Taylor and I had the ram, and when it rebounded off the door, the force jerked my arm and I dropped my elbow too low. Taylor kept coming and it bounced up and smashed Tay in the head!"

"Excuse me?" Taylor whimpered, hands clenching in the sheet he was lying on. He was definitely on a bed. Fire raced through his head, his brain agreeing with Clay's version of events. "You dropped it?"

"Sorry" was all Clay had the guts to say.

"Open your eyes, Taylor, I need to check your pupils," Brayden commanded. Taylor only did as he was told because he knew Brayden would pry them open anyway. The light hurt and his eyes watered immediately as he strained to focus on anything, but the world was swimming and he barely managed to tilt sideways before he vomited over the side of the bed, right onto Clay's shoes.

"Aw… come on! I didn't mean it!" Clay protested, but the worry was clear in his voice, and his hands weren't steady on Taylor's shoulders as he held him up.

"Lie him back down," Brayden commanded. Taylor didn't need to be told twice, letting Clay lower him back down so he could close his eyes again.

"You've got a concussion. Your skull is cracked, literally not figuratively this time. Your face is a mess, but your scans don't show any bleeding or fluid build-up…. You're damn lucky." Brayden's hand was cool and soothing on his cheek and neck, and Taylor hummed to acknowledge he'd heard.

"Thanks, Bray."

"Scared the shit out of me, Taylor. I have to go talk to Mum, she's freakin' out in the waiting room." That task no one envied. He hoped Brayden managed to convince her not to visit. His head couldn't handle it right now.

Taylor heard his footfalls recede and sighed, aware of Clay pulling a chair up beside his bed and taking his hand, rubbing soothing circles on his wrist.

"Sorry, bro."

"All good. Wanted a holiday." He could feel Clay smiling against his wrist, where he leaned down to lay a light kiss. He hadn't done that in years, though it had been a common thing when they were kids and somehow one got hurt.

"Sleep. I'm on watch."

He didn't need to be told twice.

HE WAS woken every hour, on the hour, for twenty-four hours. The result was his head still hurt, his face had time to stop swelling and start bruising, and he was tired and grouchy as hell. He also wanted to go back to the drug dealer's house and burn it to the damn ground, but apparently everyone had been so pissed that Taylor got hurt that there wasn't much left of the house anyway. They'd gutted it, and charged the man with every crime they could find evidence of guilt for, which was a lot when a team of riot squad officers put their skills together. It helped that they found an awfully large load of drugs through the house, and a lab in the garage. Not to mention the half-naked girl in the bedroom turned out to be underage.

It didn't help Taylor feel better.

"Hey." Clay yawned and stretched, still not letting go of his hand. It made Taylor smile, and he managed to squeeze a thanks back. He knew how he would feel if their positions were reversed and was glad he'd been at the back. If Clay got hurt, he was sure the drug dealer would have been murdered the second they'd managed to get the door open. Instead, apparently Clay had caught him, dragged him out of the way, and let the others do the raid, while he'd stayed at Taylor's side. They looked the same, but inside they were wired slightly different. Clay was the better of them, Taylor was the dark. Clay was air, Taylor a tumultuous ocean. Not that they ever let anyone else realise that. It was far more fun to leave people guessing and watch them choose wrong. Watching people flounder halfway through a conversation when they realised they were speaking to the wrong person was plain old funny.

"Hey." Taylor barely managed to foster the energy to reply.

"You wanna go home soon? Bray said next time you woke up, he could get the forms."

"Yeah. Go get him."

Clay agreed and squeezed his hand one more time before leaving. Taylor counted to five to make sure he really was gone before he made his first attempt at moving.

He tried leaning up on his elbows. His head pounded and his stomach protested, but he ignored it and was successful. Gritting his teeth, he sat up and had to wait a minute for the nausea to fade. His eyes were watering again, and he was sweating as he got to his feet and used the wall to wander through to the bathroom. He grabbed hold of the sink and looked in the mirror. Shades of purple mottled half of his face, and there was a huge bump on the left side of his head, visible under his hair. A few stitches ran across his forehead around several rich red and purple bruises.

"Goddamn…." He barely even remembered what had happened. He recalled getting the ram out of the truck and following orders to the door. He knew Clay went first; Clay always went first, Taylor didn't trust anyone else to have his back. And then… not much after that. He was going to get ribbed. So much was coming his way, he didn't want to go back to work. Maybe he could move to Tasmania and get a job as a lumberjack… you know, if anyone ever approved forestry again.

"Tay?" Clay's worry was thick in his voice and Taylor chuckled snidely because even if he had walked into the hospital room and found his bed empty, it had to be pretty obvious where he was. And sure enough a few seconds later, Clay's head popped around the doorway and the man heaved a huge sigh of relief.

"I'm fine. Just give me the damn forms to sign."

"Prove you can walk out here on your own, and you can sign them." Brayden's voice came through, and Taylor rolled his eyes, following orders and wearily wandering back out, gesturing at his face with a scowl.

"You call this good work?"

"I didn't mean to lower the ram…." Clay immediately looked like Taylor had drowned his non-existent puppy.

"I meant the stitches, idiot." This was why they couldn't have a dog, seriously.

"They're perfect and you know it." Brayden sniffed haughtily, handing over the forms, and Taylor hurriedly signed them, aware his signature looked off and was far messier than usual, which was saying something, since no one was ever going to accuse him of having tidy handwriting to begin with.

"There. Now get me out of here," Taylor grumbled, handing Brayden the forms and gesturing for Clay to lead the way.

"You have to go in a wheelchair." Brayden tried to stall him.

"Like hell," Taylor scowled at him, and there was no further argument. They all knew if there had been, Taylor would have been perfectly okay with beating up whatever orderly tried to make him. Clay would have felt the need to help him out and then Brayden would have had to try to explain to their boss why two police officers were arrested in a hospital while one of them was his patient. Really, it was far too much paperwork for everyone involved. Far better idea to let him walk. Or he supposed trundle was more like it. He was trundling. Joy.

"What are you smirking about? Your head looks like I attacked it with a bowling ball."

"Nothing," Taylor assured Clay, still grinning all the way to the Hilux, which was parked in a no-parking zone, with the police permit on the front.

"Not a word," Clay demanded, and Taylor obliged all the way home, dozing off and not complaining once about Clay driving.

HIS PHONE was ringing. He needed to get that damn thing disconnected. He fumbled around on the bedside and managed to answer the call, all without opening his eyes or moving anything other than his arm, which was good because he didn't want to vomit on his sheets. Mostly because that would require stripping the bed and actually doing some laundry. Washing machines were loud. His head couldn't do loud right now. Which was why he let the phone drop away from his ear almost immediately.

"So you're not dead! You're not dead, and you still couldn't think to call your mother and tell her that? What sort of son have I raised?"

Chloe blubbered through the phone at him. Taylor heard the door open, and then the bed dipped and he sighed at the gentle hand that trailed down his neck to settle in his hair while Clay picked up the phone.

"Mum, I just told you he was fine and at home and that he was sleeping. Why the hell would you wake him up?"

"He needs to be woken up, he's got a concussion. Brayden told me! I did research. You have to wake up concussed people!"

"He's been released from hospital, and it's been more than twenty-four hours, and your son the doctor said he was fine," Clay tried to point out reasonably. "I think Brayden's slightly more qualified than Wikipedia."

"Taylor's skull has a crack in it!" She screeched through the phone, so loud Taylor thought their neighbours could probably hear it.

"Which is nothing out of the ordinary," Clay stupidly reminded her. "We're always breaking stuff. It's our status quo. He's fine. I'm fine. If you stop calling him, he can get some more rest, and he'll feel better sooner and get to visit you sooner!"

"True," she conceded, and then she was yelling at them again. "You make your brother chicken soup, you hear me? If I find out you didn't, I will personally come over there and stew you myself for your brother's consumption!"

The phone went dead. They both sighed, shared a knowing look, and Clay lay down and fell back to sleep right there beside him. Taylor chuckled, winced at the shot of pain that caused, and decided sleeping some more was a very good idea.

THEY NEEDED groceries a few days later when the massive batch of chicken soup Hayley had delivered ran out. Their mother had assumed Clay wouldn't make it and had insisted Hayley do so, but it only went so far. So they went to the grocery store. Clay drove, which pissed Taylor off.

"I can drive!"

"Just because you can doesn't mean you should," Clay countered smugly.

"Yes, it does. That's exactly what it means."

"Really? So just because you can have unprotected sex with an HIV-infected individual, you should?"

"No!" Taylor cast a horrified look at Clay, and his brother smirked, as if he'd won the argument. "That is in no way the same thing at all!"

"And yet, I'm driving."

Taylor didn't bother talking to him when clearly he was deranged. He let Clay grab the basket at Woolworths, because he was an invalid and couldn't be bothered.

"Heeey.... Don't you think you're a bit big to be a Smurf? I didn't know those guys had domestic violence issues either...." Taylor groaned and turned to glare at Hale, wondering how it was possible that in a city of four and a half million, they'd somehow managed to choose to shop at the same Woolworths, at the same time.

Then he stared at Hale's bandaged arm with a dark scowl. "What happened to you?"

"Oh. Well, you went down with the ram, Clay pulled you out of the way, I ran in, tripped over your unconscious body, fell through the door, accidentally knocking the dealer over into the bookcase by the door, and the stupid thing fell on me. Bled like a bitch!"

"The dealer?" Taylor wasn't following, but then he'd been unconscious so he had an excuse. Also, he wasn't sure the conversation was actually making any sense. Hale tripped? How was that even possible?

"The bookcase," Clay and Hale said at once.

"Oh." Taylor still didn't get it. "He reads?" Somehow he hadn't expected that, though why he couldn't begin to say. "Who puts a bookcase by the door?"

"Oh, there weren't any books on it. I mean, there isn't a manual as far as I know on how to run a meth lab in your garage and not get caught...."

"So again, why?" Taylor wasn't sure if it was his head making him slow or if it was that everyone he knew really was insane and determined to drive him over the edge just to see what would happen.

"Oh. He had guns and car parts on it. I thought the guy hit me, not the bookcase... pain, you know? Does weird things to your head. So, as far as I could tell, he'd taken you out already. I freaked and grabbed the first gun I saw and shot the prick in the foot."

"How am I only learning this now?" Taylor looked at Clay, incredulous.

"You were hurt," Clay said, as if that were an explanation that made sense.

"This would have made me feel better!" Taylor argued, still incredulous.

"Well, yeah, but Brayden sewed his foot back together," Clay grumbled, clearly displeased with this fact. Taylor had to agree; Brayden should have let the man lose a toe, at least.

"Least you shot him," Taylor managed to say, disgruntled. "How long are you off duty?"

"I'm not," Hale huffed, grabbing a box of Weet-Bix from the shelf and putting it in his basket. "I'm on desk. If you fucktards do anything that requires extra paperwork, I'm going to murder you."

Taylor beamed. He was going to ticket every poor schmuck he could for the foreseeable future. Hale might be the paperwork wizard, but he'd make sure the pile had no end.

"Try it and I'll slap you upside the head, turn that fracture in your skull into a break, and you'll be on desk duty right alongside me." Hale read his mind. Taylor sighed, the wind stolen from his sails for the moment.

"You don't look like you should be getting groceries," Hale pointed out, but Taylor just shrugged.

"If Mum's letting me walk around, I think I'm fine."

"If Bray's risking Mum yelling at him about Tay falling down, he's definitely fine," Clay added.

"Fair enough. Well, I'll see you guys tomorrow, then, unless you got more leave than I did?"

"Are you kidding me? If Clay doesn't go back to work and get to punch something soon, I won't be able to let him stay at Joel's for fear of kinky crossing the line, and Mum lecturing me about whatever happens to Joel as a result...."

"TMI!" Hale bellowed at them, marching off with his hands over his ears.

"That's for the Smurf comment," Taylor muttered at his retreating back. Clay was already down the aisle, picking out chicken breasts to put in the basket. "You better not be thinking of doing kinky things with the chicken...."

THEY WERE almost back to the house, Clay driving.

"The hell...." Clay jerked on the wheel a little, waking Taylor.

Taylor forced his eyes open as they approached their apartment building, and there, standing at the gates, was Leila and none other than

Micah Salisbury. They were talking animatedly to one another, hands waving, and Leila was laughing at something he'd said. Then she spotted them and waved frantically before following them in as the gates swung open. Clay parked faster than usual.

"Leila?" Taylor looked from her to Micah and back again, the question clear on his face. Micah's brother had made it wildly apparent on the phone that he wanted nothing to do with him; *never* was hard to misinterpret. So what was his kid brother doing here—with *their* sister? How the hell did they even know each other?

"Um. Well, Micah kind of needs a favour, yeah?"

"He does," Clay replied, copying Taylor's look, from one to the other and back.

"You know, when you do that at the same time like that? You look like those clowns at the show?" She opened her mouth and mimicked, turning her head gradually from one side to the other and back until Clay slapped her lightly on the side of the head. She snickered at him. Clay and Taylor both crossed their arms over their chests and glared at her.

"What the hell happened to your face?" Micah was gaping at Taylor, and the twins huffed loudly.

"Battering ram rebounded off the door and hit him in the head." Clay was clearly still having a problem with this turn of events.

"The ram rebounded?" Micah stared at them both incredulously. "Into your face?"

"Clay dropped it," Leila clarified, and Taylor winced, seeing the colour drain from Clay's face a little.

"It was an accident. Shit happens," Taylor interjected, looking seriously at Micah. "What sort of favour?"

"Geez, I thought you looked scary before," Micah mumbled, shifting nervously and pointing back toward the gates, toward freedom.

"I uh... I need you to buy me a phone. A cheap throwaway one. You know? Leila offered, but she's not old enough. I don't need it registered or anything, just the phone and a SIM."

Leila enthusiastically backed up Micah's story. Taylor shared a look with Clay.

There were a whole slew of questions they could ask, but it could scare Micah off. They shouldn't legally buy Micah a phone, because they didn't have parental permission, but neither of them thought the phone was for Micah. He didn't need the SIM registered, which meant an adult was going to do so. Obviously, most adults could buy a phone for themselves. Taylor suspected the phone was for Sietta. They could register the SIM number with the Australian Federal Police and have the phone monitored, stating clearly who purchased it, who it was given to, and evidence for where they believed it would be going. From there, the AFP could choose to investigate further, or not. They nodded in silent agreement.

Clay put a hand on Micah's shoulder and led him to the gate. There was a supermarket down on the corner that sold cheap phones. He'd be done in a half hour, tops.

"The SIM will have to be registered to an adult. You call the phone company on the packet to do that, and it'll be in their name. We will register it with the Federal Police and it's very likely they will trace it. Do you understand what I'm saying?" Taylor crossed his arms over his chest and looked down at Micah.

Micah quickly agreed and hurried after Clay, who was already striding down the street.

Taylor put an arm across Leila's shoulders and pushed her toward the stairs. "Come on, help me up. You can wait till they get back, and Clay'll take you home. Help me with these bags."

"Oh, it's fine. Micah said he'd catch the train with me." Leila grabbed two of the stuffed shopping sacks.

"He did, did he?" So much for her being gay. "What is he, like, fourteen? Clay can drive you both."

"He's fifteen." Leila sniffed, so much like Hayley, so familiar Taylor wanted to cry. Instead he shook his head, took deep breaths, and forced himself up the stairs, carrying the remaining groceries. He was sweating again by the time they got to the top, and Leila was kind enough to say nothing when he dumped the bags by the fridge to unpack later. Leila helped him to the couch and went to put on the kettle.

"Tea?"

"Yeah. Black."

"I know."

He must have dozed off because the next thing he knew, Leila was shaking his shoulder and holding out the steaming mug. He sat up with a groan and took it, inhaling the scent.

"Are you sure you're okay? You don't look too good...."

"I'm fine," he reassured her. "Explain to me how you came to be standing outside my apartment with Micah Salisbury." Because that was far more interesting than the bruises on his face and the headache he kept getting.

"Oh. Well, I left school and went to get the train, but he was at the station. Called out to me, asked if I was Leila Jameson. I wonder how he knew my name, that's strange, right? Though I guess he knows you and I sort of look like you, at least... well, I'm pretty tall, so it's not hard to guess, right? I mean I'm taller than all my friends so that makes sense." She shrugged, as if any of that made sense. "I didn't realise who he was at first, but he was super cute, and he asked if he could catch the train with me, and I said yeah, because what sort of moron would say no, right? And so then we were going to the platform because he said he lived near me, but he stopped and asked if I could do him a favour and if I could bring him to see you instead, and then he would take me home after, and I said sure, but I was nervous too because I didn't know what he wanted, but I thought it would be okay because you and Clay are like crazy and huge, and it wasn't like he could do anything bad to you, right? But then on the way here, he explained that he needed you to get him a phone to give to Sietta, and I know you wanted to talk to him, so I figured I would help. I did the right thing, right?"

His head was swimming, and he wondered not for the first time why teenagers couldn't tell you facts, plain and simple, without all the other crazy stuff that ended up in their stories. But his head woke up at the end of her explanation, and he nodded quickly.

"Yeah, you did the right thing. The phone's for his brother?" That was fascinating. Why would Sietta need a burner phone? Because it was obvious that's what they were getting. And why would he want it to call someone he'd made it very clear he wanted nothing to do with? *Never.*

"That's what he said." Leila sipped her tea, watching him over the lip of the cup. "He is super cute, right? Do you think he likes me?"

Ah, girls. "Leila, I'm sure everyone likes you. Just... don't do anything stupid, yeah? I know where that kid lives." Not that Taylor thought Micah was a problem. Taylor suspected the kid was gay, but it was for Micah to tell Leila that, not Taylor.

She howled with laughter. She was the only one who could get away with it, and his head hurt so he let her.

His cup was mostly empty when the door opened and Clay strode in, shopping bag on his wrist, Micah on his heels.

Taylor called in to the station and gave them the number so it could be officially logged with the AFP and traced for suspicious activity. He promised to write a full report on what had taken place to justify their suspicions and reasons for purchasing the phone and hung up.

Clay made a short video of the intact packaging and filmed himself handing the bag to Micah, then slipped a police contact card with their numbers on it into the bag. Clay crossed his arms, staring down at Micah through slitted eyes. Micah squirmed. Anyone would.

"It's for Sietta," Taylor said softly, and he saw Clay's shoulders stiffen.

"Why does your brother need us to buy him a phone?" Clay demanded. Micah looked to Taylor, suddenly nervous.

"To talk to me? He made it quite clear he wanted to never speak to me…." Only he hadn't, really. Even if he had.

"Sietta doesn't have a phone. Our father, he monitors all our calls. He was standing right there," Micah whispered. "But I knew Sietta wanted to talk to you, and I can get the phone to him. I just couldn't buy it myself…." So Sietta might not even know he was getting a phone? This could be such a bad idea. Only, if their dad had been there, maybe never didn't quite mean never….

What was going on in that house that a grown man wasn't allowed to make an unmonitored phone call? That was the real question.

"It's okay," Clay interrupted, putting a hand on his shoulder and squeezing until Micah looked up at him. Clay grinned and Micah relaxed completely. "You did good, kid."

"Why does your father monitor Sietta's calls? He's not a kid…."

Micah's gaze narrowed, and he looked from one of them to the other, then gripped the phone tighter in his hand. "You didn't look at the USB." He huffed. "Dammit. I didn't give you *Vikings* episodes or anything! It was important!" He strode from the room, left the apartment altogether, but not before they saw the tears of frustration in his eyes. And fear.

"Dammit!" Leila echoed, scrambling to her feet and grabbing her bag as she ran for the door. "Wait for me! Micah!"

Clay was left standing in the living room, sharing a knowing look with Taylor. "Where is it?"

"On my desk at work."

"I'll be back," Clay called, already at the door.

Taylor looked around his empty apartment and sighed. The day had seemed so normal when it had only involved getting the groceries. How did his life keep getting weirder and weirder?

HE HADN'T been asleep more than fifteen minutes when his phone rang. His heart lurched stupidly in his chest, despite the fact he knew Micah couldn't be home yet. He grabbed it up, answering somewhat dubiously. "'Lo?"

"Okay, so what we don't get is how it hit you in the head." Ashley started in immediately, and Taylor looked up at the ceiling, wondering what he'd done in a past life. "I mean, we get that the door was reinforced and that the ram rebounded, but even if Clay dropped his end, shouldn't it have just dropped? How'd it end up in your face? We've been trying to figure it out using the hose, and we can't see how that happened...."

They were re-enacting it with a fire hose? What. The. Hell.

"Because I was behind him, and I pushed forward," Taylor grumbled, not recalling much of what had taken place but at least remembering being behind Clay and getting a run up because they'd been full of nervous energy and getting to break down a door had sounded perfect.

"Oh, he had all the momentum, like maybe they were running... yeah like that!" Ashley was far too excited to be giving someone instructions. "What else?"

"Ash... I was knocked unconscious. I don't know what happened. I don't remember it at all." There was a loud clatter in the background and someone swore.

"Wow, seriously? You have amnesia?"

"What? No! I was knocked unconscious. I don't know what happened because I wasn't awake! And what I was awake for, I didn't see because Clay was in front of me. You moron!"

"Oh. Right. That makes sense." Taylor was glad something did. "No, turn around," he called out to someone. "He said Clay was in front... yeah, like that!"

There was the sound of shuffling and cursing, and someone dropping the hose, and then much louder cursing.

"How's your head?"

"I'm fine," Taylor ground out, and Ashley made a sound that clearly said he knew Taylor wasn't.

"Dad took photos." Ashley clearly thought this was hilarious.

"He did what now?"

"While you were out of it. He took photos, I think he even filmed some of it. You were so bonkers, you even sang Clay a lullaby to try and get him to sleep, and then fell asleep in the middle of it yourself. It was pure gold."

"I did not."

"Did. There's proof."

Taylor hung up because it wasn't worth continuing the conversation when he had better things to do, like plot breaking into his father's home to steal the memory card from his camera before he thought to download it to his computer and upload to YouTube.

His phone rang again, but it was Clay, and Taylor's gut lurched this time instead.

"What's wrong?"

"Nothing," Clay replied immediately, but they both knew it was a lie. "I've got the USB. But…. Taylor, there's a lot on it. I just plugged it in to see, and… it's bad, okay? It's real bad. I'm in with the boss. We're going through it here; he's already bringing in a team."

"Define bad?" Taylor grunted. He wished he'd made a copy of the USB when he had the chance. If Clay had felt the need to go immediately to Parata, it was bad. If the boss had called in the higher-ups, something epically wrong was going on. Taylor wanted to know, and he wanted to know now. He'd never been more frustrated to be stuck at home with an injury.

"Look… I'll explain when I get back, okay? I'm gonna be a while. Get some rest. You're gonna need it."

As if he could sleep now.

HIS PHONE rang, startling him from his sleep. He reached for his bedside table, realising too late he was still on the couch, rolling off the side and hitting the ground hard, jolting his head. He moaned as he snatched up his phone and saw a random number show up.

"Hello?"

"Hey." Sietta sounded winded himself, but that voice! It was the stuff of Taylor's wet dreams. "Are you okay? Micah said you were hurt."

"I'm fine. Merely a bump."

"Uh-huh." He didn't sound convinced. It made Taylor smile.

"Are you okay?" Because Taylor couldn't hide how worried he was. Whatever had been on that USB, it had freaked out Clay, who was unshakable. And still not home, apparently.

"I'm fine."

"You're alone?"

"I believe so." Sietta's laugh was gentle, and Taylor could imagine him adjusting his nerd glasses on his nose. But the words were irritating. He believed so, but couldn't be sure, was what Taylor heard. He had to get a burner phone so his father didn't know they spoke, and his fifteen-year-old brother had to get it for him, from riot squad officers no less, because apparently he couldn't get it himself. And he wasn't even sure he was alone, at.… Taylor looked at his watch. It was two in the morning.

"It's late."

"Early," Sietta corrected. "Sorry. I didn't want to wake you, but I couldn't call earlier."

Why not? "It's fine. I've had a concussion. Probably needed to be woken up anyway," Taylor admitted. Which made it all the stranger that he hadn't been. Whatever Clay was doing, he thought it more important than calling to make sure he was breathing. That unnerved Taylor more than anything else.

"How'd you get hurt?"

"Uh.…" He didn't want to say, really, but he did want to talk, so he sighed and explained that he had been injured on the job when Clay dropped the ram. He didn't give many details, just made it clear that the injury was not his fault, because blaming Clay for things was fun.

"And it hit you in the head?" Sietta's laugh was soft, restrained probably behind his hands, but there was pure joy in it.

"Yeah, yeah, it's funny, I get it."

"Your brother must be upset," Sietta said. Calmly. Hitting the nail on the head without any thought at all.

"He is." But it said something about Sietta as a person that he knew that. That that was what he thought of first. That he understood that hurt.

"I'm sorry I was rude on the phone, last time. I just… it would have been unwise to have my father think we might be friends, or something."

Might be friends? They weren't that. They weren't anything. Yet.

"I'd like to be friends," Taylor ventured.

"Me too," Sietta agreed, and Taylor could hear the smile in his voice.

"So your dad's a control freak?" What other explanation was there for a twentysomething-year-old man being unable to have friends his parents didn't approve of, or have a phone conversation that wasn't monitored? Or have a phone?

"Uh… you could say that," Sietta agreed guardedly, as if trying out the term and attempting to fit it to the man he knew. "Something like that, anyway."

Something like that wasn't the same thing. It made Taylor want to know more about the USB, but he didn't want to hang up the phone, and he needed to if he was going to call Clay. "So you would like to get coffee with me?"

"I would," Sietta agreed, but the hesitation was immediate. "I just… I'll have to figure it out."

"Not allowed to slum it?" Taylor chuckled to take the sting out of it, mostly because his family were far from slumming it. Sure, they weren't the gazillionaires the Salisburys were, but they were certainly not anyone's idea of poor either.

Sietta seemed to know that or found something equally amusing because he lost it, laughing hard on the other end of the line. "Uh, no, more like not allowed to gay it. Or anything it, really."

"Ah," Taylor acknowledged with a grin. He supposed it wouldn't look good on Johnathan Salisbury's CV to have a gay son when the government was homophobic and still determined to be the last country on earth to legalise gay marriage. But he was pleased to hear Sietta was, as he had suspected, playing for his team. And interested, if his actions were anything to go by.

"I'll figure it out," Sietta repeated, and Taylor believed he would try. He wasn't so sure he would succeed, but Taylor found himself of the opinion he was willing to wait for a date with Sietta Salisbury. There was something about the man; it wasn't his voice alone, everything about Sietta pressed buttons Taylor hadn't known he had.

He was mindful that he was acting rather smitten, and he only recognised the signs because he'd seen them all in Clay the moment he met Joel, and those two had been inseparable for four years. While he was particularly aware of what Sietta looked like, he found himself content to simply talk, and that was new for him. He didn't usually enjoy the company of people outside family or work, but he could imagine himself sitting up and listening to Sietta ramble for hours.

"So what are you doing up so early in the morning, then?" Because it was interesting that this was the time Sietta thought it safe to call.

"One could ask you the same question." Sietta was smiling. You could hear it in his voice.

"One asked you first. Also, I wasn't awake. You woke me." He won a laugh.

"Hmm, I suppose you could say I'm a light sleeper," Sietta admitted. "And probably an insomniac. Typical musician, really. This is the best time of day."

"This is night," Taylor corrected, but he was smiling. "So you are a musician? I had heard you were a student at the Conservatorium, only it seems you're more like the Phantom of the Opera or something...."

He could listen to Sietta laugh all night.

"I do most of my work by correspondence," Sietta admitted. "My teacher comes here, when he needs to."

"Ah." Must be nice to be so rich the teacher came to you. "What do you play?"

"Piano, mostly." Mostly had other stories behind it, but he wanted to ask about those in person, where he could see the expressions on Sietta's face, instead of only imagining them.

"So you're a policeman?"

"Riot squad, yes." Taylor smirked because his job was hot and he knew it.

"Do you get hurt a lot?" That didn't sound attractive at all. Teasing. Taylor didn't do well with teasing.

"No. I do not get hurt a lot. I wouldn't have gotten hurt this time if my idiot brother hadn't dropped the ball, somewhat literally."

"Of course," Sietta placated, but he was laughing again. "And you're twins."

"That is blatantly obvious to anyone who lays eyes on us."

"But you're different," Sietta murmured. "It was you in the picture, not your brother."

Yes it was, but how had he known that? It hadn't listed his full name, only Jameson because that had been printed on his uniform. His family had known it was him, mostly because they couldn't fathom the expression on his face being on Clay's, but how had Sietta known? Because he'd left his card? Or had he simply known when he looked?

"How can you tell?"

"There's something different in your eyes. You're harder, not as kind," Sietta said with a hint of a challenge to it. Taylor inhaled slow and deep, and closed his eyes because that was it exactly, and it was ridiculous that Sietta had known. No one else ever noticed until Taylor was being an asshole to their face.

"How do you—"

"I'm good with people," Sietta cut him off. "I watch people. I see them. I listen to them. I know them."

But who had cause to watch that closely?

"Sietta, are you okay?" He was a little afraid of the answer, because the longer they spoke, the worse the feeling in the pit of his stomach became.

"I'm okay." He reassured. Soothing, as if aware Taylor knew something was wrong. "I'll think about it tonight, and I'll text you when I come up with a place to meet, okay?"

"Yeah...." That wasn't what he'd been worried about, and they both knew it. But it would do for now, a promise to meet. Taylor was going to drive out there and force Salisbury's hand the first chance he got, but Sietta could think they were waiting for a coffee date if that helped him sleep tonight.

"I like you," Sietta blurted out, and it was so random and unexpected that they both laughed.

"I like you too. I want to meet up," Taylor assured him. "I'm looking forward to it."

"Okay. Cool. Me too. So, I guess I better go. Uh... thanks, for answering in the middle of the night."

"Anytime, Sietta. You can call me anytime. I'll answer."

"Sure." Sietta was gone, the line dead.

He fell asleep again and woke the following afternoon. So much for people waking him up for the concussion! He checked his phone, and it had been twelve hours; it was late afternoon. His mouth tasted funny.

Taylor huffed loudly and forced himself to get up and have a shower. It helped soothe the ache in his head, and when he took some Nurofen, he felt almost human again. He was towelling dry when his phone rang. His heart skipped, wondering if maybe Sietta was calling back, but it was Clay's name on the screen, and Taylor scooped it up.

"What's going on?"

"Get dressed. I'll be downstairs in five. You need your overalls."

As quickly as the call had started, Clay was gone again. But Taylor moved on instinct, grabbing his work overalls and pulling them on, pushing his feet into his steel-capped boots. True to his word, the Hilux pulled up on the street, and Taylor got in.

Clay's knuckles were white on the steering wheel. His expression was dark, a rictus of anger so rare Taylor couldn't place the last time he'd seen it. It took a lot to rattle either of them, and Clay was perpetually in a good mood. Most crime amused him, plain and simple, so whatever was going on was bad. He didn't need to ask to know why.

"What was on the USB?"

Clay's hands tightened, to the point Taylor worried the steering wheel was going to break off the column.

"Better to ask what wasn't on the USB," Clay managed to grind out. "They're still cataloguing it, but we're all being called in for briefing before we get sent in tomorrow."

"That's quick." Usually things moved fast, but if they weren't doing intel, that meant they had enough to go on already.

"Tay...." Clay shook his head, trying to get a grip on his own thoughts. "The USB... there's hours of footage, thousands of photos, documents, all sorts of shit. Some of it... it's really ugly. There are medical reports, and photos, and just... It's so wrong."

"Footage of what?"

Clay shook his head and struggled to speak.

"Seriously.... You'll see."

4
FISHY

SIETTA SALISBURY was young in the video. Maybe seventeen. He still screamed when his father kicked him repeatedly, the blood pooling around him as he struggled to crawl away, but the bastard had chained him to the wall in the wine cellar, and there was nowhere to go. The beating lasted almost an hour, and Sietta didn't move at the end of the clip. The medical record attached to the file stated nine broken ribs, a punctured lung, a tear in his stomach, bruised kidneys, and a ruptured spleen that had to be removed. The operation and medical exam had been done on callout, right there in the cellar.

Sietta was a smart kid. He'd known his father wouldn't take his announcement that he was gay well, but he'd had no idea it would go as spectacularly bad as it had. Sietta had bought a spy cam, so there was evidence of whatever happened. What kid felt the need to get a spy cam to come out to his parents? That should have been the first clue to the horror that was his life, right there.

Sietta had worn it in his ear. When he wasn't wearing it, he had it pinned to the cork top of a wine bottle, which was where it had filmed the beating Taylor watched in dark silence.

Sietta had been sixteen in the video where he came out to his parents. His mother had looked cold. His father had been furious. So furious he almost killed him, and with that one beating, he committed political suicide, or he would have if anyone had found out about it. But they'd pulled Sietta from school, homeschooled him, and kept him within grasp at all times. He was allowed no contact with the outside world, everything he did was monitored because Sietta himself was the biggest threat to them. All he had to do was open his mouth....

But they couldn't kill him either. And Sietta, smart kid, had known that, and had simply spent his years gathering evidence. There was enough to send both his parents and his older brother away for many, many years. But he'd done even better; he'd followed their political careers and collected evidence of tax evasion, of backdoor deals from parliament and businesses that would see most of Salisbury's political allies immediately removed from parliament and more likely sent to prison right alongside him.

No one could have created a better undercover agent, but as the evidence was collated on the screens around him, Taylor wanted to be sick. He understood the rage he saw in Clay, but his own simmered under the surface, hotter and far more personal.

Others noticed that the information became more focussed and succinct as Sietta got older and his goal to put them all away became clearer. Sietta didn't scream anymore when his father broke his bones, as if he didn't feel it at all.

All of it tucked away on a USB in the hands of a fifteen-year-old, delivered to a police officer at a party. Why him? Why then?

"Because Micah's gay," Clay whispered by his ear, sitting down on the table beside Taylor and glaring at the screens alongside him.

"Excuse me?"

"Sietta handed in the USB now because Micah is gay and is terrified of ending up in the cellar alongside his brother. This is all, ultimately, Sietta's trump card to save his brother, not himself."

Taylor absorbed that. How long would Sietta have stayed like this? Living like a caged animal to satiate his father's rage and ambition? How long would he have tried to last, to see them all rot in prison? A while.... Sietta Salisbury was tenacious and strong and so far from stupid.

"Leila won't be pleased," he heard himself say, and Clay gaped at him before finally cracking a smile and laughing. Clay shook his head and laid a hand on his shoulder, squeezing hard.

"This is why we do what we do," he reminded Taylor. "We'll go in, we'll let the boys get what the boss needs, and we'll get Sietta. Maybe stop at a coffee shop on the way to see Bray."

"Just like that?" Taylor felt his own smirk coming hard.

"Just like that," Clay confirmed, and Taylor felt better. He turned away from the screens and forced himself to focus on the job. Someone was pulling up plans of the Point Piper mansion and its neighbours. Others were pulling up schedules and timings, and a plan was being built. Taylor let them do it, happy to be told what to do, even if it was only beat down the door, though he hoped they checked this time if it was reinforced steel.

He fingered his phone in his pocket, stroking the side and willing it to ring. It wouldn't. He knew that now, understood it. He wondered at the courage it had taken to attempt even that small risk. But then, Sietta had already sent the USB out into the world, and he had to know it was only a matter of time before the truth was out there, and he was free. But he hadn't known Taylor had thrown it on his desk and forgotten about it.

"Jameson, we need to call in a medical team for the op. Want to call in your sibs?"

"On it," Clay replied to Hale before Taylor could even react. He looked at Taylor and motioned for him to pull out his phone. "I'll get Hayley for the ground op, you get Brayden on call at the hospital?"

"Yeah," Taylor agreed, wandering into one of the small offices used for informal interrogations off the main communal space, wanting the privacy as he dialled Brayden out of habit more than anything.

"Hey, melon, how's the head?"

"Fine. We need you on call at the hospital tomorrow. Clay's getting Hay to be our Ambo."

"I didn't clear you for duty," Brayden scolded.

"And yet I get to go, since the cop doc did. Now shut up and listen to me, this is hard."

"Alright. What should I expect?"

"I don't know. It'll be two for check-ups, maybe injured. But I'm e-mailing you through records now. They're confidential, obviously. You're not going to… It's bad, okay, Bray?"

"Okay…." He could hear the tapping of computer keys and knew Brayden was checking his e-mails. The double click on the mouse was audible on the phone. Taylor could hear the scroll bar, and then Brayden gasped.

"Taylor, this…. Holy shit."

"I know."

"I'll be there. When's the op?"

"Daytime. We're hoping less people will be home. I'll keep you posted. Have your phone on."

"Not my first time, Taylor. Fuck." He hung up before Taylor could say anything else, and Taylor knew he would have the entire Salisbury family medical history memorized before they ever got anyone in an ambulance. That was why they used Brayden: he did his homework, and he did his job perfectly. The squad had been using Brayden as their medical contact even before the twins joined. The boss liked how he worked. Taylor hadn't appreciated how good Brayden was until his own cases ended up on Brayden's desk.

The doors opened and suits came in. Everyone stiffened, but Taylor had been expecting them. There was too much politics involved; of course Australian Secret Intelligence Service would be called in. The prime minister would be briefed. The chief of defence. Some powerful people were going to prison tomorrow, and there were other very important people who were going to have to be ready to handle the media fallout.

The boss went with them into a conference room, and the doors shut. The op planning continued, indifferent. Everyone had a job, and nothing outside of the rescue operation interested Taylor.

Taylor was aware he was not indifferent, that somewhere along the line since he'd first laid eyes on the man with those ridiculous geeky glasses, something had changed in him. He'd seen it happen to Clay, four years ago when they walked into that bar and he'd first seen Joel. He hadn't believed it could happen that fast, that something so fundamental to his being as not really giving a crap could be so easily altered. But he could admit he was no longer unaffected.

With each video he watched, each image he trolled through, each carefully articulated report or scan of a document evidencing criminal activity, Taylor felt himself change. He watched Sietta bleed, and thought of the sound of his laughter. He looked at a medical report and remembered the way he tilted his head and his hair tumbled over his shoulder like water. He looked at election results where the numbers didn't match up, and he remembered the way Sietta pushed his glasses up his nose.

He cared, and it terrified him. He couldn't get the sound of husky humour at the end of a phone line while he lay in the dark out of his mind.

Taylor rummaged through the images being catalogued from the USB, each another piece of evidence. Some he had no idea why they had been included, others made his chest ache, but one he paused on, staring.

Sietta was staring up at Micah, a hand on his cheek. Micah looked like he did now, so the image couldn't be more than a few months old. Sietta's leg was in a cast, a bandage up the whole length of his arm. His cheek was dark, his hair matted and hanging in filthy dreads. His other arm was in a sling. But the look on his face was pure adoration. All he saw was his brother, and the small rainbow flag he held in his hand.

Taylor snapped a shot of the photo on his phone, aware that it was illegal but wanting it. Needing to own it. He thought Sietta would want it, later. A long time later.

JOHNATHAN AND Louisa were meeting for brunch with several of Johnathan's conspirators. Jones was leading a team to pick them up. The house was relatively empty without Sietta's parents. Early morning surveillance showed the butler, Micah, a tutor, a gardener, and two security guards present at the house.

Clay and Taylor had asked to be put on extraction with the ambulance team, and it had been granted, with a warning about professionalism. The logs of his call with Sietta were on official record now, but as of yet, he had not entered into a relationship with the man. For now he was permitted to participate, but he knew that would change the moment his emotional capacity was compromised.

They still went in with the rest of the team, but their focus was different. They helped subdue the security, arresting them, leaving them cuffed with Harris and Mendel, but it wasn't their goal.

It was strange being on a PORS op. You wore black from head-to-toe, literally, which was always weird. As a kid, Taylor always thought the bad guys wore balaclavas when breaking in to homes, now here he was, with the face mask, ballistics helmet and goggles all on, rifle in hand as they cleared room after room.

They looked like the bad guys, and really it was only a matter of perspective. To the homeowner, they were the illegal entrants.

Clay smashed in a door with his shoulder and stumbled into Micah's bedroom, a large space with limited furniture; built-in wardrobes, a double bed in one corner, a desk, and a TV mounted on the wall. A few posters of science shows and a swim team of all things. Very little to give away anything about the boy who lived there.

Micah screamed at the sight of two massive black-clad armed gunmen entering his bedroom and threw himself on the floor. He looked far smaller on his bedroom floor, hands over his head, long body curled up like a snail, shaking. Clay went to him and squeezed his shoulder, and he scrunched up his nose at them when he looked up, frowning at the name on their chests. He was slow to catch on to what was happening, clearly not having expected anything to happen today.

"Clay?" He sniffled, and it damn near broke Taylor's heart. "You're way scarier than a Viking."

"Yeah, kid, sorry about that." Clay helped him up, gave him a quick reassuring hug, and then stood at his full height. "Where's Sietta?"

Micah didn't need to be told twice. He bolted down the hallway. The butler was screaming at him to stop, that his father would not be pleased, but Micah led them down to a secret door on the ground floor, behind the side kitchen wall.

Clay grabbed him and pulled him back, passing him off to Mendel, ignoring his protests. "Get him to Hayley!"

"On it," Mendel grunted, shepherding Micah out of the way and out of mind.

They didn't wait, Taylor shoving past Clay and leading the way down the dark hallway. They found a switch and the lights came on, revealing two doors. The first was a side entry to the back veranda, the opposite door revealed a corridor and stairs to the cellar.

Taylor thumped down them hard and kicked in the door, the wood shattering, the handle clattering to the floor when it collided with the steel cap of Taylor's boot.

The cellar was a stunning piece of architecture, all stone extravagance and two floor-to-ceiling walls of small wooden cubicles, filled with bottles of wine. The lights were dim, giving it an atmosphere that was probably supposed to be warm and inviting, but in a room set permanently to thirteen degrees, it was cold and terrifying, what with its prisoner inside.

Sietta was sitting on the edge of a cheap single steel-frame bed, chin in the palm of his hand, looking for all the world like he was bored out of his mind. His gaze ran from Taylor's splinter-encrusted boots to his helmet and back again.

"Well, now. That is impressive." He smiled faintly, but his hands were shaking. "You really wear that every time you break into people's houses? You must scare the shit out of people! What if it was the wrong house? Some poor innocent five-year-old, asleep with Fuzzy the Unicorn, and *wham*! Officers Jameson and Jameson, looking like the scariest ninjas in history break down the door."

Taylor didn't listen to him, lunging forward and kneeling in front of him. He broke every rule by putting his weapon down and reaching up to stroke Sietta's hair off his face, tilting his head left and right while Sietta laughed at him.

"I'm fine. You're the one with the busted head. Apparently. Should you even be here? Oh hey, it is you, right? I mean, you're the right size, right name stitched on your uniform, but it could be Clay under there, stroking my face….Coz that's not weird."

But Taylor's hands ran over him anyway, checking, and Sietta winced whenever he touched his hip and pushed the shirt out of the way to see the wild bruising across his stomach and side.

He hadn't even seen Clay leave, but he returned with bolt cutters and cut the chain close to Sietta's ankle, and before Sietta could say anything about it, Taylor had Sietta up, an arm looped around his waist, rifle back in his other hand as Clay led the way out.

"I can walk, you know!"

"I'm letting you walk!" Taylor snapped at him, anger covering the fear running through him. He wanted Sietta safe. Wanted him free of that house and that life. And he wanted to take him home. He was frustrated he had to take him to his brother instead.

He was furious he cared, more than he had realised now he had Sietta in his arms. He'd never felt that surge of protective fury for anyone outside his family.

"Sietta!" Micah barrelled into them as soon as they approached the ambulance, and Taylor regretfully handed them both over to Hayley and her crew.

The adrenaline was thunder in his limbs. He wanted to shoot something. He wanted to go back in and burn the house to the ground. He wanted to tear something apart with his bare hands.

Clay's hand on his shoulder was firm and restraining and calming.

"Just like that," Clay knocked his masked, helmeted head lightly against Taylor's. Taylor took a deep, calming breath and finally relaxed.

"Just like that."

"WHAT IS wrong with you people? I'm fine! I told your stupid brother I was fine. I told his brother I was fine. I told your sister I was fine, and now I'm telling you that I am absolutely fucking fine!" Sietta sounded at the end of his rope as Taylor came up on his door. The exasperation was cute and weirdly familiar. Really, the Jamesons exasperated themselves, let alone anyone else.

"Technically my twin brother is still his brother, as am I," Taylor pointed out as he walked into the room, waving a hand at Brayden. Sietta blinked owlishly at them.

"That is so not the point." Sietta's gaze narrowed at Taylor. "You know when Micah said you hit your head, he failed to mention you apparently tried to smash half your face off at the same time."

"Technically that was Clay's doing," Brayden pointed out, and Sietta cast him a dirty, unforgiving look.

"I'm fine!" Sietta snapped.

"He is fine," Brayden confirmed. "Lots of bruises. Everything else is old."

Taylor grabbed a chair and pulled it up beside Sietta's bed. He sank into it with a tired sigh. Brayden took the hint and left the hospital room, closing the door quietly behind him.

"Hi."

"You know, when you said you would arrange for us to meet up, this wasn't exactly what I was expecting. Still, I promised coffee, and I always deliver so…." Taylor carefully placed a steaming paper cup of hot hospital sludge on the bedside. Sietta stared at him like he had three heads.

"Is Micah okay?"

"Yes. He's with Clay. Last I checked they were watching Captain America. Micah has taken to calling Clay the Cap." He got the smile he was after.

They were quiet, staring at one another, and Taylor tried hard to convince himself it was normal for his heart to race just staring at someone. Sietta was hot; of course his pulse would race. Sietta was smart; of course he was turned on. Sietta was probably not filthy rich anymore, so he was no longer unattainable, and naturally Taylor's body was telling him to go for it.

But Taylor was terrified he was going to hurt him without trying. And he had a poker face Taylor wanted to annihilate because it was impossible to tell what the man was thinking.

He'd spoken to the man twice, once on a phone, and he suspected he was already doomed. Sietta Salisbury had somehow seduced him with nothing but words, air, and throaty laughter.

"Does the TV work?" Sietta gestured at the small LCD on the wall.

"I guess…." Taylor didn't want to turn it on, but Sietta had already reached for the remote and was fiddling with the buttons. The thing flickered to life, showing breaking news of the raid on the restaurant where Johnathan Salisbury had been lunching.

Wide-eyed, Sietta turned it up and watched avidly as his parents were arrested. As their friends were handcuffed and shoved into police cars. As the reporter detailed the lengthy list of crimes that were still coming to light. As the footage switched to an address about to be made by the prime minister, the headlines scrolling beneath mentioned the raid on their property at Point Piper, and that Sietta Salisbury had been found shackled in the basement.

"Congratulations," Taylor mumbled. "You killed Australia."

It was on every channel. Sietta flicked through them with mind-numbing intensity, and after a while, Taylor tuned out, watching Sietta instead. Sietta's gaze narrowed at strange places in the reports, he lost interest whenever his own name was mentioned and would flick to something else, seeking out what he thought was important and ignoring all else.

He fascinated Taylor. Even now, after everything, Sietta was cataloguing who had been arrested, what they were arrested for, linking the evidence he had collected to what was going on, and it was clear he was excessively pleased with what he was seeing. His smirk was dark, the look in his eyes that of vindication.

"You're strangely brave."

"Excuse me?" Sietta turned the volume down and stared at him as if the statement made no sense. Taylor smirked, liking that he had the power to draw Sietta's attention.

"Come on, you know what I mean. All of this…. It's huge. It's going to change a lot of things."

"A lot of things needed changing," Sietta pointed out, sounding ever so reasonable. "And not just marine wildlife sanctuaries, or whatever people are protesting about these days, as if protesting ever achieves anything when everyone making the decision is corrupt!" He froze, stopping before his rant could really get going, and looked up at the screen where those corrupt individuals were finally having to pay for their crimes.

As Minister for Environment and Energy, Johnathan Salisbury had continuously blocked new clean-energy legislation in the Senate to ensure support from coal and industrialised energy production magnates.

The support of the private companies gave him the financial backing he had needed to further the Liberal party's agenda to privatise education and health, ensuring the gap between working and upper-class Australia would widen and the middle class would effectively disappear. Australia's richest families already took home more than 70 percent more income than Australia's poorest. The collection of ministers Salisbury had funded in the House of Representatives and the Senate had blocked legislature for more than ten years that would have ensured all Australians continued to receive equal access to public education, health and services. They'd put the social autonomy of the country back decades to line their own pockets. Salisbury was only the head of the snake, the corruption running down through the system from federal government into state and even local organisations.

"You didn't need to do any of this," Taylor whispered, staring at the bruises and feeling the strange desire to lick them, as if he could lap the pain away and replace it with pleasure. He was of the opinion Sietta could use more pleasure in his life.

"You're wrong," Sietta answered simply, like it was a foregone conclusion. "No one else would have done it. I had to. I don't think it was brave, though, I wasn't scared. More resigned, I guess."

Taylor would have found the first person he saw after the initial beating and screamed what had happened to the world. His father would have suffered, been sent to the back bench, not prison, and no one else would have been implicated in anything. Instead, it was likely changes would be made to the very foundations of their political system.

Taylor couldn't fathom what Sietta had done, in part because he wasn't really sure what had been done. Politics had never been his thing. But he knew what Sietta had uncovered was causing havoc in government, and that he was considered too young to have known what he was doing. The news said so.

"Why'd you give me the USB?"

"Ah." Sietta chuckled, shaking his head. "Micah wasn't actually sure if he'd given it to you or Clay. Then when nothing happened, I wasn't even sure he'd given you the right USB!" He seemed to think that was terribly funny. Taylor gaped at him.

"The hell?"

"Well, I told him to hold on to it until he found a police officer he was absolutely certain he could trust. That was oh... a few weeks ago,

I guess?" He shrugged, completely nonchalant. "He said he gave it to one of you at the ferry, but he wasn't even sure who because it all got so crazy! Do you know those stoners jumped in because they thought it was a hot tub?"

"I thought it was a playlist or something weird...." Taylor was muttering.

Sietta's eyes became saucers, and he laughed so hard he got a stitch, curling over his side with eyes watering.

"It's not funny! I put it on my desk and forgot about it! What if I hadn't thought something was fishy about you?"

"You thought I was fishy?" He couldn't stop laughing.

"Oh, please, you were being kept in the wine cellar by your father. You're the fishiest fish ever."

"But you didn't know that because you didn't look at the USB," Sietta countered. Taylor was of the opinion it was the weirdest conversation he had ever had. He was sure Sietta was supposed to be freaking out, but then again what did he know? He didn't know anyone with PTSD. It was Taylor who was struggling to get a grip on it all. Still, it wasn't how he had imagined the conversation would go.

"I didn't know I was supposed to look at the USB. Maybe if you'd given it to me instead of Micah...."

"Hmm, you would have raced home to look at it immediately?" The laughter was never going to end, and Taylor was okay with that.

"Come on, it coulda been porn. Of course I woulda raced home to check it out!"

Sietta was really crying now, clutching his bruised side through the pain. Taylor reached out and put one large hand over the injured site and the other on Sietta's cheek, resting them on him and desperately holding himself back from letting them explore the way they wanted.

"God," Sietta groaned, the amusement dying hard and fast, replaced with a soft sigh, a hiccup of breath against his palms and a soft blush across warm cheeks. It took every shred of Taylor's self-control not to push him down onto the bed.

"I'm sorry," Taylor admitted. He didn't know when he'd said it last. He wasn't in the habit of apologising to anyone for anything.

"There was no time frame on it," Sietta assured him. "If nothing had happened in a week, I would've had Micah deliver another one, or given it to you myself whenever I figured out a way to meet you for coffee." He shrugged as if it was obvious, and Taylor forced himself to relax, pulling his hands off him and sitting back down beside the bed.

"It was dangerous to get the phone," Taylor noted, hoping his expression was sufficiently stern.

"I wanted to talk to you," Sietta answered benignly. "Micah knew that. I didn't realise he got it from you, but...."

"Technically, Clay got it." They both chuckled, knowing that was practically the same thing.

"So, what now?" Sietta looked at him expectantly. "I mean, I'm assuming I won't have a lot to do with the politics and crap going on, but what's next?"

"The police will come and take your statement."

"Odd, I thought they were here." Sietta grinned, because Taylor was there, and he liked that Sietta knew it.

"More important officers will come and take your statement. There will be some ASIS people." He looked like he expected that to be the way things would go, so Taylor kept going. "It'll take a while. They'll want to know how you got all the things on the USB. After that you'll have to stay in the city, there will be hearings, but it's up to you. What do you want to do?"

Sietta sighed, looking out the window at the blue sky beyond, for a moment looking far younger than he was, pale and slight and frightened. But his gaze sharpened and his scowl returned.

"I want a shower," he decided with certainty. "Then I'll talk to your police and ASIS people, but I need to find a lawyer."

That was an exceedingly good idea.

"I know a lawyer. He's very good." The best, but Taylor was biased. His father's firm Jameson, Grant, and London was regarded as one of the best in Sydney, but that didn't mean Sietta would want to hire them. "You won't have to say much in this statement. It'll be more like a fact check of events and what's on the USB. Anything you don't want to answer, just tell them you'll check with your lawyer first."

"Brilliant! So while I'm talking to police, you can call your lawyer friend, and then when I'm done, you can take me home."

Taylor stared at him with wide eyes. Sietta stared back, one brow arched. Taylor sighed and got up to stretch.

"I'll just go let those other more important officers know you're ready for them, then." He rolled his eyes and headed for the door. He was closing it when he heard Sietta's words.

"I never said they were more important."

"SIETTA SALISBURY is hot!" Hayley hissed in his ear as she grabbed Taylor's arm and hauled him farther down the corridor, away from the crowd of people waiting their turn to talk.

"Told you." Clay smirked, coming up on Taylor's other side with Brayden. Taylor sighed. Family reunions in hospital corridors were never a good sign.

"Funny too." Brayden smirked knowingly, rubbing a finger across the blush still heating Taylor's cheeks. Taylor shoved Brayden's hand away and fished his phone out of his pocket but didn't call yet, not wanting the audience.

"He's a victim," Taylor mumbled, distracted.

"Uh-huh. No one here thinks that man is a victim. Well, he is, but not in the way you'd think, but more the 'my dad beat the shit out of me and kept me prisoner in the wine cellar, but I got revenge on everyone and half the government while I was at it' kind of way," Clay clarified. Hayley was gaping, looking around at the nearby rooms and spotting one with a TV in it.

"I gotta see the news!"

"And she's gone." Clay smirked, pleased with himself.

"Why didn't I think of that." Brayden watched her hurry off and sit on the end of the poor patient's bed, settling in to watch.

"You're a father and a doctor. Sleep deprivation," Taylor surmised.

"He really is okay." Brayden knew what Taylor wanted to ask. "Physically, anyway, the only concern is his leg, which can't have been out of a cast more than two weeks and is still quite weak. There's a burn on his arm, but it's healing well and there shouldn't be much scarring. Mentally, I'm sure there's a lot going on under the surface, but taken at face value, he's ridiculously astute."

"Good word for it," Taylor grumbled.

"Micah's fine," Clay added.

"Good. I... I have to make a call."

"To who?" his brothers asked in eerie unison.

"Sietta needs a lawyer."

"Ah." Why were they doing it at the same time like that? Creepy as hell! "Good luck!" They each squeezed a shoulder and moved past him to go check on the progress of the police currently swarming Sietta's hospital room.

Taylor sighed and hurried outside, dialling and waiting for the pickup. It didn't take long, it never did.

"Tay, the raid is all over the news! You're wearing a balaclava and Clay's holding a little boy's hand!" On what planet did that statement make sense?

"I know, Dad." He sighed, wondering what it was with his family. They picked up on the strangest things. "We always wear balaclavas, and that's Micah Salisbury."

"Oh. Right. He's very pretty."

"He's very gay. Tell Leila," Taylor ordered, hoping his sister didn't take it personally. He doubted it would mean much to her at all, except that they could certainly be the best of friends forever now without any fear of him one day falling in love with her and destroying their friendship. Something like that.

"Sure. Are you alright? Should you have been on a job with a concussion?"

"I was cleared for duty. My head's fine; it's just bruised. The crack's really small."

"Nothing out of the ordinary, then," his father joked, and Taylor looked at the sky, begging for normalcy.

"Sietta needs a lawyer."

"Son, that boy needs more than one."

"Well, you have a whole damn firm. How many more do you need?" Taylor knew his father was being deliberately obtuse.

"Are you sure he doesn't want to find his own lawyer?"

"I said I knew one; he said call. I did. I figure it's up to him whether he hires you or not."

There was silence on the other end. It was pretty normal. His father liked to think about work decisions. Unfortunately, he liked to stop midconversation for indeterminate periods of time while he thought about said decisions. Taylor had once stood in front of the man for twenty-seven minutes while he silently argued the pros and cons of possible punishments, after Taylor melted Hayley's favourite My Little Ponies in the microwave because, he claimed, keeping horses in captivity was bad. In the end his mother had grounded him for a month and he'd not seen an ice cream for two.

"Chloe!" Taylor groaned and pulled the phone away from his ear at his dad's bellow. "I'm heading into the office for a while!"

Which meant he was going to go get things ready to meet his new client.

"Oh, dear, do you have to? The boys had a raid this morning, it's all over the news, you know? I was hoping we could get them over for dinner, I'm so worried about poor Tay's head."

"My head's fine," Taylor mumbled.

"He says his head's fine."

"Oh, is that Tay? Why didn't you say so!" The crashing could only mean the phone was changing hands. "Tay? Sweetheart! How's your head? Should you have been wearing a helmet like that when you're incapacitated?"

"I'm not incapacitated!"

"Well, no more than usual," his mother interrupted, and he shook his fist at the sky.

"I'm fine! We're not coming over for dinner. There's too much clean up to do on this job; we won't finish early."

"Oh, alright, oh… your father needs his phone. He said he's going to the office for a few hours."

"I know, Mum! I asked him to!"

"Oh, well, no one told me!"

"Because it has nothing to do with you!"

"Taylor Jameson, how dare you presume that anything that involves your father does not involve me? I'll have you know…." The phone disconnected, and Taylor slumped, shoving his phone back in his pocket and turning to find Clay grinning by the door.

"ASIS kicked everyone out. Spoke to the boss quick when he came out. He said they won't release Sietta and Micah to family. He said Sietta told him quite firmly he and Micah were going home with us."

"Uh… yeah, sorry. He just said it." And Taylor wanted it too badly to argue, too much to even think he should check with Clay.

"Nah, it's good. I was just gonna say I'm happy to go to Joel's tonight. And he's happy to have Micah with us, if you want. The boss thinks it's best to split them up for safety, but only if they're both okay with it."

Blinking, because he had no idea what anyone else thought he was going to do with a guy he'd only had three conversations with, but clearly it wasn't what he was thinking was going to happen, all Taylor could think to do was agree.

"Sure. That'll work." It would give Sietta time to sit down and talk with their dad. After some sleep.

Clay bumped their shoulders together. "Come on, stupid. Boss wanted to talk to you. Give you feeding instructions for your new pet and all that."

5
MILK AND APPLES

"I'M GOING with him because he thinks I'm suspect," Sietta reiterated so loudly, Taylor and Clay shared a disgruntled look in the hallway outside. Their boss was inside Sietta's hospital room, checking for the last time that Sietta really wanted to go home with the Jamesons, which the boss actually thought was a good idea and just wanted to make sure Sietta thought so too.

He'd also warned Taylor that nothing could happen that wasn't above board. They weren't dating at the time events occurred, and it was highly unlikely Taylor would ever personally be required to offer testimony on what had occurred in the lead up to Sietta's emancipation, as he hadn't been involved in the op. But just to be on the safe side, he'd felt the need to lecture Taylor. It was Sietta's decision where he went, but it was in Sietta's best interests to offer him some form of protection. Sietta wanting to go home with Taylor made protecting him a more straightforward procedure, provided Taylor didn't complicate it by doing anything too left of field, like sleeping with the victim. The boss had been supremely clear on that. He'd obviously listened to the phone call Taylor had shared with Sietta, but Taylor didn't bother to comment on it because he was being lectured and he was getting what he wanted. It was awkward, knowing strangers at the AFP had overheard him hitting on Sietta.

"He thinks you're suspect?" Nikau Parata enquired. He was better known as 'boss.' Taylor was certain he'd never used the man's name in conversation. Parata wasn't a small man, but then most of the squad weren't. They needed to be intimidating, and capable of taking down hard criminals who had no compulsion to be gentle. But it wasn't just the man's size that made him intimidating. Nikau Parata carried himself like he was Jesus and the sea would part around him. Taylor knew how hard it was to sit under his gaze, but Sietta appeared completely unfazed.

"Fishy, then. He thinks I'm fishy. That was his word for it too. I'm fishy," Sietta announced proudly.

"You're fishy...." Their boss clearly didn't understand. "You want to go with the Jamesons because they think you're suspect-fishy?"

"Yes." He sounded so completely sure of his decision and a little peeved that anyone would dare to suggest he shouldn't be.

"You're certain—"

"Enough! Yes, I am completely certain. Everyone else on the damn planet thought it was completely fucking normal that everyone thought I was dead or MIA or whatever! Taylor Jameson is the only person in six years who thought I was fishy! So yes, I am bloody well going home with him, and no, I don't think there is anything suspect about that at all!"

Clay looked sideways at Taylor, smug, and Taylor bumped his shoulder, and they walked into the small hospital room together. Sietta didn't know it yet, but he was one of them. That conversation was straight out of Saturday barbeque.

"Boss."

"Boys," he sighed, waving a hand at a furious-looking Salisbury. "Just go home!"

Now that the raid was done, their reports would be handed over to ASIS and the Australian Federal Police, who would take over the case. All they had to do was sign the paperwork when they went in to the office and they would be little more than glorified self-appointed bodyguards.

Clay and Taylor parted so the boss could leave and then closed ranks again, looking at Sietta, who sat on the edge of the bed, long legs hanging down to scrape the floor. He was dressed in the clothes they had found him in, and he looked worn and tired as he glared at them, as if daring them to say he couldn't go with them.

"Micah's waiting by the car with Brayden," Clay said, and the transformation was immediate. Sietta smiled brightly at them and hopped off the edge of the bed, running a hand through his messy hair and waving at the door as if to say "lead the way."

They had arranged a back-end exit, using Brayden's car to avoid the media circus camped out front. They took the emergency exit stairs down to the ambulance bay and found the Holden station wagon hiding behind two ambulances in the wash bay. Brayden was there talking quietly to a laughing Micah, but as soon as Micah caught sight of them, he sprinted across the cement floor and threw himself at his brother.

"I can't believe this is happening," he whispered into Sietta's neck, but his brother held on tight and stroked his hair and crab-walked them back toward the car.

"Everything's gonna be okay, Micah. I promise. I'll get it all sorted."

"Like I'm worried about that!" Micah tugged on the ends of Sietta's hair to make him look down and meet his gaze. "I'm really happy we're free."

Clay got them into the car, putting Micah in the front with Brayden, a baseball hat low on his head, Sietta hidden between Clay and Taylor on the back seat. Taylor didn't miss the way Sietta pressed in against his side but barely touched Clay, and it made him smile.

"Your place first?" Brayden asked Taylor, after buckling up and getting them away from the hospital.

"Nah, drop Clay at Joel's first," Taylor replied, looking at Sietta. "We were thinking Micah could stay with Clay and Joel tonight, until you know what's happening next?"

"Who's Joel?" Micah asked immediately, and Sietta looked to Clay for an answer, appearing as perplexed as his brother.

"My boyfriend?" Clay seemed confused by the answer, because everyone else always knew about Joel, as if by magic. In reality Chloe Jameson happened to know a lot of people and didn't often stop talking about her children, so anyone who knew them always already knew everything. "He's a professor at Macquarie University."

"He can't come home with us?" Sietta asked.

"He can if you want him to," Taylor replied quickly. "It could be a legal issue later. Joel's a registered foster carer for emergency cases, particularly for gay children. Our boss was concerned about Micah being underage. He needs to be with a registered carer, and it can't be you, because a court could attest you haven't been cleared as sound in mind. Yet," Taylor clarified in case Sietta took that to mean Taylor thought he was nuts. "But we could all stay at Joel's, it'll just be crowded. Or we can go to Joel's tomorrow."

"Okay," Sietta agreed. "He can stay at Joel's. But I want to see him tomorrow, as soon as possible." He nodded to Micah, and the kid grinned like he was going to a sleepover, apparently reassured by Sietta's demand to see him in the morning.

"Is Leila gonna come over?" Maybe he was having a sleepover, after all.

"I thought you were gay?" Taylor squinted at the kid.

"I don't see how that matters," Micah protested, turning in his chair to look questioningly at all three of them in the back seat.

"It matters in so far as you're in a car with three older brothers who get to decide whether you get to see said girl, to what degree, frequency, and duration. And said big brothers look like they could tear your head off and eat your brains should you upset the fair maiden." Sietta snickered.

"Oh. Right." Micah bit his lip, clearly reconsidering his response. "I'm gay. Leila knows. She wants to be BFFs. I think it's a stellar idea. Can she come and stay at Joel's house too?"

"Sure thing," Clay agreed, apparently liking this response more, if his pleased tone was anything to go by.

"Much better." Sietta smiled at them all, and Taylor wondered what he was getting himself into. Sietta was far from the simple rich kid-cum-musician he liked to pretend he was. He seemed to control conversations flawlessly, with whoever he came across, and he recalled Sietta saying as much on the phone. He watched people. Saw them. Listened to them. He'd simply omitted the "I control them" part. Taylor had to admit that part sounded creepy, he would have left it off too.

"How many brothers and sisters do you have, anyway?" Micah asked Brayden, as if he were a safer option. It was probably true. But he was wide-eyed and fascinated, as if their family were in some way unusual.

"How many do you have?" Brayden asked, even though the twins both knew he was aware of the answer. He was simply being the older brother. Annoying.

"Three. Anders, Viola, and Sietta. Anders is getting married soon."

"Was," Sietta corrected idly, and Micah spun to stare at him. "Well, I doubt a socialite's going to want to marry a guy who's likely going to prison along with the rest of his 'suddenly famed for all the wrong reasons' family." There was ice in his tone, and Taylor ran a soothing hand down his arm. Sietta clearly disapproved of Anders getting anything besides a long prison sentence, but there was more to it than that. A touch of melancholy for Micah and himself because they were forever tainted with the same brush, perhaps.

"Ah… true." Micah pondered this a minute. "Poor Anders. I mean, I think he really likes her?"

The expression on Sietta's face clearly said he didn't feel sorry for their older brother at all. Taylor wondered what Anders had done to so completely alienate Sietta, but it sadly wasn't hard to guess.

"She's better off finding out now. She can get away clean," Sietta mumbled, and while his expression was hard to read, the way he pressed in harder against Taylor's side, subconsciously seeking shelter, was not. Taylor gave in to temptation and laid an arm over the back of the seats and Sietta's shoulders, warm and heavy. Sietta tensed at first but then relaxed underneath him.

"I have five siblings," Brayden interrupted with a chuckle. "I'm the oldest, and then there are Clay and Taylor, Hayley, Ashley, and Leila."

"Oh, cool! So it's just Ashley I haven't met yet!" Micah exclaimed excitedly.

They all froze and realised it was true. It was a miracle the kid was alive.

"Waaaaait." Sietta leaned forward in his seat and squinted at each of them in turn. "Bray, Clay, Tay, Hay, and Lei? Seriously?"

"Our mum had a C-section for Ash…. Dad named him while she was unconscious." Clay appeared amused as ever by his mother's ridiculous penchant for rhyme.

"Mum's a writer," Brayden admitted softly. "She thought it was funny."

"That's so fucked up," Micah exhaled, awed.

"Language," Sietta snapped, still eyeing them all as if he wasn't sure he should believe them.

"Brayden named his son Jay…." Taylor added, deliberately to make things worse.

"You're shitting me!" Sietta exhaled loudly, gaping at the man.

"Language," Micah mimicked, and the brothers shared a dark look before Micah turned back to Brayden, apparently still of the opinion he was the one with answers. "Is Ashley also a giant? Are your parents? I mean, even Leila is, like, six feet tall! She's all freaked out about it because her graduation formal photos will look super strange if she can't find a guy taller than her. I don't think that really matters, though? I mean aren't all supermodels taller than guys in photos?"

"Leila is not a supermodel," Taylor snapped immediately. Over his dead body would she be such an image-obsessed lackey of modern culture.

"She could be, though…." Clay mused. "Do you think she wants to be?" Micah was nodding. It was a bad sign.

"And she doesn't graduate until next year! That's a next-year problem!" Taylor intervened. "And she has four brothers. One of us can be her date!" That would be fine, they were all taller than her and would have her home way before midnight, so Mum would be pleased.

"Social suicide," Clay countered, glaring at him. Clay would allow him to ruin Leila's night over his dead body. Taylor was still keeping it as an option.

"Ashley's a fireman," Brayden finally managed to reply, and Micah let out an explosive sigh as he flopped back into his seat.

"So he's huge."

"He's not that big," Clay and Taylor rumbled together, looking out their windows. They'd spent their whole lives ribbing Ashley. They weren't about to stop just because he was finally filling out.

They turned off the main highway, and Brayden wove through Killara's backstreets until he pulled up on the curb by a cute terrace house with an immaculate façade and beautiful trellis courtyard at the front.

"Oh my God, you live here?" Micah was already out the door, not expecting an answer.

"Joel lives here," Clay corrected anyway, getting out as the front door opened and Joel appeared. He was only six foot tall, which was tall enough but still looked tiny when surrounded by Jamesons. His brown hair was kept long around his ears and curled gently at the ends, framing his face. He was far more tan than Clay, and his grey eyes always seemed amused. His glasses never quite sat straight on his nose, and his clothes were forever slightly askew from the messenger bag he carried everywhere. He wasn't pretty, but he was pleasing to look at, and underneath his clothes was a compact body that he forced to the gym every day. Taylor waved through the window, watched Clay kiss the man hungrily, and then each man put a hand on Micah's shoulder and squeezed. Micah looked perfectly happy to be there, already asking Joel questions about the terrace.

"He'll be fine," Brayden said to Sietta.

"Safest place for him," Sietta agreed, waving that they could go, and Brayden wasted no time pulling out. "But how come Joel's able to be registered with child services? I thought that wasn't permitted when you weren't married, and well… that's not legal for us?"

"Yeah, but we petitioned years ago for a legal compensation on the condition that all children fostered with Joel were LGBT, since they were heavily represented in the system but also misrepresented in availability of homes. My lawyer friend's really good and had him registered on the condition he passed an insane number of police checks. And that all his references were police checked." Taylor rolled his eyes, because really… they were the police. Getting police checked. It was hilarious, really.

"So you do this a lot," Sietta surmised.

"Oh, I wouldn't say that." Brayden mused, but failed to elaborate.

"But Micah's okay here, yeah? I mean, Clay's there to protect him and Joel's a good guy?" He couldn't hide the big brother concern.

"Joel's the best. Micah's not the first at-risk kid to stay there. He's a teacher; he's really good with teenagers. Taught high school before switching to university lecturing. Sets boundaries, curfews, homework, chores… the whole shebang," Brayden assured him.

"And he'll be safe." Sietta still wanted clarification.

"I promise," Taylor agreed, pulling him in close and squeezing his shoulder gently in reassurance. "It's unlikely any retaliation would be directed at Micah anyway. His name hasn't even come up in the news reports, but it's safer this way, just until the media attention dies down."

"Okay." Sietta didn't sound as though he was trying to convince himself anymore. Taylor figured that was a good thing.

Even though the back seat was partly evacuated, Sietta didn't move away, staying close, tucked in against Taylor's side, and watching the world pass by them through the window as Brayden pulled away from the curb and headed toward Crows Nest. The conversation died, but everyone seemed fine with that, and it didn't take them long to get to North Sydney. Brayden took them down into the carport in case any media had thought to look there, but no one even knew the Jamesons had been involved in the raid on the Salisbury property, so the place was quiet.

"Give me a call if you need anything," Brayden ordered, and Taylor agreed, watching Sietta climb wearily out of the car, then waving Brayden off as they both headed for the stairs.

"Your place is nice," Sietta murmured as he wandered into the living room. Taylor just smiled, wry, because people always expected a pigsty, but he and Clay kept an immaculate apartment. The front door had a small entry area, but it opened quickly into a large kitchen area with two living spaces coming off it; a dining area to the left of the kitchen and a lounge at the far end. It was all white tiled and white walled, with silver appliances and a black marble bench top. The dining area was glass walled and opened out to a large balcony with views over several buildings to the ocean. It wasn't a great view, but the balcony caught the sea breeze, and that was really all they had been interested in. Off the right side of the lounge sat a short hallway, to the left of it lay Clay's room, to the right Taylor's. A bathroom was tucked between them, an en suite off Taylor's bedroom. The bathroom with the same black and white tile as the rest of the apartment. The bedrooms had a pale grey carpet and white walls. All the pictures hanging had matching black frames, and the few bookcases around were black and white, and kept clean and tidy. Nothing was ever left on the floor, and they had no problem putting time aside together to clean. They'd always lived together, two sides of the same coin, and it showed in their living space.

"Thanks." He smiled, still pleased that Sietta liked it. "You should lie down. It's been a long day."

"Will you sleep with me?"

Taylor nearly choked but managed to nod. That had not been what he was expecting at all, and it must have showed on his face.

"Not like that! I don't want to do anything," Sietta clarified. "I want to stay with you. If that's okay. I want to listen to someone else breathe. I don't... I don't sleep well, at night. It would help, I think. If someone's breathing here with me, then I know I'm not there." In the cellar.

"It's okay," Taylor agreed immediately. He would have agreed to anything Sietta asked for at that point. Nothing, everything, anything in between, it was all fine.

"Okay." He stood there, expectantly. Awkward.

"This way." Taylor rolled his eyes at both of them, leading the way through to his bedroom. It was a nice space; large and airy, with a huge, heavy ebony king-size bed and thick white quilt, white sheets, and a large black-and-white framed photo of a lighthouse by an ocean surrounded by dark rocks on the shoreline. He hadn't taken the photo; it was an image he'd seen that resonated in him. The image on the wall was only one half of a two piece work, the other showing more water, the sun, and a seagull soaring through the grey sky. That half was in Clay's room.

There were two large floor-to-ceiling windows, but the view was nothing special, they were there for light, and he'd hung heavy white blackout curtains along the length of the wall that he went over and closed.

"There's a shower in the en suite. The towels in there are clean. You can borrow anything of mine from the closet. I'm gonna make some tea, okay?"

"That'd be great," Sietta agreed, already walking toward the shower, as if drawn by a siren. Taylor watched him disappear, noted that Sietta didn't close the door the whole way, and smiled. Trust. They didn't have much between them, but there was a great deal of trust, and from Sietta, Taylor suspected, that was the greatest gift of all.

He went out to put the kettle on.

TAYLOR PUT a steaming mug of pear green tea on either side of the bed, and went and showered in the main bathroom, putting on a pair of boxers and cautiously going back to his room. Sietta was in one of his T-shirts. A grey monstrosity with RIOT in giant black letters across the back. It looked like a dress on him and made Taylor bite his tongue to keep from laughing, but his grin was huge. Sietta chuckled at him, low and wry, and waved a hand at the bed.

"I think maybe our clothes sizing is entirely incompatible."

"Oh, I don't know, I could get used to this." Taylor smirked. And he could. He really liked what he was seeing; liked Sietta in his shirt, on his bed, and his mouth went dry when he saw the long length of gold thighs, crossed through his sheets and realised Sietta was only wearing the shirt, nothing else. But then he had nothing else that would have fit him anyway. He went and collected Sietta's clothes and put them in the wash before coming back in and climbing in beside him on the bed, propping himself up against the headboard and watching Sietta sip the tea.

All Sietta's height was in his legs, his torso slender but lightly muscled with not a scrap of fat on him. That made Taylor want to punch things because it was obvious the man hadn't had a decent meal in a long, long time. His arms were long and slender, and he moved them with an effortless grace that came naturally to him. His neck was so long, Taylor wanted to lick his way up it to the man's full lips, a perfectly balanced bow of redder-than-usual skin that called to Taylor. But everything on

Sietta's face was in perfect symmetry, not just his lips, and Taylor's gaze was drawn, as always, to those eyes, such an intensely bright blue, like the ocean in the sunlight, framed with thick black lashes and slender brows. His hair was loose and hung wet around his shoulders, sticking to his skin in wild patterns.

"It's nice to be clean," Sietta admitted. "I only got to have a hot shower when they needed me to go to an event, and then I wasn't doing it for me, you know? And cold showers suck."

Taylor didn't trust his voice. He wanted to murder Johnathan Salisbury and had to settle for watching him go to prison. That didn't sit well with him at all.

"The tea's really nice," Sietta said, softer this time. Taylor sighed heavily, wondering if Sietta had had much of anything he enjoyed over the years. He doubted it.

"Did you call your lawyer friend?"

"Yeah," Taylor managed to agree, sighing because he didn't want to talk. Talking would lead to getting angry, and he didn't want to be angry around Sietta. He wanted to keep him safe. Realising that was almost as horrifying as being angry. "Yeah… he'll come see you tomorrow."

"Okay."

Sietta stared at him while they drank their tea. When Sietta put the mug down, Taylor did the same, and he didn't wait for permission, simply wrapped his large hand around one small wrist and pulled Sietta to him. Sietta stiffened, but Taylor shifted until he was lying, propped up against all the pillows, with Sietta tucked in against his side, safe in the hollow of his body and the sheets. And only then did Sietta relax.

Listening to Sietta breathe, Taylor fell asleep, hoping Sietta found a way to do the same.

THE PHONE was ringing. Taylor groaned and pulled his pillow over his head. Then he realised he was alone and sat up quickly, searching the room, but Sietta was nowhere to be seen. Sighing, he forced himself to get up and wandered into the main living area.

Sietta was sitting at the bench, Taylor's laptop in front of him, a cup of tea beside him, half empty. He looked Taylor up and down, and Taylor could see him swallow, mouth dry. It made him smirk, and he wandered over and, without thinking about what he was doing, gently stroked Sietta's cheek before reaching past him for his phone.

"You can use anything you like." He nodded to the laptop, ignoring the stunned look on Sietta's face, liking that he'd put it there as he redialled.

"I'm chatting to Micah on Skype..." But Sietta was still looking him over.

Taylor liked that Sietta had helped himself to some of his clothes. Sietta was wearing another oversized shirt over the scuffed trousers he'd been wearing at the time of the raid.

"Oh, Tay, it's all good. I was just calling to make sure you were home. When you didn't answer, I assumed you were still in bed." His father sounded slightly winded, as if he'd been walking up stairs. Of course, because that was the natural assumption. Taylor sighed, ready to say something else, when there was a knock on the door.

"Come let me in."

"You have a key," Taylor grumbled, heading to the door anyway.

"No, your mother has a key, and if I'd asked for it, she would have asked why, and then she would be here as well. I thought it better to get you to let me in."

Taylor opened the door, and his father was there, in his suit. He had a briefcase and a stern look on his face that was all business and no father.

Daniel handed him the morning paper, his expression dark. When Taylor looked down at it, he understood why. Johnathan Salisbury's face was the last thing he wanted to see before he'd even had a cup of coffee. The headline was typical rage fodder for the masses. Exposed! Conspiracy! Lies! He shoved it under his armpit and made a mental note to call the office and see what police presence they thought was needed.

Taylor led him back through the house to where Sietta was looking from one of them to the other. It was exceedingly obvious they were related.

"Your father is a lawyer." Just stating the facts.

"It's a pleasure to meet you, Sietta."

"If you say so." Sietta waved a hand at the chairs surrounding them. "Please, sit down somewhere, or I'm going to get a crick in my neck. Apples, trees, all that jazz." Whatever the hell that was supposed to mean.

"I'm Daniel Jameson."

"Of Jameson, Grant, and London." Sietta knew immediately. "Wow. That's a big firm…." He eyed Taylor with renewed interest, squinting as if trying to see something invisible. "It's strange, you don't look like a rich kid. Did you go to public school?" He said it like public schools were the devil, and he had Daniel in stitches already.

"Of course I went to public school," Taylor grumbled, tossing the paper on the table so Sietta could read it if he wanted. "There shouldn't be any private schools! And I'm not a rich kid! I'm a police officer!"

"Hey, wait, so a famous lawyer and a writer had six kids, and every last one of them decides to take a job in the public sector?" He was gaping at Daniel now. "What did you feed them?"

"Milk," Daniel and Taylor said at the same time. It was the same answer Taylor had given Micah, and the one they always gave to that same question, which they seemed to get a lot. It also had something to do with Brayden having been in a Milkybar Kid commercial when he was little, and then getting fired when he couldn't say *delicious* properly because he had a lisp. Of course, getting fired had only made the lisp worse until he finally grew out of when his adult teeth came in.

"Ha." Sietta frowned at them both.

"Technically, Leila's undecided," Taylor offered, because they still had two years before Leila would finish school and have to decide what she wanted to do with her life.

"Please, Mister Salisbury. We have a lot to discuss. Are you certain you're ready for this?" Daniel seemed unconvinced, but that he was there at all said he was ready if Sietta was.

"I've been ready for this for years," Sietta replied immediately, all the softness and humour evaporating, leaving a dark look on his face and colouring his voice with distance. Sietta looked at the headline on the paper, but his expression was unreadable. Daniel blinked but took the change in stride, sitting beside Sietta at the coffee table and pulling out his files.

"Well, then…. Let's start with the charges and what's likely to happen there."

Taylor ignored them, going in to the bedroom and putting on some shorts and a T-shirt, then leaving the apartment. It was not his place to listen to Sietta's legal proceedings. If the man wanted to talk about it, he could fill him in later. For now, Taylor was happy knowing the only man he really trusted to handle it had everything in hand.

He ran his usual track, a twenty-kilometre circuit through Crows Nest and the surrounds, making sure he spent as much time in view of the ocean as possible. They'd gotten Sietta and Micah free of that house, and Sietta seemed fine, but underneath, Taylor knew that couldn't be true. And he was trying extremely hard to just be present and not say anything or push, but he wanted nothing more than to lock the door and never allow the world in. That was exactly what Johnathan Salisbury had done. So all Taylor could do was run, and try to burn off the anger.

CLAY WAS sitting on the fence when he got back. He hopped off and fell into step beside him, gesturing to their father's car on the street and rolling his eyes when Taylor pointed up toward their apartment. They went to the small pool in their complex, and Taylor didn't bother taking off his clothes. He walked into the water and sighed in relief at the cool chill that sank through him.

"Micah had nightmares," Clay said softly. "Nothing too extreme, he woke screaming a few times. Joel sat with him, made him Milo. He's better at it than me. Doesn't get angry."

"He doesn't know what we know," Taylor countered, knowing how Clay felt.

"I rang the boss, told him they were fine. He said the child services paperwork was all there, so Joel went in to sign it all with Micah, dropped me off here on the way."

Taylor didn't ask why Joel went. Joel was the safer option. Joel wouldn't have to drop everything and run to work to do a raid. Joel wouldn't be recognised by criminals. Joel had been a foster child himself and understood the mind frame of the dispossessed. Joel had a nine-to-five job and worked with kids every day. Joel knew what the hell he was doing, and Micah trusted him. All of that went unsaid, but Taylor saw the feeling of quiet inadequacy in the way Clay's shoulders slumped and knew it for what it was.

"Hurts not to be able to do anything," he said darkly, and Clay grunted in agreement.

"It's all over the news."

"That was always gonna happen," Taylor noted wryly. "I just want to keep him out of it for as long as possible. He doesn't.... This shouldn't have happened to him."

Clay was quiet, watching him, clearly unsure what to say, but also with a lot of things he wanted to say. "Was he okay last night?"

"I guess? I don't really know. I fell asleep before him and he was already up when I woke up. Hard to say, I sleep like the dead...." A fact they both knew well. Clay was a lighter sleeper, but even he usually had a perfectly sound night's sleep. It came with the job; you took sleep when you could get it, and it didn't matter what was going on around you; you slept. Sietta was different. He'd said on the phone he had insomnia, and Taylor could well understand why. He wasn't surprised he hadn't seen Sietta asleep, if the man had slept at all.

"He trusts you," Clay mumbled, sounding a little surprised, which irked Taylor. He was a dependable guy. Sure, he was an asshole, but he could be relied on for anything. If Taylor Jameson said he was going to do something, it got done. Simple as that, and Clay knew it. So it hurt that he seemed so surprised.

"Don't look at me like that!" Clay scowled darkly. "I'm just.... He's gotta be freaking out, right? I mean, I know he's playing it all calm on the surface, but really, he's been a prisoner since he was sixteen! It's a miracle he even knows what trust is, let alone that he trusts a complete stranger."

That was all very true. That didn't mean he had to stop scowling.

"You're really into him," Clay murmured, a hint of amazement in his voice, but he looked happy with the concept. Taylor felt his ears heating, but he didn't bother denying it. He was interested. He didn't think he'd been interested like this, ever.

"He's different." As if that explained everything. Maybe it did.

"You're different with him," Clay pointed out, as if nervous what Taylor would think of it. But Taylor absorbed it, knowing if it was Clay saying so, it must be true.

"How so?"

"Not so much an ass." Clay grinned at him, and Taylor rolled his eyes, grabbed his brother's wrist, and hauled him fully dressed into the pool, the both of them wrestling and washing away the dirt of it, at least for the moment. It was easy to let the job get to you, but they were good at pushing it aside as well.

"You think it was safe to leave him with the old man?"

"I think if he had a problem with it, we would have found Dad on the street when we got here." Taylor smirked. Sietta didn't seem the type to put up with much if he wasn't being forced to. He'd had enough of that, or something.

"Maybe so," Clay agreed, but his face was a mask of concentration. "What if he's just waiting for his chance to kill you in your sleep? Kid could be completely bonkers."

"Then I guess I've got five or six years to find out," Taylor deadpanned. "Maybe longer. I mean, it took him that long to find a way out of the wine cellar, so I figure I've got at least that long." Clay gaped at him before the laughter bellowed out of him, and he dragged them both from the pool.

6
WHOOSH, NO PANTS

LAUGHTER FILTERED loud and bright even through the door. Clay and Taylor shared a look and entered warily, finding Daniel and Sietta on the floor, surrounded by sheets from the case file, a mug of tea in each of their hands. They looked up a little guiltily to where Clay and Taylor stood shoulder to shoulder.

"Do you even, just for a moment, think maybe you're drunk and seeing double?" Sietta looked between them.

"I wish that were true," Daniel sighed, shaking his head. "Sadly, there has never been a day I was not completely aware there were two of them. Four hands are so much more troublesome than two."

"Excuse me?" Clay frowned at them both. Taylor didn't bother to reply.

"See what I have to live with? This, multiplied six times!" Daniel looked to Sietta for sympathy, but Sietta was staring at Taylor, a strange mix of wistful longing and amusement on his face.

"Horrifying," Sietta agreed quietly, clearly still amused.

"Hilarious," Taylor finally snorted. "You're both just hilarious. Did you actually do any work, or did you just have a chat?"

"Oh, we worked," Daniel assured him. "I'll go down to the courthouse to file everything this afternoon, but it's really just a formality. The Salisburys will be going to prison regardless, what with the terror laws the way they are now, but this way Sietta and Micah should walk away with a significant fund to set themselves up with."

"That's good," Taylor grumbled, not sure why Daniel Jameson looked so pleased with himself, and knowing it was rarely a good thing.

Clay put the kettle on, and Taylor found himself migrating to Sietta's side, reaching down to tangle his fingers through the raven-dark hair, amazed at the soft, silky quality of it. Fine strands that stuck to his skin and tangled on his limbs. He could get used to that. He thoroughly approved of the way Sietta subconsciously leaned into the touch, looking up at him with a quiet smile.

"I wrote a book," he admitted timidly. "Your dad's going to take it to a few publishers for me, see if anyone's interested."

"Are you shitting me?" Clay dropped the mug he had just picked up, caught it before it shattered on the tiles, and continued to gape at them all. "Interested? I want to read the damn thing, and every publisher in the stupid country's going to want it. You'll make a fortune!"

"Yes, he will," Daniel agreed, laughing at Clay as he attempted and failed to regain his composure as he grumbled around the kettle. "But I get to read it first. I need to check he can't be sued for anything in it, but I doubt that will be a problem, and I can still scout publishers while I'm reading. They'll be held on a gag order until sentencing finishes for the trial, but we can still do the groundwork now."

"When did you write it?" Taylor was looking at the top of Sietta's head as if he could see into it, like a magic eight ball, wondering how he wasn't completely crazy. Maybe he was, and he was just really good at hiding it? Time would tell. Maybe.

"I started it more as a journal, I guess? I wanted to keep a record, to write it down so it wasn't going around and around in my head? After a year or so, I started to realise it could be worth something one day. Evidence if nothing else, but also... I don't know, people find that stuff interesting, right? And if I could get paid for it, I'd have something if I got free." He shrugged, as if it had seemed a little irrelevant at the time, and as if it maybe still was. But Taylor heard the small things Sietta tried not to say. After the first year, when Sietta had started giving up hope of being free. All he'd wanted was to get it out of his head, because he wasn't going to get to tell anyone else. The despair behind it was the elephant in the room, and one he forced himself to push aside, because Sietta was choosing to do the same. He only hoped the damn thing didn't go all water for elephants on their asses and stampede them into an early grave when they least expected it.

"Well, if it's alright with all of you, I need to go back to my office and finish all this paperwork, get things rolling."

"Thank you," Sietta cut in immediately, but Daniel put his hand up to stall him from saying anything else. His smile was tinged with sadness as he reached out to take Sietta's hand, squeezing it gently.

"It is my pleasure. I'm very pleased you've chosen to trust me with your affairs." And Taylor knew it was true; nothing touched their father more than trust. Whenever they had done something stupid as children, they'd felt little fear, knowing if they told the truth, admitted what they'd done, and asked for help in fixing it, their father would be pleased. Their mother would scream the house down and ground them for months, but that was to be expected.

Clay came over with steaming mugs as Daniel was getting up to leave, and they hugged briefly before Daniel left with a promise to call that evening to let Sietta know what he had gotten done. It seemed soon, but none of them had any illusions. With such a high-profile case, everything would move quickly. The government would want to be seen to be decisive and unforgiving, and the public would be demanding and relentless. The upside was that things would be over sooner, and Sietta and Micah could have lives that didn't involve being dogged by paparazzi and endless public appearances.

"Micah's doing fine," Clay told Sietta immediately, and they both saw his shoulders relax. "He's already unpacked his things in Joel's spare room and helps himself to everything in the fridge just like we told him to. He's also thrilled to see Joel has a PlayStation, and I think they were going to try and go by the house and get some more of Micah's things this afternoon, if Joel could get the police to send an escort with them."

"That's a good idea," Sietta mumbled, and it was clear he wondered for a moment why he hadn't thought of it before he'd looked at his watch and realised the day wasn't even half over yet.

"We can go by later, if you want?" Taylor asked hesitantly and wasn't at all surprised when Sietta shook his head in a vehement "no."

"I don't want anything from there."

"You need clean clothes. I know you don't want a handout or anything, but can I take you shopping and grab you some basic stuff later? Even if it's just from Kmart?"

"Thanks." Sietta hesitated briefly, something about the idea not sitting well, but then he looked up at him, and Taylor knew he'd hit the nail on the head. Sietta wanted clothes, but he wanted nothing of his old life. Cheap threads didn't bother him. As long as they fit, he was good to go. Sietta didn't seem thrilled with the idea of going to the shops, but he couldn't sit around in Taylor's shirts indefinitely, much to Taylor's chagrin.

"You're welcome. I'd give you Ash's clothes or something, but…."

"But even Leila's would be a tough fit," Clay finished, no doubt laughing at the thought of Sietta Salisbury in his sister's clothes. "Man, that'd be pure gold!"

Sietta and Taylor were both glaring at him, and Clay blushed but otherwise remained unrepentant as he sipped his tea.

"I can't believe you didn't tell me your dad was Daniel Jameson!" Sietta suddenly blurted, and they both stared at him as if he had grown a second head.

"How do you even know who Dad is?" Clay countered, and Taylor had to agree that was a good question.

"Are you kidding me? Jameson, Grant, and London are the most prestigious law firm in Sydney! My parents were always trying to use them, but Benjamin Grant kept refusing, I'm guessing because he knew my dad was dirty."

"Ben's got a nose for stuff like that," Taylor agreed. His use of "Ben" made Sietta smile, bright and unguarded, as if Taylor had set off fireworks in the house. "Ben's like an uncle to us."

"If uncles set up trust fund accounts for your fifteenth birthday present. And give you advice on contracts you should get one-night stands to sign before sleeping with them," Clay recalled darkly.

"No way…." Sietta breathed softly, and both Clay and Taylor shook their heads in dismay at the memory.

"It was awful," Taylor admitted.

"We had to tell him we were gay." Clay picked up the paper from the coffee table and read through the headlines with a scowl before tossing it back face down on the glass once more. "And then he said that didn't mean we didn't need a pre-nup," Taylor continued. They both sighed glumly, as if this fact upset them greatly, even if they'd known Benjamin was right and had meant well.

"Well, it's true…." Sietta was looking from one of them to the other, trying to gauge what reaction they were expecting.

"Oh, we know. We just didn't really understand it all when we were teenagers." Clay scowled, and Sietta laughed. Hard. For a while Taylor was nervous the laughter wasn't going to stop, or that it would morph into tears, but Sietta reined it in and settled, drinking his tea in larger gulps.

"So Dad's filing the court work and looking into a book deal.... What about Micah? I mean you're legal, so you're allowed to do what you like, but...." Clay trailed off, waving a hand.

"Daniel said the best thing to do would be to have Joel apply to be his permanent carer until Micah is eighteen. It's only a few years. He said it would take them years to declare me mentally fit for custody, and then another year to actually give me custody, but by then Micah would be a legal adult anyway. And he can claim emancipation from the family once he's sixteen regardless. He said Joel would help us work things the way we wanted them."

"Joel's the best," Clay agreed immediately.

"Says the fan club," Taylor muttered, but he agreed. Joel was the best, especially with kids. Taylor had never seen him anything but patient with anyone, but with kids he was something else. He functioned on the same wavelength or something; he got teens, which was rare as unicorns.

"I agreed with him." Sietta shrugged, as if he didn't need to think about it at all. "He said they had to wait three months anyway, and that Joel had already filed to keep Micah for that time, so we'd just file the next lot of paperwork when it's time."

"Okay, then." Clay was no doubt letting the information sink in for a moment before relaxing, because there really wasn't anything left for them to do. It was in their dad's hands now.

"So. Shopping?" Taylor didn't want to push, but if they went now, they would beat the afternoon crazy. People weren't usually shopping when they could be eating, and it was nearly lunchtime.

"Sure," Sietta agreed, the hesitation still there. He finished his tea and got up to put the mug in the sink. Taylor snagged his wrist on the way back and pulled him down beside him on the couch, aware of Clay quietly slipping into his bedroom and closing the door, giving them a little privacy.

"Are you okay?" He didn't know how else to ask and figured Sietta would tell him if blunt wasn't okay.

"I'm fine." Sietta shrugged, but his lips turned up in the corners, clearly pleased Taylor was asking. "I mean... it's not a surprise or anything? This was all going to happen one day, and it's not like I didn't know how it would all happen, really." He shrugged again, and Taylor could only stare, wondering how anyone could be so calm about it all, but then Sietta didn't seem the type to get riled up about much of anything. So far.

"You'll tell me if you need something. Right?"

"Sure," Sietta agreed easily, mostly because it was obvious they both had their doubts about the agreement, but each knew Sietta had all the power, and he'd make whatever decision he felt best at the time, whether it involved Taylor or not. Weirdly, that was okay with Taylor, mostly because Taylor knew he was big enough to step in and interfere if he decided he needed to.

He opened the front door for them, but Sietta hesitated, ghosts of fears flittering across his expression before he took a deep breath and moved past. Taylor slammed it harder than he needed to, so Clay would know they were gone and he could run around naked if he wanted to. Taylor didn't care, his gaze fixed on the way Sietta waited for him at the top of the stairs, eyes watching every move he made as if he were somehow fascinating. Really, it was just nice to know he wasn't alone in his odd infatuation.

"What's your favourite food?" Sietta called back up from where he was winding his way down the stairs.

"Food."

"Colour?"

"Blue."

"Ah, police blue?"

Taylor smirked and was rewarded with a roll of Sietta's eyes.

"What about… favourite sport?"

"Sport." Taylor smirked, loving the laugh and the way Sietta visibly relaxed as he wandered out into the garage and over to Taylor's monster truck, not Clay's.

"How did you know this was mine?"

Sietta only shrugged and climbed in when Taylor unlocked the doors.

"What's your favourite food?" Taylor asked.

Sietta stared at him for a long time. "Food." The same answer, but for such different reasons. Taylor didn't feel bad for asking, though, only felt a driving need to make sure Sietta didn't go hungry again.

"Colour?"

"Blue's growing on me." Sietta chuckled, opening the glove box and then closing it because the only contents were the service manual and a few receipts.

"Sport?" Taylor backed out of the car space and unlocked the gates with the fob hanging on his keys.

"Yeah... I am not a sport person," Sietta admitted. "Studying music, remember?"

"You're actually studying? I thought it was a front or whatever...."

The look Sietta gave him was dark, incredulous, and yet somehow still amused. Taylor wasn't sure if Sietta hadn't expected Taylor to be quite that blunt, or if he was peeved someone was dissing his studies, but whatever the reason, Taylor found he liked the look anyway. Sietta was taking things so easily, it was good to know the guy could get angry. That there were things he cared about.

"I work hard," Sietta managed to ground out, holding up his hands and wriggling his long, slender fingers. "For hours, every day."

"You were allowed to do that?" Taylor had pictured him chained up in the wine cellar all day, every day, brought out for the occasional public appearance as required.

"Ah... I was, perhaps a little literally, chained to the piano."

"How can you be a little literally chained to anything? What does that even mean?" Taylor's anger was ignited. He wanted Johnathan Salisbury's face in front of him, so he could shove his fist into the man's flesh, repeatedly.

"You're very attractive when you're angry," Sietta observed.

Taylor snorted, the anger fading as quickly as it came. "A little literally?"

"Mmm," Sietta mused. "Well, figuratively, then, but I felt chained to it."

"So they didn't install a chain on a piano?"

"Well it would be sacrilege, you know. I think Mozart's father might have invented it first though anyway, and you know my dad's not really one to copy." How Sietta could sit there and laugh about it was beyond Taylor. He gripped the wheel tightly and silently fumed.

"You don't fume silently, you know?"

Taylor glared at him, but Sietta was grinning from ear to ear, and it was stunning.

"You fume. You know, like heavy breathing and nostrils flaring, and it's like you can almost hear your muscles creaking...." Sietta demonstrated, and it looked so ridiculous that the fury fled Taylor, just like that, leaving him feeling drained and amused and a thousand other things he couldn't be bothered thinking about.

"You look like a gorilla with rabies." Taylor scowled.

"Seen a lot of those, have you? I guess you look in the mirror a lot...."

"No need, I just look at Clay." He liked how easily Sietta laughed, how relaxed he was with him, as if they were old friends. He wondered if it was simply the way Sietta was, or if it was unique to him. He was selfish enough to wish for the latter, but also curious because Sietta hadn't exactly had a lot of company since he was a teenager. Where did his sense of humour come from, if it wasn't simply something innate in him?

It wasn't far to the nearest shopping centre with a Kmart, and he pulled into a park close to the store, rummaged in his gym bag on the back seat, and found his sunglasses and a cap, holding them out to Sietta, who didn't question him at all, just obediently put them on his head.

Sietta still needed a moment before he was willing to get out of the car, so Taylor waited patiently until he was ready.

The store was relatively empty, and Sietta wasn't a fussy shopper, apparently. He walked to the men's section, grabbed two pairs of cheap jeans, a black T-shirt and a white T-shirt, two pairs of underwear, and a belt, and shoved them in a basket. Taylor frowned down at the meagre pile, but he knew better than to argue. He watched a five-dollar pair of black canvas shoes go in, and sighed, but Sietta was still grinning so whatever. A cheap black cap joined the pile, and a cheap pair of thick black-rimmed sunglasses. A pair of boxers, and then some socks. A single dark hoodie.

"That is the saddest wardrobe I have ever seen." Taylor snatched up the basket and rummaged through it as if the contents might change.

"I don't need anything else," Sietta sounded a little confused.

"Except maybe a sense of style," Taylor muttered. Sietta's eyes widened, and he stared down into the basket alongside Taylor, as if searching for what was so wrong. It was his complete lack of ability to care about his clothes that sealed the deal for Taylor. He stroked a hand down one of the locks of hair that had escaped his hat on Sietta's head, tugged gently, and then led the way back to the register.

The whole lot cost less than a hundred dollars, and they packed it themselves at the self-serve checkout, in a brown paper bag. Sietta clung to it like a lifeline, and Taylor made sure he said nothing, leading them back out to the car and sighing a little in relief. Apparently middle-aged mothers frantically doing the groceries had far more important things to do than recognise and harass a recovered kidnap victim.

"Thank you," Sietta said softly from the passenger seat, and Taylor managed a wry smile because they both knew there was no point to thanking him.

Despite the austere nature of the clothing, Taylor had to admit that when Sietta emerged from the bathroom an hour later, freshly showered and laundered, he looked good. The jeans were loose in all the right ways, hanging low on his hips, and the shirt wasn't tight but fit snugly, moving with his lithe form as he sat down beside Taylor on the couch and waved a hand at the television.

"Reckon we can watch a movie? I haven't seen anything in... well...." He was laughing, but it had that hint of brittle to it, and Taylor didn't bother answering with words, reaching out to ruffle Sietta's hair. Then he got up to boot up the computer attached to the television.

"Preference of genre?"

"Not a thriller," Sietta grumbled. Taylor looked at the ceiling and quietly asked for a little help. But he found a simple comedy from a few years ago and got it playing, moving back to the couch, but sitting closer to Sietta, wrapping an arm around his shoulders, and hauling him over with him as he lay down and settled in to watch.

It was like holding a wooden plank at first, but gradually Sietta relaxed, and eventually Taylor was treated to the gentle vibrations of Sietta's laughter against his chest. He liked that Sietta smelt like him: his shampoo, his deodorant, his home. He liked the way Sietta's hair tangled between them, tickling his neck and shoulder where Sietta rested his head. He liked how warm Sietta was, and the weight of him. He liked a lot of things, apparently.

He fell asleep. When he woke, it was not Sietta's eyes staring at him, nor Sietta's face. Little flecks of brown, completely out of place in the eyes of any Jameson, which told him exactly who it was. Not that he needed that to tell him, when there was that much fruit on the kid's breath.

"Emma... back off."

"Give her a break, ever since she heard Uncle Tay was let out of the hospital, she's wanted to come and make sure your face was okay." Brayden's voice came from somewhere near the kitchen.

"My face is fine, Em," Taylor grumbled in response, reaching down to haul her into his lap as he sat up and searched the living room. He spotted Brayden by the couch, handing Sietta a steaming mug of what smelled like ginger tea.

"You let him in?"

Sietta froze, eyes flicking from one brother to the other before settling on Taylor. "Was I not supposed to?"

Taylor shook his head, and Brayden laughed, going to collapse on the other couch, looking tired, as usual. "Don't mind Taylor, he prefers to avoid family as much as possible."

"But…. Clay lives here," Sietta pointed out, less confusion in his voice and more amusement as he sipped his tea.

"Uncle Clay and Uncle Tay are the same soul split in two bodies," Emma settled in Taylor's lap like a small princess. Somewhat literally, as she was dressed as Elsa, her favourite Disney princess, along with the rest of the world under six.

"I don't think that's quite right," Brayden told his daughter, but she scrunched up her nose at him.

"Nanna said it!" As if that would magically make it saner.

"See, not right, then," Taylor agreed with Brayden.

"Well, she was right about your face!" Emma reached up to poke the dark purple bruises on the side of his head, making him hiss and bat her hands away. "Why did Uncle Clay let the thing hurt your face?"

"What's your preoccupation with my face?"

"Jay says if you pull a funny face and the wind changes, it'll stay that way. What if now your face stays this way? Then everyone will know Uncle Clay is the nice one just by looking at you, and no one will ever talk to you again."

There was one of those strange silent moments before the shock wore off and they were all laughing with Emma shaking her head at Taylor and continuing to try to poke his bruises, before he grabbed her hands and folded them in her lap for her.

"My face is going to be fine, they're just bruises and bruises fade. You know that. Remember when you hit your knee last month? And now it's all gone, right?"

"Yeah, but… I'm a nice person."

They were probably never going to stop laughing at him, and Taylor really couldn't blame them. From the mouths of babes and all that.

"I'll still be Taylor's friend," Sietta said from across the room, and Emma seemed to notice him for the first time. Her eyes went wide and she leaned closer, as if trying to get a better look at him. Sizing him up for her next victim, perhaps.

"Is he paying you?"

"What?" That tea almost went everywhere. Sietta was clearly struggling to swallow the hot brew and not spray it.

"Emma... no, Taylor is not paying Sietta to be his friend." Brayden struggled to explain, clearly wanting nothing more than to laugh hysterically. "Sietta was hurt, and I helped him at the hospital, and then Uncle Taylor agreed to let Sietta stay here while his brother is staying with Uncle Clay and Uncle Joel."

"Oh." Yeah, oh.

Sietta was still struggling with his tea.

"How come I don't get to stay with Uncle Joel?"

"Because you live with me. You know, your father," Brayden pointed out. It was like he had these conversations every day. They didn't seem to faze him at all.

"Oh. That makes sense."

He was a doctor. Of course it made sense. But Taylor wasn't stupid enough to tell her that.

"Is Uncle Tay's head really going to be okay? I don't want him to have no friends."

"Yes, Emma, Uncle Tay's head is like a rock, remember? So his head's fine, and his face will get better. It's just God's way of telling him he's horrible and needs to be nicer to people. His face will go back to normal when he's learned his lesson."

"Bray, what the...." Taylor gaped at Brayden, but he was sitting there looking smug and sickeningly in control of the situation, and Taylor let him have the win. It wasn't like he really cared, anyway, Brayden hated that Taylor was Emma's favourite. Supposedly because Taylor needed whatever friends he could get, but Taylor suspected it had more to do with the secret stash of lollies he gave her under the table at Saturday lunches.

"You should learn faster, it's pretty ugly," Emma told him resolutely, and Sietta was laughing again. At least something good was coming from his pint-sized emasculation.

"I'll try," Taylor looked at Brayden. "What are you doing here?"

"I came to check on my patients. Mostly because Mum wouldn't stop harping on about you dying of brain damage or something. But also because I have duty of care and Emma wanted to see you."

"There are these things called telephones," Taylor reminded snidely, letting Emma play with his hair, happy he kept no glitter in his apartment. They'd all learnt that lesson pretty quick.

"You don't answer yours when you don't want to." Brayden shrugged.

"Or I'm busy? Or at work? What if I'm on a raid and my phone starts ringing and I've got to answer it because my mum's calling?"

"Why would you take your phone on a raid?" Brayden scoffed, and Taylor scowled at him because he was deliberately missing the point. Not that Taylor actually cared.

"Were you on a raid with Uncle Tay?"

All sets of eyes returned to Emma. Taylor wondered if it wasn't her superpower; coming up with the most awkward thing to say in any given situation to ensure all attention was purely on her.

"Oddly enough, I was." Sietta was snickering. He seriously had issues. Serious issues. Seriously serious issues. If Taylor hadn't known it already, the look on Brayden's face would have told him, clearly and succinctly. And yet he didn't care about that either. He cared that Sietta was laughing, not in the slightly manic way he had been, but openly and naturally. Genuine.

"He was in the wine cellar," Taylor told her in a soft, serious tone he knew she would listen to, and her eyes went wide in fascination while Brayden groaned.

"Were you drinking?" So serious.

"Well, not when Taylor found me, no, but sure, I would drink down there. I mean… it's hard to survive if you don't drink something." She was nodding along to everything Sietta said, as if it made perfect sense to her. It didn't, but it was cute that she tried.

"Uncle Clay takes his clothes off when he's drunk."

Dead. Silence. Brayden sank into the couch as if he thought it could eat him. Sietta sat gaping at her. Taylor looked at the ceiling and prayed for a reprieve from his whole family, Clay included.

"He… what?" Sietta was still struggling. It was cute as hell, and something Sietta would have to get used to if he intended to continue to hang around Jamesons. Which, considering Micah was fostered at Joel's, he was going to have to.

"It's a Clay thing. One too many and whoosh, off go his pants and he runs around naked until he passes out or I arrest him, which I try not to do because then he thinks we're playing cops and robbers, and he tries to steal my stuff." Taylor shifted Emma off his lap to snuggle in against his side.

"Oh... my... God..." Sietta's eyes couldn't get any bigger. Emma was shaking her head, clearly recalling their last Christmas party, where Clay had overindulged. Taylor had convinced Clay to lie on the lilo in the pool, he'd passed out and gotten so sunburned he'd had to go to hospital, where Brayden had made him stay overnight. Emma had been kind enough to go read Uncle Clay a bedtime story or fifteen while he was stuck in hospital.

"He only tries to steal Taylor's stuff, though," Brayden thought to add. "The rest of us apparently aren't in the game. Or we just plain don't exist if Clay's drunk. It's like Tay's his whole world."

Taylor went to stick his finger up before he remembered Emma was in his lap and covered it by shoving his fingers into his hair instead, glaring at his brother.

"Taylor drunk is just funny," Brayden offered, and the light of curiosity lit that quickly in Sietta's eyes as he turned to listen. Brayden smirked knowingly, and Taylor groaned and wondered if there was any way to claim brain damage and scare them all out of his house. Unlikely; it would be more likely to land him back in hospital under Brayden's care, and he did not want to be there. "He sings. So badly. It's amazing." Those eyes were like saucers.

"When you say badly...."

"I mean dogs howl loudly in an effort to drown him out and run away to hide and whimper when they fail."

Well, at least Sietta was getting a laugh out of it.

"Why do you sing, then?" Sietta asked a little breathlessly. Taylor could think of ten things right off the top of his head that would have made him equally breathless and been far more fun than Brayden telling stories. Oh well.

"Apparently drunk me thinks he's a superstar," Taylor muttered.

"Oh, no... drunk Taylor is awesome." Brayden got up and went to the kitchen, taking a bag of frozen vegetables out. He shoved them against the bruising on Taylor's face, amused when Emma took over holding them in place so he could return to his couch.

"He's nice!" Emma piped in, and Taylor gave up, because if it wasn't going to be Brayden and his pint-sized niece, everyone else in the family would ensure all his secrets were revealed and he remained single for life.

"Drunk Taylor is nice?" Sietta looked around the room for clarification.

"Will agree to do pretty much anything," Brayden acknowledged, and even he seemed surprised by this.

"Just about?" Sietta was looking at Taylor now, smirking.

"Well, there was this one time when a girl tried to get him to go home with her...."

He could jump off the balcony.... Right? Run down the street.... The train station wasn't that far away, and he was sure he had a few coins in his pocket. He could get to Joel's and beg asylum?

7
LEMONADE BARBEQUE

THE DOOR clicked shut, and Taylor fell back against it, closing his eyes briefly and counting to ten to make sure they were really gone. He locked it for good measure before he dared to push away, looking up and meeting Sietta's incredulous look where he still sat on the edge of the couch, as if he might fall off if anyone told him one more ridiculous thing.

"Your whole family is like that," he noted a little breathlessly. "I mean... even the small ones!"

Taylor went to sit beside him on the couch, noticing Sietta didn't flinch or pull away in the slightest, that he visibly relaxed instead and leaned back into the curve of Taylor's body, making it that much easier for Taylor to settle a heavy arm around his shoulders and pull him even closer. Everything about Sietta felt easy and comfortable.

"Even the small ones," Taylor agreed.

"I need to go to Saturday Barbeque" was the last thing Taylor had expected to come out of Sietta's mouth, which had to be obvious when all he could do was gape at him.

"Oh, come on, how bad could it be? Your dad invited me, said Leila has invited Micah, and that Joel was going, so I could meet him and everything."

"I don't think you understand...." How could he? He had brunches, not barbeques, and for those, he'd likely still been chained to the chair, so no one had expected him to do anything. Brunch was a whole different beast to barbeque. Brunch was avocado toast and coffee at a café where everyone had to be on their best behaviour. Barbeque was sausage sandwiches and beer and your family getting all up in your business and telling embarrassing stories. These two things were not the same!

"Have you already forgotten that I was rescued by *Vikings* extras, handed off to your seriously loony sister, who delivered me to the medical devil himself, who let me go home with the *Vikings*?"

"What's your obsession with *Vikings*?"

"Micah loves that show."

Taylor suspected he'd lost whatever semiargument they'd been having. But really, he'd lost the moment his father handed out the invite, and really... what *could* go wrong? "Just remember I warned you."

But Sietta was smiling, and that was all that mattered. Taylor let the matter drop and went about putting something together for dinner, scrounging some chicken breasts from the freezer, a packet of stir fry veg, and some Hokkien noodles and making a stir fry in the wok. Fast and simple, it was one of his favourite things to make.

"That smells really good...." Sietta came over to see what he was doing and stared wide-eyed at the full wok and the herbs Taylor was throwing in.

"You didn't think I could cook, did you?"

"Actually, I figured one of you could, I mean...." He gestured at Taylor idly, and it made Taylor preen a little, happy because Sietta liked what he saw. It was obvious in the hint of red on his cheeks and the way his gaze never shifted away from him.

"But you assumed it was Clay?"

"No, I figured he'd make you trade off, so you both had to be able to."

"You're right." Taylor swirled the noodles in the wok, not surprised by the correct assumption, but delighted, as usual, by Sietta seeing things for what they were. "Are you allergic to anything?" He should have asked that beforehand.

"Not a thing," Sietta assured him, moving around the bench and rummaging in the cupboard, getting out two bowls and forks and putting the kettle on for another cup of tea.

"You drink a lot of tea," Taylor observed, trying not to judge.

"I haven't had hot drinks in years," Sietta confessed, and Taylor bit his lip and watched Sietta flick through the few boxes of tea they had, choosing a green variety Joel had brought over.

"Sorry. Not... not for pointing it out, I just... I'm sorry you couldn't even have simple things. I'm not sorry for sticking my foot in it, because honestly I think you need that, and obviously no one else is saying anything so...."

"Thank you," Sietta interrupted, and the wide smile on his face did strange things to Taylor's stomach, twisting it into all kinds of pretzels. Taylor forced himself to count backward until the throbbing in his groin eased.

"No, really… what you've done is amazing and might actually change the way politics work in this country, force things to be more public and transparent, but… I wish it hadn't been you, anyway. Not that I wish it was someone else, just…."

"I get it! Geez, stop talking!" But he'd gotten a laugh from Sietta, who served up his tea when the kettle boiled and went to sit on the couch, still chuckling and stealing glances over at Taylor. "I'm not sorry, either, you know? I could have run, or figured something out a long time ago. It was my choice to stay. I wanted to damn him, and I did." There was no question as to who "he" was. Taylor finished dishing up the food into two bowls, and carried them over, not bothering to ask, then sitting beside Sietta and putting a bowl in his lap.

"Eat. I think the wine cellar stunted your growth." Another laugh, and Taylor smirked, delighted when Sietta curled in against his side and happily ate everything put in front of him.

"JUST REMEMBER… you chose to come," Taylor muttered under his breath. Sietta sat calmly beside him in the passenger seat of Taylor's black Hilux, which only made Sietta look small and fragile. It made Taylor nervous, and he scolded himself again for ever agreeing to bring Sietta along. But it really hadn't been his choice; his father had invited him, and Sietta had made a point of reminding him every hour the day before, and again at six that morning. Today was Saturday. Which was family barbeque day. Worse, the boss had demanded they take the day off after the raids while the AFP worked through all the paperwork. He'd also told Taylor to somehow magically heal his face, as the boss's boss had asked about it and made him nervous. How he was supposed to achieve this, Taylor had no idea.

"It's only lunch. Right?"

"If someone gave me the choice between being locked in the wine cellar and attending lunch?" Taylor nodded into the silence. Hell yes, he would take the wine cellar. But to hear Sietta laugh like that, he could be convinced to go to lunch, sure.

He pulled onto his parents' street, right behind Clay, who was in Joel's car. Micah was in the rear seat, face pressed to the back window, waving at them like a maniac. Sietta waved back with equal enthusiasm but didn't bother trying for more, because they were pulling up to the curb anyway, and before Taylor could get the engine turned off, Micah was out of Joel's car and at Sietta's window, waiting impatiently for Sietta to open the door.

"Hey." Taylor met Clay and Joel on the kerb, shaking his head at Clay's uncharacteristically wild hair. "Couldn't find a brush at the Professor's house?"

"I'm sorry, do you think I have any possessions left now I've got a gay teenage son in my house?" Joel quirked a brow at him, but he looked as calm and put together as always, and Taylor knew he had no complaints about the situation.

Taylor liked Joel. If he'd had to imagine the perfect partner for Clay, Joel was not a thing like what he would have thought of. But he was perfect. He had no interest at all in the law, as long as he didn't have to break it. He didn't care about shift work, as long as he knew what time someone was going to be at his house. He was calm, had a wicked sense of humour, was way smarter than Taylor understood anything about, and he was nice on the eyes. But the best part was simply that Clay adored him. Was, quite simply, besotted with the man, and had been from the moment they met. If Joel ever cheated, he was dead, but he understood that loud and clear, so they were all good.

Ashley's car pulled up behind where he'd parked, and Taylor gaped at it. The bumper held on for dear life, though how he couldn't quite figure out. The roof completely caved in at the back in a suspiciously man-shaped gouge. One of the tyres was so flat, he shouldn't have been driving on it, and one side of the paint was peeling off, black and melted from a fire. Ashley climbed out in his overalls, and Taylor could smell him easily. It wasn't pleasant.

"Ash... the hell?" Clay waved at the car. Joel, smartly, was covering his amazement with his hands on his face. Micah was already bolting over to get a good look when another car screeched around the corner.

"No plates," Taylor squinted at the windscreen, but he couldn't see much through the glare.

"Gun!" Clay bellowed at the same moment Taylor saw the glint of sunlight on metal through the open passenger window. The crack of gunfire shattered the relative quiet of the neighbourhood, and the whole place fell into chaos.

Instincts were strange things. Too engrained, and as soon as the word gun was vocalised, he and Clay were moving in synch, racing for loved ones. Clay body slammed Joel into the ground, rolled, and reached for Micah's ankle, but the kid was already on the ground, wide-eyed and terrified. Taylor lunged for Sietta, who had been leaning on the side of the Hilux, grabbing his wrist and tossing him to the ground as the gun fired again.

Someone screamed in pain, there was shouting coming from the house, doors opening and slamming, but Taylor had eyes only for Sietta, who was staring up at him from where he'd tossed him on the ground, looking as stunned by the action as Joel.

Brayden's familiar white doctor shoes appeared near Sietta's head, sliding to a halt on the freshly mowed lawn.

All Taylor did was check Sietta was okay, and then he was off, trusting Brayden to get everyone safely out of the way. Taylor sprinted down the road after the car, Clay in perfect harmony beside him.

"Duck!" Ashley bellowed from back near the driveway.

They hit the asphalt, and Taylor watched in horrified fascination as an axe sailed past where he'd been, and slammed into the back tyre of the fleeing car. The blowout caused it to careen off the road, slamming through the neighbours' fence and smashing into their shiny Commodore.

The front doors of the car opened and two men tried to get out, but Clay and Taylor were already up, leaping over the fence. The driver didn't even manage to get out of the car. Taylor threw himself against the door and trapped him inside, while Clay hauled his accomplice from the car and slammed him into the ground face first, grabbing his hands and holding them in a lock against his back. Taylor tried to get a look over the car at what was going on, but the driver grabbed the gun off the passenger-side floor and shot at Taylor through the glass, and he was forced to duck behind the door.

Furious, Taylor grabbed the handle, opened the door, and when the idiot aimed the gun out the gap, he slammed the door back on the dumb prick's arm, smirking at the satisfying crunch that followed.

"Clay! What on earth are you doing to that poor man?" Their mother bellowed from her house, and they groaned together.

"Mum! Call the damn cops! We're arresting the fuckers! You know, because they shot at us? Are you deaf or something?" Taylor watched Clay drag the driver, and his broken arm, from the car and got him on the ground beside his derelict friend.

"Oh! I thought it was a car backfiring!"

"Nope!" Clay was sweating now that the adrenaline was starting to wear off.

"I called the cops!" Brayden bellowed down the road. "They'll be here in ten!"

"Okay!" Clay looked at Taylor over the car and shook his head. "Do you think they could maybe not yell at us down the damn street?"

"Do you boys want some lemonade?"

"No!" They bellowed in unison. "Just… go wait out the back of the house, Mum!" Taylor wandered around the car to Clay, shaking his head and pushing the driver's face harder into the cement when he dared laugh at them.

"Where did you even get a freakin' gun," Taylor asked him darkly. "And why did you decide to come try and shoot me?"

"Weren't trying to shoot you," the driver grumbled, and Taylor twisted his broken arm to shut him up. He could explain what the hell he'd thought he was doing to the boss; Taylor wasn't supposed to be working today.

"Shit…. Tay…." Clay was gaping at him, and Taylor frowned, looked down at his shirt, and realised there was a large red splash seeping down his chest. Now that he was looking at it, he realised it hurt. A whole lot. And that was actually a lot of blood….

"Ah, fuck. You shot me!" He kicked the driver in the hip, annoyed more than anything. The driver yelped, trying to say something, but Taylor wasn't listening to him, looking at Clay and trying to be reassuring even as he was starting to feel decidedly woozy. "It's not that bad, Clay."

Clay had that look on his face Taylor knew meant he was trying to decide something, and then Taylor's day got a thousand times worse.

"Brayden!" Clay bellowed down the street.

"What?"

"Are we seriously going to keep screaming down the street?" Taylor muttered, looking at the hole in his shoulder and moving it back and forth to see where the pain was. The bullet seemed to have grazed over his collarbone and through the far edge of his trap. It really wasn't that bad, which sort of amused him because everyone was yelling about it.

"Tay's shot!" Clay screeched. There was nothing manly about the sound, and it was followed by more screeching off down the road, and then Brayden and Hayley were sprinting up the road, a first aid kit hanging off Hayley's shoulder.

"Great. Now look what you've done." Taylor scowled at Clay, but his brother glared at him.

"I'm not the one who got shot! What, couldn't see the damn gun past your black eye?" Oh, so now it was fine to make fun of his face? Clay must be more worried than Taylor had thought. It made him pause and look down at his shirt again. Maybe if he hadn't worn a white T-shirt it wouldn't have looked as bad.

"Shit, Taylor… you need to lie down," Brayden ordered as soon as he came around his side of the car.

"Oh sure, let me just let the driver go, and I'll get right on that, yeah?"

"Shut up, you don't get to be a smartass while you're bleeding on everything!"

"Who the hell cares if I bleed on the guy who shot me?" Taylor asked, incredulous. His siblings were terrible people, that was all there was to it.

"Technically, this guy shot you… I think." Clay pointed out from his side of the car. "I dunno… which bullet do you think got you? I'm thinking the second one, back down the street? That's a lot of blood for it to have been just before…."

"How the hell should I know which bullet shot me?" Taylor snapped, annoyed that he couldn't swat Brayden's hands away as he came and started poking at the wet shirt, trying to see how bad it was.

"I think it went straight through… yeah, there's an exit wound… hold still." He was poking and prodding, and Taylor forced himself to remain still and quiet as Brayden and Hayley tried to stop the bleeding and get some kind of bandage in place while he and Clay stood guard over the shooters. The driver kept demanding his own medical attention, and everyone ignored him. His friend had the sense to stay quiet.

It wasn't ten minutes when the familiar sound of sirens filled the air, and then the black van Taylor considered a home away from home rounded the corner.

"What the… you called the riot squad?" Taylor ground out through the pain, glaring at Brayden, who ignored him and bandaged Taylor's shoulder with gauze and tape.

"I have your office on speed dial. It's faster than calling triple zero."

"Do you see a riot?" Taylor tried to make him see his point, wondering how he was the only sane person present.

"You're here," Hayley pointed out. Taylor was starting to feel light-headed.

Uniforms filled the street, and suddenly Ben Harris, youngest member of their team, was in front of Taylor in full riot squad uniform, looking as out of place as ever. He looked like he should be on a beach with a board under his arm.

Ben forced Taylor off the driver, letting Brayden haul him away, back down the street to their parents' house. Clay moved ahead of him, leaving their squad to take care of the criminals.

Joel was still on the ground, though he'd managed to get himself into a sitting position. Sietta was rubbing his knee, also on the ground, Micah at his side, wide-eyed and clearly stunned by the proceedings.

"You got shot?" Sietta asked weakly, though it was obvious he didn't expect an answer; he was simply stating the obvious in his shock.

"It's not that bad." Taylor shrugged with the shoulder that didn't have a hole in it, and tried to avoid the scowls of his siblings. "Brayden'll stitch me up. It'll be fine."

"Oh God, Tay, you're covered in blood!" His mother gasped, and Taylor looked heavenward, praying for some kind of miracle. Like another drive-by with a better shooter to put him out of his misery.

"He got shot, Mum. Of course he's covered in blood!" Hayley was pulling open his car door, and Taylor sighed because he didn't want to go to the hospital. He just wanted to go home and sleep, preferably with Sietta.

"I don't need to go to the hospital!"

"Excuse me?" His mother was suspiciously quiet, so Taylor let them sit him in the passenger seat, though he insisted on a towel to protect his interior from the blood. That stuff never came out.

"What happened to your knee?" Taylor looked over at Sietta where he was still on the ground, rubbing it, Micah at his side. He got a frown in reply, and Joel snorted. Taylor looked from one to the other and sighed, realising he and Clay had each thrown their loved ones with a little too much force in their need to get them to the ground.

"It's fine, we'll just have bruises," Joel soothed quietly, looking amused now that things were calming down, and letting Clay help him to his feet while Micah did the same. Taylor was relieved when Sietta immediately stepped up beside the car, leaning in to tentatively stroke the makeshift bandage, meeting his gaze solemnly.

"I'll be fine," Taylor assured him, genuinely unconcerned. Brayden would fix him up; he had no doubts about that.

Brayden's wife, Kelly, appeared in the doorway, holding Jay against her side, but Emma ran out into the yard, looking around with wide eyes and mouth agape at all the things going on. Brayden was about to yell at her to go back into the house, but Emma suddenly threw her hands in the air, so much like her father, and the most disgusted snort possible came from her mouth.

"Uncle Ash, what the hell did you do to your car?" You would think Emma had paid for the car herself, with the amount of indignation in her voice.

All attention turned back to Ashley, who was still standing in the driveway, in his yellow overalls and blue T-shirt. His car stood behind him, completely black down one side, missing windows now Taylor took the time to look at it, the back end flattened and the tyre still close to dead. Dead silence reigned on the street, even the riot squad had turned to stare.

Ashley looked from Emma, over his shoulder to the car, and then back to Emma, and the grin that split his face was ecstatic.

"I got to fight a fire, Em! It was huge! I got sent in to save this guy stuck on the second floor, but then the fire collapsed the stairs and we couldn't get out, and the ladder stuck, so we jumped from the window and landed on my car! See?" He pointed to the flattened bit, apparently oblivious to Emma's widening eyes and mouth and the way she leaned forward in horror at his story. "And then the windows exploded and my car lit on fire! Because I was just leaving when the fire got called in, and I thought I would go make sure they didn't need my help, so I'd followed the truck and parked behind it...."

"You're an idiot!" Emma bellowed, standing there in her crisp white summer dress, hair immaculately tied up in pigtails, pink sandals on her feet.

One of the riot squad officers snickered. Then another, then everyone was yelling. Emma stormed back over to Kelly, who smartly took her children back inside, informing Brayden he could pick her up when he got back from the hospital.

"Ash... the hell?" Clay was doing Emma's thing with his hands, as if he couldn't think of quite what gesture he should make.

"Oh, come on! Look at that shot!" Ash was still beaming, pointing off at the crashed car, and Taylor looked over and finally remembered the axe that had flown past them.

Well, that explained how the car crashed. "Nice shot!" Taylor managed to bark out, keeping his laughter to a minimum so he didn't jolt his shoulder, and Ashley puffed his chest out proudly. Brayden groaned and demanded Taylor stop encouraging that kind of nonsense.

"Nice shot? You nearly chopped my damn leg off!" Clay bellowed, but it was worry, for both Taylor and Ashley, and he stormed over to get a better look at the dilapidated car, muttering under his breath.

"Micah, you wanna come to the hospital with us?" Sietta hugged his brother close and kept checking him over for injuries, but he didn't even have a graze.

"Is it okay if I stay? I'm hungry, and Leila said we could swim in the pool." He was also looking queasy at all the blood.

Priorities.

"Alright, I'll call you later." Sietta climbed in the back of the Hilux, not bothering to ask anyone's permission, and Brayden checked with the riot squad before climbing into the driver's seat and starting the ignition.

"They'll come get your statements in a day or so." Brayden was still stealing glances at Ash's car. "What the hell was he thinking?"

"Oh come on, he just had the best day of his life." Taylor chuckled.

"His brother was shot!"

"And he saved the day. Twice. Cut him some slack." Taylor leaned back into the seat, sighing heavily. The pain was really setting in. He was nauseous and the light was starting to bother him.

"You're worse off than I thought if you're complimenting Ash," Brayden muttered, but he pulled away from the curb and got them out of there.

"So." Sietta looked at each of them deliberately. "We're doing Saturday barbeque again next week... right?"

8
SNOW WHITE PICKET FENCE

"IT'S VERY hard to tell when you wake up," Sietta noted from somewhere to Taylor's left. Taylor forced an eye open and grunted at him, the light stinging his eyes. He was not on enough morphine, and he searched for Brayden as a result. Sietta knowingly pressed a button but made little other movement.

"How long?"

"Not long, actually. Brayden said it would be longer—"

"Because he's all civilian now," Taylor mumbled. "Was tougher when he was in the army." It was true. Brayden played by rules that hadn't existed when he was military. Stop the bleeding, make sure they don't die. Those had been the rules. Now he had to make sure the patient was comfortable and consented to treatment and didn't die but also didn't sue you for not dying or for being uncomfortable. Taylor knew; everything these days was paperwork.

"Or because you're ridiculous," Sietta countered, looking tired.

"Excuse me?"

"You didn't even know you got shot." Sietta was laughing at him, and Taylor was glad for it. His own family would not see the humour in it until it had healed, so it was nice that someone could see the funny side of it. Besides, Sietta's laugh made him feel warm in all the right ways.

"To be fair, it's not a bad wound," Taylor pointed out, and Sietta kept laughing, though he had the grace to nod in agreement. As gunshots went, it wasn't a big deal. Straight through his trap, right above the collarbone on his left side, the very definition of a flesh wound. A knife would have done more damage. Brayden had calmed as soon as they'd gotten to the hospital, and he'd had a good look at it. He had put him under more to shut him up than anything, the surgery taking less than fifteen minutes.

"How's the knee?" Taylor asked.

"You got shot, I scraped my knee." Sietta examined the bandage as if he could see through it to the stitches beneath and lifted his knee in comparison. "Pretty sure we're both gonna live, and that shot trumps knee scrape, yeah?" Yeah.

"Can we go home soon?"

"Honestly, I didn't ask...." Sietta turned to the door, as if expecting Brayden to show up so he could ask. Taylor took the distraction and quickly sat up, grunting at the pain that shot through his chest, but when Sietta turned to stare at him, Taylor pulled him in, closing his eyes as he finally gave in to the urge to kiss the man.

Sietta's lips were softer than he'd expected, dry and smooth like flower petals that opened to the soft push of his tongue, letting him inside where Sietta was warmer and wet. Taylor sighed in pleasure at the gentle pressure Sietta finally gave, pushing back against him as a soft moan escaped.

Taylor let him go only because his chest ached and he needed to flop back onto the pillows, which he did with a wide smile, taking in Sietta's flushed cheeks and stunned expression.

"You... oh...." Sietta looked panicked for a moment, and then tears started to build on his lashes, and for a moment Taylor's sense of achievement slipped, but Brayden appeared in the doorway and he couldn't ask about it.

"Seriously? You couldn't stay under for an hour? Are you for real?" Brayden scowled and came to check him over, but Taylor was fine and they both knew it. Taylor was much more concerned about Sietta, who had retreated a step from the bed, and while he wasn't crying, he was just standing there, fingers grazing his lips as he stared at Taylor on the bed.

"I want to go home." Taylor would accept no arguments.

"Yeah, yeah, I figured as much. I've got a few scripts for some medication I'm sending home with you. I've left them with the nurse. I'll be coming to check on you after my shift, though."

"Of course." Taylor rolled his eyes, but he took the pills Brayden offered, and swallowed them obediently. Brayden seemed to hesitate then, looking him up and down and sighing heavily.

"Just... please, stay in the house? Don't do anything stupid? If anything else happens to you, Mum's going to kill someone, most likely me because I'm the oldest and should apparently be able to control you."

It was nice that Brayden was worried, but it was also completely unwarranted.

"Clay dropped the ram." Taylor felt the need to remind him.

"I know."

"I didn't shoot myself."

"I know."

"Mum still worries when I get a papercut," Taylor grumbled. Really, there was nothing he could do to stop the woman from worrying. He was built like a tank. How much more reassuring could he be?

"Oh, I'm not worried about Mum. Emma's in the waiting room, insisting she be allowed to see for herself that you're not dead. Apparently she trusts no one else to arrange your funeral. Something about you having given her very specific instructions about how that should go?" Brayden was glaring darkly now, but he left the room, no doubt to go and get said small child.

Sietta watched the man leave and moved immediately to the side of the bed. Taylor went to apologise, or check he was okay, or something, but his words were swallowed, pushed back down his throat by the press of Sietta's tongue into his mouth, Sietta's warm breath exploding against his lips as they both smiled into the heat of it.

"Uh...." was the intelligent reply Taylor finally managed when Sietta pulled away. It was, apparently, Sietta's turn to smirk, but Taylor didn't care, wrapping his fingers in Sietta's shirt and pulling him in for another searing kiss.

The door slammed open.

"No fair! Uncle Taylor got woked up like Snow White!"

Sietta pulled away like a cat who'd had a bucket of water poured over it, standing ram-rod straight and staring at Emma's indignant expression. She stomped her foot and crossed her arms angrily over her chest, and Brayden had the sense not to laugh at them all.

"I'm sure Uncle Taylor won't mind closing his eyes so you can be the prince, okay?" Brayden followed Emma into the room but hovered by the door, writing on Taylor's chart.

Her eyes widened and the hopeful expression on her face did him in. Taylor ignored the hand Sietta placed over his mouth to hide his mirth, and obediently closed his eyes. Emma's squeal was followed by the patter of her shoes across the floor, then the bed creaked and tilted to one side as she threw herself up onto it, and she planted the sloppiest kiss on his cheek ever.

His eyes flew open and he reached out with his good arm to tickle her side, her squeals filling the room and chasing away the last of the cobwebs in his brain.

"You're awake!" Emma beamed with pride, watching him from the side of the bed as if expecting him to tickle her again when she least expected.

"Thanks to you, Princess Emma." She preened a little and eyed Sietta dubiously where he stood beside Brayden, but she didn't comment on what she had seen, for which Taylor was grateful. Instead, she gently patted the huge bandage on his shoulder, staring at him solemnly.

"Uncle Taylor... if you die, are you absolutely sure you want me to play 'Kiss from a Rose'? Uncle Clay loves that song! It'll ruin him forever." She was oh so serious. It was oh so hard not to react inappropriately.

"I'm absolutely sure, pumpkin."

"Well." She threw up her hands as if to say "what can you do." "Alright, then! But he's gonna cry." And she fled the bedside and threw herself against Brayden's legs instead, shifting to put her feet on his so he had to penguin walk her around the room.

"I'm supposed to start work in an hour anyway, so I'm going to stay here. Dad's out there, though. He brought Em. He's going to take you all home...."

"Bullshit he is! He's going to take me back to the damn house so Mum can make sure I'm alright, and then we'll never get to leave! It'll be the 'Hotel California', only worse!" Taylor protested. "You can't leave me with them!"

"Oh, please, it won't be that bad." Brayden waved off his concerns. "Besides, it was the only way anyone could get Clay to go in and give his report and not chase you to the hospital. We promised we'd get you back to the house, and he could take care of you from there. If you think Mum's the worried one, you're in for a shock...."

"Uncle Clay was crying," Emma whispered conspiratorially. "It's how I knew you were going to die."

"I'm not going to die, Emma, Clay's just a sook."

"He broke your face," Brayden corrected. "And now you've been shot. He's allowed to worry. He's never seen you hurt like this before."

"It's not even a bad wound!" Taylor protested, already exhausted and knowing it was going to be a thousand times worse when they were all there trying to coddle him. "Please, Bray... you can't make me go there! They'll never let me leave!"

"You got shot," Brayden noted coldly. "If we make the punishment harsh enough, maybe you won't do it again."

"I didn't get shot on purpose!" Taylor was protesting, but they weren't listening. Brayden was penguin walking Emma back out the door, and they were mumbling about how you had to be excessively harsh when punishing boys or they would turn out bad.

Sietta was standing by the bed, one hand absently rubbing Taylor's ankle through the sheet, staring after them, humming.

"Are you humming the 'Hotel California'?"

"What? It's a good song."

TAYLOR SPENT the car ride in silence. His dad had taken one look at him, hugged him hard, refused to cry, bundled him up as best he could when he stood a head taller than the man, and put him in the passenger seat of the car. He kept looking at him strangely, but Taylor didn't care; his dad could do whatever he needed to feel okay with it. Taylor was busy staring at Sietta in the back seat. He was quiet, and in the afternoon light, his skin looked paler than usual, the circles under his eyes darker. His hair had been tied back in a loose ponytail, but strands had escaped and now stuck out in all directions. He didn't seem to notice. He blinked, often and slowly, in that way people did when they were starting to fall asleep in the car, but his eyes never remained closed.

"Tired?" Daniel cast a glance at Sietta in the rear-view mirror.

"No more so than usual. Just... not used to being in cars so much. Puts me to sleep."

"And yet, you're not asleep," Daniel mused, but his smile let Sietta know he was teasing. Sietta simply shrugged in response.

Cars overflowed from the yard when they got to the house. A police car sat out the front, and another was down the street, helping the family clean up their broken fence. It took effort to get out of the car, and not only because he didn't want to. Taylor had to admit that despite the injury not being awful, it still hurt like crazy, and he had to be careful not to jostle his chest too much or it pinched horribly now the pain medication was beginning to wear off. He was much happier once he was on his own two feet.

The front door slammed open, and Clay barged out, Joel following far more sedately. Clay nearly grabbed him in a bear hug, stopping at the last second, hands hovering before carefully settling one over the thick bandage, the other on the back of Taylor's neck. He pulled Taylor in close, until their foreheads were pressed close together and he could feel Clay's breath on his cheek.

"Fuck, Tay...."

Taylor sighed and pulled him in with his good arm, holding him close despite the pain that shot through him at the action. "I'm fine, Clay. Really. Clean shot, minimal damage, should heal up in a few weeks just fine. Sorry I scared you."

Clay didn't say anything, but he didn't move away either, and Taylor met Joel's bemused expression over Clay's shoulder. Taylor let Clay linger, holding him tight and waiting it out, knowing he would have needed the same if their positions were reversed.

"I kissed Sietta," Taylor whispered in Clay's ear, and that finally got him moving. Clay jerked back, looking hard into Taylor's face and then slowly grinning with him, seeing the heat of it in Taylor's eyes.

"And you liked it," Clay noticed, his smile only widening, and Taylor dared to steal a glance at Sietta, who was talking by the car with Daniel. "Well. I suppose if it got you kisses, getting shot's not so bad." It was still bad, Taylor knew, in Clay's eyes, but if this helped him deal, then great. Clay glanced at the house then and winced.

Taylor just sighed. "Can we please go home now?"

"Are you kidding? I like having sex. No way am I giving Mum a reason to have me castrated. We'll go in, let her fuss, give her a minute to realise you're as solid as ever, and then we'll sort out some kind of distraction to get free...."

They both knew there would be no distraction, but it was nice, conspiring together as always. He'd missed Clay's presence at his side of late, and was grateful for the gentle press of the identical shoulder against his own.

They headed through the house.

"How's Joel?" Taylor still kept his voice down, leaning closer so they wouldn't be overheard, not because Clay was divulging sensitive information but because it was easier than the family overhearing and deciding they needed their opinions heard.

"He's fine." Clay winked at his beau when he looked up and spotted them through the glass doors of the living room. "He said Micah was freaked out a bit, but he seems okay now." He pointed to where Micah was lazing on the grass with Leila, both on their backs playing the cloud game.

"Hey Sietta." Taylor turned to him and pointed to their younger siblings through the window. "You wanna check Micah's okay? Joel said he was freaked out before…"

No further prompting was required. Sietta lunged past them and went to check on his brother.

"Where did he even get the gun?" Hayley was saying as they emerged onto the back patio. "This isn't America. We have laws, you know?"

"Boss man is looking into it," Clay mumbled as he helped Taylor to a lounger his mother had set up with extra pillows. Taylor snorted at it but didn't dare protest when Clay glared at him with suspiciously wet-looking eyes.

"Tay, honey, you should stay in the guest bedroom, I can make you dinner," Chloe jumped in immediately, and Taylor scowled.

"I'm going to be very clear. It's not bad. It would have been worse if someone stabbed me with a screwdriver. It's so not bad. In fact, Brayden only put me under to shut me up while he worked. It's so not bad I can go back to work as soon as the stitches come out. It won't even require any rehab. So I'll be staying at home, in my own damn bed, and no one who doesn't live there is staying with me! Understood?"

"But Sietta…." Chloe immediately began to protest, and Sietta just laughed as he returned from checking on Micah, who had shooed him away. Sietta went immediately to the lounger, sitting beside Taylor as if it were completely normal.

"I live there." Sietta shrugged, not even acknowledging the way Taylor jerked in response. "Well, for now anyway. The police paperwork says so." It won a laugh from Clay, who ignored his mother's raised eyebrow.

"Well… at least you'll have someone there to look after you," Chloe mumbled, clearly annoyed that Taylor wasn't giving in to her wishes, but not wanting to push him.

"Oh, Joel and I will be there," Clay reassured her, and he glared at Taylor before he could respond. "And Micah. Micah can sleep on the couch…."

"Oh no he will not!" Chloe protested immediately, eyeing the boy on the grass with Leila. "He can have a sleepover with Leila. I'm not having that poor child on your couch! Besides, the cops are out front, he's safer here."

"A what now?" Hayley eyed them all dubiously.

"Oh please, that boy is gay as a go-go dancer!" Chloe waved them all off. "He's safe as houses for sleepovers."

"With Leila maybe," Sietta muttered, but he made no protests, so Taylor let it drop because there was certainly no telling Clay he couldn't stay in his own apartment, and honestly Taylor wanted him there.

"Do they know who the shooter was?" Hayley tried to steer the conversation back to the morning's events. Taylor didn't bother commenting. Even if he knew something, he wasn't allowed to say, and she knew that. She just needed to ask. She always needed to ask.

"Ash." Taylor drew attention to their brother, needing the distraction and honestly wanting to hear what he had to say. "What the hell, man? Please tell me you have insurance."

"How dumb do you think I am, exactly?" Ashley bristled, but he couldn't keep the excitement out of his expression either, clearly recalling his day. "I needed a new car, anyway."

"What was wrong with your old one?" Daniel protested from where he'd taken a seat beside Chloe, Emma in his lap. "It was a perfectly sound car!" He knew because he'd had every legal check done on it before he had bought it for Ashley's eighteenth birthday.

"Nothing was wrong with it." Ashley rolled his eyes, sinking down in his chair as he realised the family's attention was shifting. "Taylor got shot!" he tried to remind them.

"And you torched your car!" Hayley snapped at him.

"I did not! I just parked it behind the truck. It's not my fault the fire exploded out those particular windows!" He was so indignant, it was taking all of Taylor's willpower not to laugh at him, and a glance at Clay revealed he was in a similar predicament. It was great that Ashley had finally fought his first big fire, but how his car had ended up at said fire and been so badly damaged was what really interested Taylor. Ashley had a knack for getting himself into awkward situations. He would have felt compelled to go help because he was a genuinely good guy who loved his job as a firefighter.

"And you couldn't have jumped onto the fire truck? You had to jump out a window onto your car instead?" Hayley was clearly unimpressed with whatever version of events Ashley had given so far.

"No, I just thought the car would have more give than the truck! I didn't feel like being splattered!"

"So you did intend to damage the car!" Daniel scowled darkly. "Insurance won't cover intentional damage!"

"It wasn't intentional…." Ashley ran frustrated hands over his face. "Insurance is already paying for it, so there!"

"So there?" Joel blinked at him from his seat beside Clay, clearly astounded Ashley thought that was the end of it. But then, Joel probably heard that a lot. Or didn't, because he didn't allow those sorts of childish antics in his classroom. Clay was guffawing outright.

"I stopped the shooter!" Ashley threw in as an afterthought. "Can't we remember that instead?"

"You mean when you nearly cut your brothers down and sent a car barrelling through the Thompsons' fence, damaging their car, destroying their petunias, and giving their poor sausage dog PTSD?" Chloe had her unreadable face on; the one where it was impossible to tell if she was being serious. They were all quiet in the aftermath of her question.

"Uh…."

"Uh…." Joel mimicked, clearly unimpressed with Ashley's response.

"I did not try to cut them down! I told them to duck!" Ashley finally protested, looking to them for help.

"To be fair, he did," Taylor agreed, but he was distracted, enjoying the way Sietta's whole body shook where he snickered against him.

"And I don't think dogs can get PTSD," Daniel mused, but he was looking so adoringly at Chloe you would think she had suggested he hung the moon.

"Have you seen that dog? Probably got PTSD the first time it barked and realised it was a possum not a dog." Hayley scowled, and they were all humming in agreement.

"Besides, you've done nothing but whinge about that fence since they put it up!" Ashley huffed. "I did you a favour!"

"Oh whatever, if I wanted it gone, I could have dug it up any time I wanted," Chloe scoffed at them, and Daniel almost spat out his water. "Please, I wouldn't expect you to represent me or anything! Besides, I wouldn't even get caught…. Just look at what they let into the police these days! Taylor's face is still purple and now he's full of holes. He's like a rotting eggplant. I'll expect his hair to fall out next."

"Mum!" Clay and Taylor gaped at her in matching indignation, and no doubt it was the mental imagery that won a laugh from Joel.

"In all seriousness, sweetheart, if you do anything else stupid, I'm probably going to murder you myself." Chloe cast him a look that said she would take no argument, as if that ever actually worked.

"I did not get shot on purpose!" Really, did she think he deliberately threw himself in front of the bullet? He wasn't even sure which bullet hit him! He was just glad it had been him, and not Sietta or Clay or Micah or Joel…. What if Emma had been outside? Much better it had been him.

"I'm still not sure which bullet hit you," Clay mused, and Taylor stiffened when Sietta sighed heavily beside him.

"The first one" was not what anyone had expected to hear. The conversation stopped entirely, something only Emma seemed to manage regularly, and everyone stared at Sietta with varying degrees of curiosity. All he did was wave a hand at his black shirt, which didn't help everyone else, but in the sunlight Taylor realised it was stained with red. With blood. For a brief second, he panicked, thinking Sietta was hurt.

"Moron, it's yours. Must have got it on me when you decided to audition for the Rugby World Cup on the front lawn!"

"Oh, that just won't do! Leila, sweetheart? Can you go find a shirt for Sietta? Oh, and one for Ash while you're at it!"

"Sure, Mum!" Leila had no complaints as she scrambled to her feet, leapt over Micah and ran inside to fetch the requested items.

"No offence, Ash, honey, but you stink."

"I was in a fire—"

"Do not remind me!" She held up her hand and actioned that he shouldn't even talk to it. Frighteningly, Emma copied her. She had the mime down perfectly, and she was only five.

"They shot you!" Clay was fuming again. "I mean, it wasn't even an accident, they got you with the first bullet!" But Joel laid a firm hand on his shoulder and shared a knowing look with Daniel, silencing Clay's protests with the dark frowns on their faces.

"I know." Sietta shrugged, looking guilty for the most part. That was when it started to make sense to Taylor, and he froze, staring at Sietta's profile, wishing he could crawl inside his head and figure out what he was thinking.

"They were shooting at Sietta," Hayley realised what they were all carefully not saying. She frowned then and looked up at Daniel as if he had the answers. "Why?"

"That's for the police to figure out," Daniel replied softly. "A lot's happened in the last few days. A lot of things are going to change. People don't like change, and a lot of people aren't happy with what's happened."

The Governor-General had stepped in and divested more than thirty senators of their positions, including members of the cabinet and shadow cabinet. Usually people protested the Governor-General interfering, but this time the general public seemed unanimously approving of the intervention. Polling dates had been set for re-elections in those seats, and Independents were likely to win. There was the possibility that for the first time in history Independents might hold more seats than the major parties.

"They're looking for someone to blame, and the media has made Sietta the face of this whole thing. He's an easy target." Daniel took a long swig of his beer while they let that sink in.

Trust Daniel to put it all out there on the table. Joel nodded in agreement, his hand still firm on Clay's shoulder, reining in his temper with just that touch. Taylor longed for something similar as his limbs turned cold and heavy. Someone had tried to murder Sietta. After everything Sietta had already been through, it was such a dick move, Taylor wanted to go down to the station and beat the two men until the breath rattled from burning lungs and they begged him to stop with their last breaths.

Unfortunately, that was illegal. So he had to settle for sitting next to Sietta, who had apparently figured it all out much earlier and seemed completely unconcerned. It was a front, Taylor knew, and he wanted to get home where he could hide them away in his room and ask Sietta the questions he wouldn't give anyone else the answers to.

Leila appeared with a pile of clothes, dumping a police shirt in Ashley's lap before going to the lounger, handing Sietta the rest of the clothes.

"What the hell?" The protest came from Ash, holding up a navy-coloured shirt in distaste.

"You've outgrown most of the others," Leila argued. "Besides, maybe no one will pull you over in that trash can of a car now!" Their mother, at least, thought that was funny.

Sietta looked at the blue shirt she had handed him with a raised brow.

"I know, it's not black." Leila rolled her eyes. "Micah said to pick something colourful, so I did. The hoodie's for Tay. No one here needs to be looking at that." Leila waved a hand at his bloodied shirt.

"He could just take it off! I don't mind looking at that!" Micah called out from the lawn, winning a spectacular glare from Sietta and a blush from Taylor, who made quick work of pulling the hoodie up his good arm and tossing it over his bad shoulder, covering up as best he could.

"Teenagers," Joel bemoaned, but he looked mostly amused and didn't scold Micah at all.

Sietta got up and went inside to change his shirt, and while he was gone, Ashley made quick work of swapping his shirt over, tossing the smoky one into the pool where it floated for a moment before sinking.

"I want to go home, Mum," Taylor said softly, and for once his mother gave no protest. She'd seen he was fine, but he needed rest. Sietta definitely needed some downtime, and he needed to have trouble away from his family, in a place he could control it.

"I'll drive," Hayley offered, but Joel waved her off.

"I'll drive. Clay and I are staying there tonight anyway. I'll leave my car in the drive if that's okay?" He waited until Daniel nodded. "Micah has a change of clothes in the back of the car, so he's fine if you're sure it's okay for him to stay over?" Again with the nod. "Alright, then we'll be off."

And just like that, because reasonable Joel had said it, no one argued. Sietta came back to find everyone getting up, and he fell into step beside Taylor, ready to help if he needed, even though he had to know Taylor wasn't going to need it. Joel went to check Micah was okay as they meandered their way to the front lawn.

9
THE MANY (MORONIC) FACES OF JOEL

"IS ANYONE hungry? I can get some takeout?" Joel parked the car and looked in the rear-view. He was rewarded with Taylor and Clay's stomachs' growling loudly in perfect unison.

"We'll go for a wander and grab some Thai from down on the corner." Clay waited for anyone to protest. No one did. "You guys get settled upstairs. Maybe put the kettle on."

"Sure." Taylor rolled his eyes. "Can't believe we went to all the trouble of going to Saturday barbeque and she didn't even feed us."

"I think you getting shot may have derailed Chloe's plans somewhat." Joel rolled his eyes as he waited until they were all out before locking the car up and heading for the gates while Taylor headed for the stairs.

"See you in a bit." Clay waved, and they were gone. Sietta frowned at the stairs, went to offer him a hand, thought better of it, and hurried up the stairs. Taylor had barely reached the fourth-floor landing when Sietta pinned Taylor to the wall, one hand on his good shoulder, the other on his hip, lips pressed firm and warm against Taylor's and tongue demanding entrance. Such an easy thing to grant when it was what he wanted. Taylor opened, feeling the thrust of Sietta's tongue against his own, tickling as it stroked the roof of his mouth. He was instantly hard, all tiredness forgotten.

Sietta pulled away reluctantly and fished the keys from Taylor's pocket, marching to the front door and pushing it open as if it had offended him somehow. Taylor let him lock it behind them, mostly because it gave him time to wrap his good arm around Sietta's waist, lifting him easily from his feet, tucking him under his arm, and carting him to the bedroom, then dropping him on the bed and kicking the door shut.

"You shouldn't do that," Sietta grumbled, but he didn't seem to have disliked it. He rolled his eyes at the confusion on Taylor's face. "Because of your shoulder, you moron!" Oh, right. Taylor smirked and prowled onto the bed, straddling Sietta's hips and putting his good hand down beside Sietta's head to support himself as he leaned in and rubbed his nose against Sietta's throat, inhaling the scent of him, and God, but the man did things to him.

"Are you smelling me?"

"Yes," he murmured, completely unabashed.

Sietta's hands came up to rest on his chest, his long fingers touching lightly at first, but growing bolder when Taylor only leaned in closer.

"Kiss me?" He wanted Sietta to initiate, needed to know he wanted it. He didn't need to wait; Sietta's hands came up to frame his face, tilt his head the way Sietta wanted it, and then their tongues were stroking, teasing, and playing in a way Taylor could never get his previous partners to stop and achieve. They saw muscles and a nice face, and they wanted it for a night. They didn't see Taylor, or the things he didn't like, or what he wanted. Not that Taylor had ever wanted foreplay, but this wasn't going anywhere tonight. This was just for fun, and that was different.

"Feels so good," Sietta whispered against his lips. "I only kissed one person before," he admitted, his hair framing their faces, closing them into their own world where his secrets seemed safer. "I know that's completely lame. I'm probably terrible at this, but I don't care. I want more…."

"You're not lame." Taylor chuckled at him, leaning in for more kisses because he wasn't sure he would ever get enough of those. Sietta tasted sweet and a little watery, as if his skin were infused with all that tea he drank. He was warm and pushed up against him without even noticing what he was doing, until Taylor worried he would come in his pants from the vague friction alone.

"Only one person?" His brain caught up a little, realising Sietta probably hadn't had much chance before his imprisonment, and certainly hadn't been given the opportunity during. And now… well, now Taylor was more than happy to give the man whatever the hell he wanted. As long as it really was what he wanted.

"Are you sure? I mean… me?" Even Clay wouldn't recommend *him* as boyfriend material, but even as he thought it, he realised that was exactly what he wanted. He wanted Sietta to be his boyfriend. He wanted Sietta to be his partner. His whatever. His everything, because if anyone else got to lay a hand on him, he was going to lose his mind. But Sietta had to want it too, and the fear that maybe he was only hurting and damaged cut so deep, Taylor could barely acknowledge it.

"I've never been surer of anything in my life," Sietta said, his voice gentle but firm. "I was in the hospital… you were in surgery, you know? I knew you were fine, but I went to the bathroom, and I realised I was wet. I had your blood on me. I had to wash it off, but I didn't want to wash even that much of you away. I liked it on me. I wanted you so badly I couldn't think straight. I just knew, right then. I know I probably sound batshit crazy, but I don't care. You're mine. I want you. I've never wanted anything the way I want you. You make me crazy and sane, all at the same time."

"Yeah." Taylor reached up and pushed Sietta's hair back behind his ear, stroking his thumb over Sietta's temple. "I know that feeling." He wondered if that was how Clay had felt, that first time he spotted Joel. He'd certainly seemed crazy when he finally came home the next day, raving about the love of his life. But Taylor wondered if maybe he understood a little better now.

"You're like a walking wet dream," Sietta mumbled. "It's ridiculous." His hands were still stroking over Taylor's pectoral, down his abs, pinching his hip. Sietta seemed fascinated by every line of him. It made Taylor chuckle, soft and low, and harder when Sietta glared at him.

"Si… you're the sexiest thing I've ever seen in my life. Guess we have different wet dreams, but as long as they match up, we're good, yeah?"

"Just… I'm not gonna be good at this, you know?" Sietta's eyes were wet, and he bit his lower lip to keep from saying more, but he didn't need to. Taylor smiled and pulled him in for more kisses.

"Look, I know you have no clue, but you're kind of good at everything." Taylor chuckled at him, silencing his protests with another kiss. "And even if you're not, you're perfect for me. But while we're pointing out our faults to one another, I suppose I'll help you out and admit I've only ever had two serious partners, and by serious I mean they lasted more than a week. They both dumped me. They both to this day would tell you I'm an asshole, and they would both be right."

That made Sietta pause, blinking and looking up at him as if he had suddenly grown a spectacularly fascinating second head.

"You're pretty blunt sometimes, but honestly… your family is nuts. I defy anyone to have a conversation with them that doesn't end with you acting like an asshole to get away…."

And right then Taylor knew he was in love. He pinned Sietta to the bed and showered him in enough kisses to make up for the time Sietta had lost he could have spent getting kissed.

"If you're having sex in there, I just want to remind you there's a hole in your shoulder you shouldn't be putting any pressure on, so Sietta better be on top! And I mean that in the physical sense, not the sexual sense, I really don't care or want to know who's got their dick in who, okay?" Clay bellowed from the other side of the bedroom door.

Taylor had a short moment of dismay before Sietta was howling with laughter, and only because of that did Taylor not storm out and castrate his twin.

"There's food when you're ready," Joel added through the door. "And fresh bandages for your shoulder if you wanted to have a shower." Great, they were both listening to Taylor and Sietta make out. That wasn't embarrassing at all.

"Food first." Sietta's words were almost lost against his throat. "Then I want to shower with you." Startled, Taylor pulled back to get a better look at Sietta's face, not surprised to see his cheeks flushed dark with heat, his eyes heavy with desire. "If that's okay—"

"I'm only going to say this once, Si. Absolutely anything you want to do with me is fine. You do not need permission to do anything, at all. Well, except do not ask me for faecal play. That shit is nasty!"

Sietta gaped at him, and was nodding and shaking his head at the same time.

"I'm taking that as a *yes* you understand what I've said and a *no* you're not into that sort of thing because, yes, it is disgusting." Just nods now. Perfect.

Taylor managed to extricate himself from the tangle of limbs he'd made of their bodies, groaning as he got himself standing, partly because his shoulder ached, but mostly because he was hard and wanting to shower naked with Sietta was definitely higher on his list of wants than food. But if he took care of food first, he would have longer with Sietta later. Sietta was right; that was a better plan.

"I like the nickname," Sietta admitted, sitting up and pulling his shirt straight. "I've never had one before. Well, other than 'rich kid', or 'faggot'…. Si. It's kinda funny." He shrugged as if he hadn't just punched Taylor in the guts, and all Taylor could do was lean in to kiss his temple and go to open the bedroom door.

"HOW MUCH freakin' food do you think we can eat?" Sietta swept his gaze over the coffee table, which was quite literally covered in small takeaway containers. Thirteen dishes, if Taylor's quick scan of it was correct. He double-checked, and yeah there were thirteen. And a bag of spring rolls and a few dipping sauces. It was the usual order, with one extra dish. He looked at Sietta in confusion and went to sit on the floor opposite where Joel and Clay were seated. They'd given him the couch side, so he could lean back against it if he wanted, but his back felt too tender for that. He gratefully took the offered cushion, though, propping it up against his lower back.

"Are you eating on the floor?" Sietta was still standing there, taking in the table of food with a judgemental sweep.

"Gets kept chained to a wine cellar for years, balks at eating on the floor. Can you believe this guy?" Clay waved his chopsticks in Sietta's direction.

"To be fair, I don't think he saw this much food in all the years he was kept in the cellar," Joel reasoned, and they both turned to look up at him. Taylor smiled and patted the floor at his side, amused as Sietta dazedly wandered over and sat down, still gaping at the containers.

"Why did you order so much?"

"When Clay and Taylor are hungry, they'll easily eat five or six containers themselves," Joel replied softly, looking amused and more than a little pleased to have someone to commiserate with at last. "And then if I'm hungry, honestly I always want a bit more than one. And just in case, we order a spare or two so they have some leftovers for lunch if they're working the next day, or just a midnight snack. Oh, then you need rice, so a few containers of that. And everyone likes spring rolls, so we got some of those. But we had no idea what sort of sauce you like, so we just got one of each...." He looked a little helpless himself at the array of food.

"This is ridiculous." Sietta's eyes were wide as he looked from one dish to the next, leaning in to sniff at something he couldn't immediately identify. "You are ridiculous," he turned to tell Taylor, as if he hadn't already said it numerous times today.

"Hey, Odin needs his banquet."

"Ew! I do not have a daddy fetish," Sietta objected immediately. "Thor all the way, thank you very much!"

They all stared at him as he carefully dished some rice up onto a plate, looking up at them when he realised they were all staring.

"What? Micah raves about that guy, showed me pics on his phone. That guy is hot!"

"And now his presence here makes sense." Joel winked at Sietta to show he was only joking. He understood all too well how someone could be attracted to Clay and Taylor. He started dishing himself up some food, and Taylor and Clay waited only long enough for them to have what they wanted before digging in themselves.

"Micah says you're an amazing piano player," Joel noted conversationally. Taylor loved the way Sietta's cheeks immediately darkened and he ducked his head nervously, suddenly shy.

"I'm okay" was the mumbled response.

"Uh… I think you have to be better than okay to win the Sydney International Piano Competition?" Joel, as per usual, dropped an academic bombshell.

"That sounds prestigious and wanky," Clay observed, looking from Joel to Sietta and back again. "It's prestigious and wanky, right?"

"It's one of the world's great piano competitions," Joel agreed, still watching Sietta.

"Definitely prestigious and wanky." Clay shoved a spring roll in his mouth whole. That wasn't surprising, since Clay had tried to learn the guitar once and succeeded only in smashing it over Brayden's head in a fit of rage when Taylor dared point out the strings would keep breaking if he continued plucking them so hard. At least it had provided good kindling for the bonfire they had that weekend camping. Since then, Clay had thought anyone who successfully learned a musical instrument was a genius.

"It's not that big of a deal," Sietta mumbled, his blush darkening. He shovelled food into his mouth as if it would mean he wouldn't have to contribute any further to the conversation.

"Considering there are auditions held worldwide for thirty-two positions in the competition, and you won twenty-five thousand dollars, and your Gala recital is considered the most stunning performance of the decade, I'd say not that big of a deal is not exactly true," Joel reasoned, and Taylor finally clued in that this thing Sietta had won was a big deal. To somebody. He had no idea how playing the piano could be important, but whatever the deal was, Sietta had aced it.

"They made me do it," Sietta blurted out, and Taylor finally realised there were tears in Sietta's eyes when he turned to look up at him, searching for help or a way out of the conversation. Or maybe someone to listen and understand. "I didn't want to go in it, but they thought even just auditioning would look good for them, participation in the arts, you know?"

Taylor stared at the long, bony fingers gripping the chopsticks too tightly and wondered how it hadn't registered that they were musician's hands. A pianist's hands. Apparently an exceptionally gifted pianist's hands. But hands that didn't want to play in a competition, nonetheless. He closed his own hand over Sietta's and lifted it to his lips, kissing the back, then his fingers, and then stealing the piece of chicken from the end of the chopsticks and chewing it thoughtfully while Sietta fumed.

"That was mine!"

"And there's plenty where it came from, as you pointed out," Taylor reasoned, smirking.

"The university has a grand piano in one of its practise rooms. I can book you some time, if you'd like to play," Joel said, and Sietta looked back at him, still looking upset, but the offer seemed to calm something in him. Taylor realised it was something Sietta missed. Not the competition, but playing. If he'd listened better, he would have remembered Sietta was studying music; that it was one of the few things he was permitted to do. He'd joked that they had chained him to the piano, and Taylor realised it was able to be joked about because he enjoyed playing it.

"I'd like that," Sietta admitted. "Just, not when there are lots of people there."

"At night, then," Joel agreed, smiling. "I'll book a few sessions tomorrow and send you the times. Clay said you have a phone?"

Sietta looked so pleased with it when he pulled it out that Taylor felt guilty. It was the cheapest prepaid Clay could get from the corner store. It didn't even have wireless, let alone a touch screen or any of the other things they considered a "necessity" on a phone these days.

"Is that a Nokia 3310? They don't even make those anymore. How old is that thing? Where the hell did you get it?" Joel reached for it, but Sietta refused to hand it over.

"You need a new phone," Clay muttered, looking embarrassed, but Sietta clutched it to his chest as if afraid Clay would take it off him there and then.

"No! I love this phone!" Sietta blurted out. "I just... I like this one. I'm keeping it."

"O-kay." Clay blinked at him, glancing at Taylor as if he wasn't sure Taylor understood he was crazy, but not bothering to say anything. Sietta liked this one because they had bought it for him, and if he wanted to keep it, Taylor sure as hell wasn't going to deny him. At this point he wasn't prepared to deny Sietta anything, soul included. The little imp had already taken it, he was sure.

Joel put his number in Sietta's phone and handed it back. It disappeared into Sietta's pocket before anyone could try to snatch it away. As if Sietta expected it to be taken. As if he was used to it. Sietta looked up at him, amused as he quietly nibbled on a spring roll.

"Why would they try and shoot you?" Clay grumbled, not for the first time, except this time he was staring at Sietta, his frown dark in contemplation.

"Revenge?" Taylor didn't think that it was something they needed to think about. The boss had all the information, and it had been handed over to ASIS and the AFP. No doubt someone was working on the case. For once they got to sit and eat and not have to deal with paperwork. That suited him just fine.

"Unless it's related to something else?" Joel had his thinking face on. Taylor didn't think anything good ever came from Joel having that expression. Usually, things that followed were things Taylor did not understand…. A lot of the time maths was involved, and Taylor didn't like maths unless it involved bullet trajectories or speed, and really that was physics.

"What do you mean?" Sietta was quiet, chopsticks poised over the fried rice, frozen as he watched Joel and then looked up at Taylor. "What's with his face?"

"Excuse me?" Joel frowned at him.

"That's his thinking face," Taylor noted sagely.

"I do not have a thinking face!" Joel's expression morphed.

"That's his angry face. I bring it out in him a lot." Taylor gestured to Joel with his chopsticks.

"I do not have an angry face! What the…. Clay?"

But Clay was nodding in agreement, and Joel's face morphed again.

"That's his 'I can't believe this is happening' face," Taylor whispered deliberately loud, and Joel gave up and shovelled food in his mouth.

"Joel has many faces." Clay beamed at him. "Many, beautiful, adorable faces. He can't play poker for shit."

Joel continued to shovel food in his mouth while Clay watched him lovingly.

"What did the thinking face mean?" Sietta prompted when everyone kept eating. His own chopsticks remained poised over his fried rice.

"Well, you've exposed a lot of people. A lot of them are going to prison, especially the ministers who are proven to have taken bribes from oil and gas companies. Even more will lose their jobs, on top of those who the Governor G already removed, which was badass by the way. So far the arrests have focussed on Federal Government, but ASIS will work their way down through the state government soon, and then local. People are demanding full transparency, and they're getting it." Joel licked the sauce off the end of his chopsticks and then waved them at Sietta when a new idea came to him. "What if this wasn't about any of the things that have been exposed, but instead was something they thought you knew but hadn't exposed yet?"

"But anything I knew or found out, I put on the USB." Sietta looked adorable when he was confused, frowning with a line between his brows and his lips pouting slightly.

"But no one else knows that," Joel pointed out reasonably. "For all they know, this is just the first information you dumped. What else do you know?"

"Nothing. I seriously don't even remember half of what was on the USB. I just kept collecting stuff, and honestly I had my head beat so many times, I'd forget a lot of it afterward if I didn't write it down or save stuff...."

Taylor flinched, and Sietta hunched over a little, as if embarrassed when he realised what he'd said. Everyone was quiet again, forcing themselves to eat instead of comment. Taylor knew it was something he was going to have to get used to. Sietta was still in shock. Taylor expected Sietta to let random facts tumble out at unexpected times, and that the things he revealed would not be pleasant. It was important not to allow Sietta to feel victimised or blamed in any way. Just let it happen and become his normal. Somehow.

"I could be wrong," Joel said softly. "But it takes a lot to get your hands on a gun, and you have to be pretty determined to go hunt someone down at a weekend barbeque and try to shoot them. The thugs didn't seem like the kind of people who would take offence to the political anarchy you've caused. I'm assuming they've been hired, or convinced it's in their best interests to get rid of you. Or just threaten you."

Taylor shoved enough sweet and sour pork in his mouth to keep from commenting. He didn't like that idea at all. So it was probably right, since it was coming from Joel's mouth. That meant whoever was behind the attempt might try again. Taylor hated that, but at least he was sure he would be able to keep Sietta with him, and subsequently safe.

"We'll have to see what the boss says," Taylor managed to grumble.

"You mean I'll have to see," Clay corrected, pointing chopsticks at Taylor with his brow arched. "You don't honestly think they're going to let you work with a bullet hole in you. Do you?"

"But I'm fine…."

They were all laughing at him. Taylor tried to think of anything at all he could say in reply, but his mind remained blank. He had been shot. He was definitely going to be on desk duty for some time. There would be evaluations, physical and mental, and they would make him write reports. Quitting almost sounded better, and definitely easier. He sighed and ate his dinner a little more glumly.

Joel and Clay offered to clean everything away, so Taylor took Sietta back into his bedroom and sat quietly on the edge of the bed, watching Sietta move around the space, examining it all quietly, picking things up and putting them down again. Not that there was a lot, but there was enough for someone who'd been locked in a wine cellar to find interesting.

"Do you want a shower?"

"Yes. After you." Sietta glanced shyly at the door to the en suite, and Taylor didn't hesitate, grabbing some boxers from a drawer on the tallboy and leaving Sietta to his perusal of the bedroom. Sure, Sietta had proposed showering together, but suggesting something and following through with it after you'd calmed down a bit were two entirely different things. He was happy Sietta was thinking about it.

The shower was hot and cleansing, and he managed not to get his bandages wet. It felt good to wash the scent of iodine off his skin. He dried off, pulled the boxers on, and towel dried his hair quickly before wandering back out, amused when Sietta froze, his gaze trailing up and down his body before meeting Taylor's, a rich blush creeping up his cheeks.

"You're allowed to look." Taylor stepped under the light where he would see him better, and Sietta's soft chuckle in response was dry.

"There's a lot to look at," he mumbled, slipping past Taylor and shutting the bathroom door.

The bed lured Taylor in, and as soon as he lay down to wait for Sietta, sleep pulled him under.

10
COCONUT MILK AND ALZHEIMER'S

FINGERS TRAILING over a hardened nipple pulled him from his dreams. Taylor moaned in response and opened one eye to peer at Sietta, taking in the dark circles under his eyes but also the bright light of curiosity behind them. He bit his lip when Sietta pinched, watching Taylor's reactions, but didn't interfere.

Sietta's fingers were soft, long, and languid as they explored, rolling over the ridges of each of his abs to the waistband of his boxers, turning and scraping back toward Taylor's belly button.

"Exactly how much of your day is wasted pushing heavy things?"

"A few hours." Taylor smirked. "Though some of it's spent pulling as well, or running or swimming or riding...." He could think of something he'd like to be riding, but he shoved those thoughts aside for the moment. "I wouldn't say it's wasted?"

That blush was beautiful, streaking over Sietta's cheeks and down his throat.

"No... wasted was definitely the wrong word," Sietta faintly admitted.

The fingers had been teasing enough, but all Taylor could manage was a strangled moan when Sietta's head bowed low and his soft, warm tongue tentatively licked at his hardened nipple. For a moment Taylor hesitated, not sure he should react, but he didn't want to treat Sietta with kid gloves, and doubted that was what Sietta wanted either. A second after he came to that conclusion, Sietta was on his back, pinned to the bed with all of Taylor's weight pressing him into the mattress while Taylor thoroughly explored Sietta's mouth with his tongue.

It was all the little things that drove Taylor to distraction. Attractive people were not rare, especially not in Sydney. Fun people were not unique. Intelligence even, was not that uncommon, especially in business circles. But kindness, that was limited. Courage, sparser still. But it was smaller things, like the way Sietta gasped as if the air had run out, or the way his fingers jerked slightly whenever something felt particularly good, as if he'd been electrocuted slightly. The way he smelt and tasted and pressed up against him, needing more. Those things made Taylor lose all sense of time and place until the world was only a sense named Sietta.

The demanding pounding at the front door made Taylor groan, and he looked up at the ceiling, incredulous while Sietta huffed in annoyance underneath him.

"Seriously?" Taylor smirked down at him, carefully moving off the bed and offering a hand down to Sietta. Sietta took it and pulled it closer, sucking his first finger into his mouth and wrapping his tongue around it, until Taylor was afraid he was going to come in his pants for the first time since leaving puberty.

"I was enjoying that," Sietta mumbled, but he forced himself up and went to the en suite, closing the door. The shower started a moment later. Taylor suspected Sietta was going to be addicted to bathing for some time, and left him to it.

Unfortunately, there was only one person he knew who pounded that hard on his front door, waited exactly ten seconds, and pounded again. Waited ten seconds… the man was like a clock, it was so precise every time. Taylor took a deep calming breath before opening the front door and stepping back.

"Please, come in." Because Benjamin Grant would, regardless. Even if he hadn't been one third of Daniel Jameson's law firm, as Taylor's godfather he seemed to think entry into any Jameson household was a given right.

Dark brown eyes looked him up and down, a slight downturn of lips marring an otherwise flawless face on a surprisingly tall Asian gentleman, in a suit Taylor knew cost a month of his salary. His hair was long enough to be pulled back into a sculpted man bun Taylor still insisted looked ridiculous, mostly because it didn't at all. There was no briefcase or messenger bag or anything in his hands, only a phone tucked neatly in his inside jacket pocket, as usual. There was no need to take notes when one had an eidetic memory.

"Ben…."

"I don't know why I still hold out hope that one day you'll answer the door, clothed." Benjamin Grant shook his head at him and strolled into the apartment as if he owned it. Taylor sighed again and closed the door.

"It's seven in the morning," Taylor pointed out. "And I pulled myself out of bed to answer the door for you." As if any excuse would cut it. Ben arched one flawless brow at him and went and perched himself on one of the kitchen stools to wait.

Taylor walked into the kitchen and immediately put the kettle on to make tea if Sietta emerged, and turned on the Breville coffee maker. He worked as quietly as possible, which was hard when the machine insisted on being loud, especially the milk frother. He tried to make it exactly the way Ben liked it, because if it wasn't perfect, the lecture was going to be epic, and an expensive coffee machine would likely find its way to his doorstep. Again. With a Barista's manual and Ben's venti latte instructions highlighted. Again.

"You're looking better than I expected. Daniel mentioned you've fractured your skull. Why were you not placed on light duties?" The man could sniff a lawsuit, as if Taylor would ever charge Brayden for negligence, especially when it was his own.

"It's not a bad fracture. It's in an area protected by the helmet I wear, and it's not a place likely to cause any damage if I were to hit it again. Also, it's tiny. Like a centimetre or something. My eye is worse, and even that's healing fine." He waved a hand at his face and the bruising that, while still purple, was far lighter than the bloody mess it had been a few days prior.

Benjamin was staring at him like he was a moron. There was a crack in his skull, after all. "So it was your decision."

"Yes."

"You're a moron."

Obviously. He continued making the coffee.

The bedroom door opened, and Sietta emerged in loose jeans, a black T-shirt, and his loose black jumper, hair wet and tied up loosely in a far messier version of Ben's bun, feet bare. Taylor wanted to shove him back in the bedroom, strip him naked, and get back to business. As if that was going to happen today.

"Mister Salisbury, it's a pleasure to meet you." Ben held out his hand, and Sietta stared at it, looked at Taylor in amusement, and reached out to shake it.

"Uh…."

"Benjamin Grant," Taylor offered.

Sietta carefully took a seat on the stool beside Ben. "I didn't know we had an appointment."

"Ben doesn't tend to make them," Taylor informed him, and once again Sietta looked between them but stayed quiet. Ben had that effect on people.

"Your father's legal team attempted to lay charges against you last night. Daniel had me step in on your behalf."

"What?" Taylor slammed his hand down on the top of the coffee maker, startled by the news, but Sietta looked as if he had expected it.

"It is illegal to record phone conversations in New South Wales," Benjamin explained. "However, recording for the purposes of exposing criminal activity is treated differently, and in this case the judge agreed with me and threw out all charges. I'll finish having the rest of it dealt with when the courts open today. I suspect they will keep trying, but no judge is going to accept charges against a kidnapped child. That's just absurd. They're just trying to buy time and distract from the charges they are facing themselves."

Taylor placed the latte in front of Ben and put a cup of hot water in front of Sietta, watching him quietly peruse the tea box until he chose a green and lemon bag. Taylor made himself a strong black, figuring he was going to need it.

"Thank you, for helping me," Sietta spoke, but it was clear he meant what he said, and Benjamin actually smiled at him in response before turning a dark glare toward Taylor.

"What is this supposed to be? Is this full cream milk?"

"No, it's light... ah, fuck." He'd forgotten to use coconut milk. Sighing, he fetched the barista frothing coconut milk from the fridge and got to work remaking the coffee, taking a long sip of his own to get him going. At least Sietta seemed amused.

"I'm assuming your other half is at work? And Micah's still at Daniel's?"

"Yup." Taylor frowned as he tried to get the coconut milk exactly right, refusing to be stuck making a third coffee for the pedantic prick.

"Let Clay know I'm monitoring the charges for the shooting, but I doubt there will be any trouble from it. You're both giving your statements today?"

He'd forgotten about it, but he nodded now he'd been reminded. It was probably a good idea to take Sietta in to the office so he could catch up on everything as well, with people who actually knew what was going on. As far as he knew, ASIS were still using the riot squad offices as their base for the case because it made things move faster to have the riot squad act on warrants as soon as they were issued. Besides, the office was safe. Safer... something.

"You forgot, didn't you?" It was not really a question, and Ben was looking at him as if he were a moron.

"I got shot! I'm entitled to forget about paperwork."

"You forgot you got shot, didn't you?" That tone spoke volumes.

"I...." Yeah, he forgot. It wasn't like it hurt more than anything else.

"You're a moron."

He put the coffee in front of Benjamin and watched him tentatively sip before smirking and taking a larger gulp. Taylor thanked whatever god and finished off his own coffee before starting in on Ben's discarded one.

"Is it really possible they might charge him?" Taylor was turning the idea over in his mind, unable to come up with any way it was sane, which meant it was probably true.

"They'll try, as a stalling tactic mostly, but there's no way the public will agree to even allowing the charges to be laid, so no, it's not possible. No one is going to agree to that kind of public backlash just to delay proceedings for a lynching they do want to see happen. Don't stress about it, I will take care of it."

Which was as good as saying it would never happen to begin with. Benjamin Grant was never to be taken lightly, and if he said not to worry, there was nothing to worry about.

They stopped worrying.

THE PUBLIC Order and Riot Squad offices were eerily quiet when they entered. Sietta looked uncomfortable and stuck closer to Taylor's side than usual, aware of people looking up and just as quickly looking away. It was not what ordinarily happened when Taylor arrived at work, but then he wasn't really sure what usual was, since normal meant Clay at his side, whining about whatever was scheduled for the day. Sietta was contrastingly silent.

"What the hell are you doing here?"

Taylor dropped into his chair, in front of his desk, and spun it around to glare at Hale. "I work here."

"Not when you get shot, you don't." Mendel shoved a spare chair over for Sietta. "Boss is going to flip it if he sees you. He's already lost it a million times this morning."

"A, I didn't mean to get shot. B, I wasn't working when I got shot. C, it's not bad. I was home in two hours. D, he's the one who told me to come in."

"Mmm… bet he meant Clay." Hale looked at Mendel, who nodded in immediate agreement.

"Your boss can't tell the difference?" Sietta asked quietly.

"Not unless one of them's injured." Hale waved a hand at Taylor, indicating the fading bruises on his face and the bandage peeking out from under his shirt, and smirked at the dark look Taylor tossed in response. "Besides, Clay always hands out Taylor's number for work stuff, so boss probably rang 'Jameson' in his speed dial and had no clue he'd called Taylor."

"But…." Sietta was frowning, and it made Taylor smile. He liked that Sietta had no trouble at all telling them apart, even if it was his voice. The only person other than family capable of that was Joel, and even he had struggled in the beginning. Taylor hoped that meant something.

"Don't let it worry you," Mendel was consoling Sietta. "We usually tell them apart by Taylor's terrible personality."

"With an attitude like that, I'm surprised he's not always showering you with a placid disposition," Sietta grumbled, and the startled looks on their faces had Taylor laughing in delight, which only made them gape more. Sure, he was rarely in a good mood at work, but they dealt with scum on a daily basis, and his teammates seemed to go out of their way to make him feel worse. Combine that with trying to deal with his siblings, and was it really any wonder he wasn't the most polite human? Sure, Clay dealt with it better, but Taylor also kind of liked making everyone think he was an asshole. It was… well, fun. Which probably meant he was an asshole, but that was okay.

"This is Finn Hale, and Chris Mendel." He introduced them, motioning to Sietta. "Guys, Sietta Salisbury."

"No shit." Mendel frowned at them as if convinced they were conspiring against him. Mendel was a strange guy; taller than Taylor, and wider, obsessed with bench press in the gym, and convinced if he ate chicken for breakfast, lunch, and tea he'd somehow grow a few more inches. He was worth having in a firefight, an ex-military sniper, but he'd been friends with Brayden in the army, and he knew far too many embarrassing stories of their childhood for Taylor's comfort. Taylor tended to steer clear, while Clay hung out at the watercooler with him like he was their long-lost brother. It was plain weird.

Hale was one of those quiet guys who waited, absorbed everything, and then slapped you in the face with a solution to the unsolvable. If Taylor was going to be stuck in a life or death situation, other than Clay, Hale was the man he wanted at his side. He actually reminded him a little of Sietta, though far less sneaky. Also, the man could shoot anything.

"It's okay to meet you." Sietta smirked at them, and they groaned, looking sideways at Taylor.

"He's been around you too long already," Hale muttered.

"Or not long enough." Taylor shuffled papers around on his desk, trying to tidy it a little since Sietta was there and it was a mess. "Though, he has been to Saturday lunch and he's still here. I'm not sure he's sane."

Mendel choked on his coffee, and Hale laughed harder than Taylor thought was strictly necessary.

"Well, I was locked in a wine cellar for a while. I suspect I'm socially stunted. I mean, I have this thing for showers at the moment? They're pretty much the best thing ever...."

"That's not abnormal." Taylor gave up on his desk. It was never going to be tidy. "I mean if you were bathing in wine, maybe? But everyone likes to be clean, and it's kind of a novelty for you at the moment."

"We get it." Mendel scowled. "We're leaving. You can stop being weird and talking crazy now!" Taylor watched them leave, more amused by the smirk on Sietta's face than anything. It was almost like having Clay around, but different. Not better, certainly not worse, just different. Taylor liked it, a lot.

"Jameson, what the hell do you think you're doing here?" His boss's voice boomed across the room. Sietta jerked and almost fell off his chair, startled, while Taylor spun lazily around to face the man, amused to see Clay standing right beside him, looking perplexed.

"Sir, I seriously just gave you my report. You sure you don't have Alzheimer's? Short-term memory loss? Something?" Clay seemed truly confused.

"I'm here to give my report," Taylor called over, trying hard not to laugh at the crimson rising in their boss's face as he turned to glare at Clay, who was looking between them as realisation dawned.

"Oh, you meant *that* Jameson…."

"Yes, I meant *that* Jameson." The boss pointed over at Taylor and glared at Clay, who shrugged as if to silently say "my bad" and turned to Taylor with a dark scowl.

"What the hell are you doing here?"

"I think I work here?" Taylor reminded his brother. "You sure you don't have short-term memory loss? I thought it was me that hit my head, but maybe you clonked both our noggins? Wouldn't be the first time…."

"I said I was sorry!" Clay stormed over, the rest of the men in the office chuckling under their breaths, trying to keep it in while the boss was watching. Taylor had to give them credit; he'd have been laughing in their faces by now, the boss be damned.

"Forget your face, you've got a hole in you, Jameson! Go home and e-mail me your damn statement!" The Feds must have been giving Nikau a hard time. He had circles under his eyes so dark they were starting to resemble war paint, and Taylor was certain there was more grey at his temples than usual. His temper was even shorter than normal.

"But I'm right here and can do it in person. I'll give it to Hale and he can give it to you, while you talk to Sietta. Since I brought him along to see you?" He waved a hand at Sietta and put on his best innocent expression.

Maori men could be frightening when mad. The Haka was considered intimidating for a reason. It would not have surprised Taylor at all if the man had launched into a war dance right there in the office; he certainly looked pissed enough. He appeared angrier than that time Clay broke the squad truck when he tried to pick it up in a Hulk challenge when they were visiting in a school. Instead Clay had managed to push it forward and it rolled through the windows of the science lab, knocked over a Bunsen burner into a beaker of chemicals, and blew a hole in the floor. An expensive mishap for the school, and he hadn't even managed to lift the truck.

Clay had been on desk for over a month, and the boss's face had looked just like it did now. He was a scarily quiet fumer, eyes dark and teeth showing. He wasn't the sort of man you should joke with; it was dangerous. Maybe that was why Taylor took such pleasure in it.

"Mister Salisbury, join me in my office. ASIS can speak to you while you're here." He was already heading back in himself, and Sietta hurried to catch up. "Hale, write the moron's statement!"

"I don't think you're allowed to call your employee a moron," Sietta muttered as he slipped into the office and the door closed behind him. Nikau gave Taylor the filthiest scowl before following. Taylor waited for several seconds after the office door closed with Sietta on the other side of it before getting up and wheeling his chair over to Hale's desk, dropping into it smugly while Hale banged his head on the desk.

"Why me...."

"Because you type faster than Mendel. It's those huge fingers, you know? Hits like five keys at once, and the report reads like gibberish. Not sure he can spell anyways...."

"Fuck you, Jameson!" Mendel snapped from the watercooler, where Clay had gone to have a bros catch-up.

Hale booted up his computer and opened the file, glaring at him as he leaned back in his chair and waited. Taylor sighed and started his report, aware of Hale's fingers hurriedly inputting the information.

"Wait... your mother offered them lemonade?" Hale's fingers paused, rereading the information on the screen as if it might change before his eyes and actually make sense.

"Yes, my mother, Chloe... you know, the crazy one who birthed me?"

"I don't know why I'm surprised." Hale waved for Taylor to continue.

"Emma was chastising Ash about his car? What happened to the car? You mentioned that was why you were distracted when you first noticed the perps' car had no plates...."

So Taylor went into a lengthy description of what happened with Ash, even though it had little to do with the report.

"Aw, baby bro got his first big fire! That's awesome! Tell him I said congrats!"

"That's... a super weird thing to be congratulating someone on...."

"I don't mean... he saved a life, right? He must be stoked! Don't tell me you guys just gave him a hard time about that rust-bucket car your dad made him buy?" Hale looked completely heartbroken on Ashley's behalf.

"He needed to learn to respect his belongings! You should've seen the first car he made me buy!"

"On what planet does your dad think that forcing a teenage boy to own the shittiest, ugliest car at the shop is going to encourage them to love and care for it?"

"Mechanically, it was sound," Taylor argued, though he had to admit, Hale had a point, and that really made no sense, yet they'd all fallen for his argument at the time.

"Yeah. That totally works when you get handed a Nokia when everyone else has the latest iPhone." Hale rolled his eyes. "There's something seriously wrong with your family."

"I've been saying that for years," Taylor mumbled, but got back to his report.

"Wait, I'm still confused. Brayden let Emma run out the front, after you got shot?" Nothing he said seemed to surprise Hale.

Well, now that he mentioned it, that was sort of weird.

"I don't think it was Brayden, I mean he was with Hayley giving me first aid, so it must have been Kelly... but there's no way she would have let Emma out, so I'm assuming Jay was up to something stupid and Emma escaped...."

"And the fact a small child has to 'escape' your house doesn't concern you?"

"Not really." It was a pretty normal event during their childhood. Taylor and Clay had escaped so many times, there was a contact list on the fridge for the most likely houses they could turn up at, for use by babysitters.... That probably wasn't a good thing, now that he thought about it... "I don't know why Em was out there. I was shot, remember?"

"I'm putting that in the report." Hale nodded to himself, typing away, and Taylor sighed. It wasn't like the report was going on his record or anything. Hale could write whatever he wanted, as long as it was true. As long as there was no note to contact child services, he wasn't concerned. If that happened, Bray would kill him, Kelly would eat him, and Emma would become a psychopath and later destroy the world. But as long as he wasn't around to see it....

"Okay, we're done." Hale saved and submitted the report, closed his laptop, and then sat there staring at him.

"What?"

"Are you really okay? I mean...." He waved a hand at Taylor.

"I'm fine! It's a black eye and a graze!"

"No, a graze is when the bullet rubs up against you and tickles your fancy, not when it nails you hard and leaves you bleeding all over the place while your mum offers the guy who nailed you lemonade."

Clay's laughter filled the office, and when Hale and Taylor turned in their chairs to glare at him, he laughed until he cried. "Sorry, just... imagining Sietta's face when Mum walks in on him the first time...."

Hale gaped and turned back to Taylor, leaning in and whispering disturbingly loud.

"You're banging the vic?"

"He's not a victim!" Taylor growled.

"Oh. My. God! You're banging Salisbury!" Hale hissed even louder. Just loud enough for Mendel to overhear, apparently.

"That's so wrong, man! Not the gay thing, you know I'm so cool with that, but... dude, is he even legal?"

"What?" Taylor threw his stapler at Mendel, trying to process that Mendel thought he could even look at an underage and think a dirty thought, let alone act on it. "Are you two fucking serious? Dammit, Sietta is twenty-two, completely sane, and FYI we haven't moved past first base!"

"Ooooh, wining and dining," Hale cooed, clutching his hands to his chest over his heart and kissing air.

"Fuck you." Taylor rolled his chair back over to his desk and glared at Clay, who looked far too smug for words.

"Aw, come on, you remember how much shit you all gave me for dating a doctor of science! You are fair game, brother!"

"So... he's sane?" Mendel still looked confused.

"Just be careful, Jameson. If you're involved with him, you should tell Parata," Hale pointed out reasonably. "As long as the boss knows what's going on, he can make good decisions. If you make him make crap decisions, he might actually kill you."

"I wouldn't put it past him." Mendel sipped his water.

"Don't give him a reason to kill you. Tell him if you're in a relationship so it doesn't come back to bite him in the ass." Hale was adamant he do something, apparently.

Taylor gave him the finger but didn't bother replying, distracted when Sietta came out of the boss's office, shaking his hand and thanking him with a hard smile before looking across the room and meeting Taylor's gaze.

"I don't want to see your face for the rest of the week, Jameson!"

"Woohoo!" Clay fist bumped the air.

The look the boss gave Clay was withering. Nobody dared to move, unsure if perhaps they'd finally crossed some invisible line that marked the end of his sanity.

"I know you know exactly what I meant." His voice was too controlled, each word clipped, and he was far too careful closing the door, deliberately making the soft click of its closure audible in the large room.

"One day he's gonna snap, and you're gonna die. And I'm going to watch, and it's going to be glorious. Your wee little bones will snap, like twigs." Hale snapped his pencil in half, dumped the remains on his desk in front of Taylor, and went to get himself a cup of water.

Taylor wondered, every now and then, if Hale was sane.

"Meet you for a run after work?" Clay asked hopefully, and Taylor thought about his shoulder for a moment, rolling it tentatively to test how painful it was, but it only bit a little so he nodded. It wasn't like they ran fast anyway. He got up and reached out absent-mindedly to tuck a strand of Sietta's loose hair behind his ear.

"We'll meet you at Joel's. Sietta can hang with Micah while we run."

Clay shoved him out the door. He hated working apart, so Taylor left him to it, knowing he would be in a strange mood and happy to let the rest of the team deal with it.

"How'd it go with the boss?" he asked Sietta as they made their way down to the underground carpark.

"It was okay," Sietta mumbled, fumbling at his side, catching up Taylor's hand and holding tight to it, seeking contact in a way Taylor definitely approved. Sietta relaxed a little and thought a moment. "It's easier than I expected, ASIS have taken care of everything. They're just keeping me in the loop, but I don't really have to do anything, and there's a lot they're not able to tell me, which is fine, but… I don't know. It doesn't feel like I thought it would. I don't feel happy, just… tired, I guess. I didn't expect to feel drained."

"Si…." Taylor sighed and pushed him out the hall door before shoving him hard up against the wall of the garage. He pushed Sietta's hair back, away from his face and stayed there, cupping Sietta's head as he leaned in and pressed their foreheads together, taking a few deep breaths, enjoying sharing the same air and feeling the warmth of Sietta's breathing against his own.

"You're allowed to be tired. You're allowed to feel like you don't know what's going on, or like you don't know what to do now, or like you're lost. You can feel anything you want to, or nothing at all. You did the hard work, now it's someone else's turn. All you have to do is breathe. The rest you can take your time with. Have showers, drink tea, pick on Clay, play with my dick, whatever you want...."

He won the laugh he was hoping for, and Sietta's hands smoothed over his chest, ran over his shoulders, and looped behind his neck, pulling him in and sealing their mouths together. His tongue teased, and Taylor let him in, pushing him harder into the wall and tasting him thoroughly, exploring his mouth with deliberately slow languor. He let Sietta steal breaths, amused and hungry every time Sietta pulled him back in for more.

Minutes passed until Sietta pushed him away suddenly, holding him at arm's length and taking several deep breaths, looking up at him and shaking his head. "Can we go home?"

"Anything you want. I mean it." Maybe he was going to have to repeat that, a lot.

"Good." Sietta drew heavy breaths as he looked Taylor up and down and slipped past him to head hurriedly to the car. "Because I definitely want to play with your dick."

Taylor laughed hard and followed.

MAKING OUT was becoming one of Taylor's favourite things. He'd never really seen the point before. It had seemed boring, a waste of time when he could be out doing something, anything really that was more exciting than sticking his tongue down someone's throat. There was a reason his lovers had always called him selfish, and it was largely that sex had had a singular purpose: to get off. Making out while watching a movie had seemed a distraction from watching the movie. Making out before sex had seemed like wasting a whole bunch of time before having sex, time that could have been spent watching a movie. Making out while making dinner was distracting, made the cooking process take longer, and could result in imperfect food, and if it took more time, that was time he could have spent doing something else.

But that was before he was lying under a curious Sietta, while those long, slender fingers teased at all of his weaknesses until he wanted to scream, but he didn't feel the driving need to roll over and have his way. Instead, he was happy to lie there and squirm because Sietta was enjoying himself.

It should have terrified him, but instead Taylor felt excited, happy, and oddly at peace with the situation. That, really, was what should have been terrifying, but it wasn't because he suspected it meant Sietta had done something no one outside the family had managed.

He got Taylor to care.

"How'd you get this one?" Sietta was stroking a faint scar on the inside of his thigh, little licks of pleasurable sensation tickling up to his groin, making Taylor gasp.

"Uh...." He had to think about it. There were a lot of small scars from their childhood escapades, and more dark scars, heavier and newer from his adult reality. But this was older, the memory somehow sweeter, though maybe that was only because it was Sietta asking. "A bike accident. Clay wanted to go down these dirt tracks, he stacked it and hit my back wheel, sent me into a tree. I went over the handlebars. One of the spokes broke and got me in the leg."

"Serious?" Sietta was staring at it as if it were amazing he survived, when in reality the spoke had stuck in about five centimetres and then torn its way out through the skin. It had bled like a geyser when it first happened and needed fifteen stitches, but Taylor had barely felt it and only remembered that it had been fun and they'd tried to hide it from their parents when they got home by tossing their clothes straight in the wash and walking around the house in a towel. It all came out when Brayden asked how Taylor got his period.

"Serious." He was amused by Sietta's perusal. "May I?" He grabbed the bottom of Sietta's shirt and carefully pulled it off while Sietta bit his lip, his only sign of nerves. Taylor was careful, spinning him in his hands and switching places, laying Sietta out beneath him. He deliberately went about peeling off Sietta's jeans as well until Sietta was lying there in only briefs and a stray sock that hadn't come off with the jeans. His dark hair spread around him in a black halo, his skin looking paler than usual against the navy bed sheets.

"We're very different," Sietta managed to whisper, stroking Taylor's cheek with the back of his hand.

"Different's good. I don't want to sleep with my brother."

He loved Sietta's laugh, the soft, throaty chuckle that shook both of their bodies and had him hard in seconds. He loved the way it made Sietta's eyes crinkle in the corners and his nose scrunch as if he couldn't quite understand what he was laughing at. Taylor wanted to listen to that sound for the rest of his life. The thought was sobering, but did nothing to halt his hands as they traced the lines of Sietta's body.

"But you want to sleep with me?" Sietta sounded unsure, but not at the act. Just who it was with.

"Yes. I want to sleep with you." Taylor tried to be as clear as possible, wanting no misunderstandings, needing Sietta to know he was serious. He'd never been so serious in his life. Well, except for maybe when he warned Joel exactly how he would dismember him if Joel ever hurt Clay, but that was different.

"Now?"

Taylor froze, wondering if all the air had been sucked from the room, listening to his pulse roaring in his ears as he searched Sietta's face for any sign that it wasn't what he wanted.

Instead of answering, Taylor leaned down and teased Sietta's mouth open with his tongue, exploring as he let his weight slowly fall completely onto the slender body beneath him, letting himself feel the warmth of Sietta's skin, the strong muscles in his long legs, the fine layer of hair that rubbed and tangled against his own. Sietta was too thin, bones protruding in ways that made his chest ache, but that was fixable and already Sietta's colour had changed, less pale, pinker in his cheeks, dark circles softening.

He took his time, exploring Sietta's body as thoroughly as Sietta had explored his own, seeking out each fine scar and laying his lips to the mark, or swiping his tongue across the smooth skin to taste. But he didn't ask because the scars were not the fond childhood memories of Taylor's past. He'd seen some of these scars and knew their origins, and he wouldn't ask Sietta to recall pain when he could instead replace it with pleasure.

He rolled the briefs from Sietta's body and was faster with his own, shifting to lie against Sietta's side to keep from squashing him, aware suddenly of his own size. Sietta rolled to face him and wrapped his hand around the back of Taylor's neck, eyes wide as Taylor's fist wrapped around their cocks, enclosing them in heat and rubbing them together.

"Oh," Sietta gasped.

Taylor loved the way Sietta's hair went everywhere, creating a pillow under their heads, wrapping around his neck, over his shoulders, tying them up together and refusing to let go. He slid his free arm under Sietta's head and pulled him against him, needing him as close as possible while he carefully stroked and rubbed, feeling the pressure building in his groin and watching the same feeling flush Sietta's throat scarlet, his eyes closing on each stuttered breath.

"I want to see you come," Taylor murmured in his ear. Sietta moaned, looking pained in his disbelief before his eyes opened again, lips demanding kisses. Sietta pushed in against him, using Taylor's mouth to muffle his cries as wet heat erupted over Taylor's fingers, slicking his own cock for the last few strokes he needed before he was spilling between them.

Taylor's pulse slowed gradually, but he barely noticed, barely breathed, too absorbed in watching Sietta calm, his body relaxing, his breath evening out, his skin cooling, and that ridiculous smile stretching from ear to ear.

"You know what's next?"

Taylor felt warmth spread through his chest at the excitement in Sietta's voice and nodded in agreement, forcing himself to get up.

"Your favourite thing."

"My favourite thing," Sietta agreed, laughing as he hurried into the bathroom and turned on the shower. Taylor looked down at the mess on his stomach and curiously swiped a finger through the mess. He had a new favourite thing.

11
NASCAR GUCCI

RUNNING WAS one of Taylor's favourite things. It cleared his head, left him feeling tired but energised at the same time, and made him feel connected to the place he ran. He and Clay had been running together their whole lives, their steps in perfect synch, even their breaths matching. They'd invited Hale once, but they'd been too slow for him, and he'd been creeped out by how identical they were, running side by side. He said it made him feel like he was seeing double, and at one point, he even stopped and gagged, shaking his head as if that would help clear it. Taylor was quietly glad it hadn't worked out. He liked it being just them, and Clay felt the same. He'd banned Joel from joining them, not that Joel liked to run with them anyway, but that was not the point. Running was their "together with no one else" time, and Joel understood they needed that.

Taylor often joked that Joel owned the smallest house in his suburb of Killara. Sometimes he didn't think it was much of a joke. They ran down narrow streets with high fences closing in wide open yards with mammoth two- and three-story homes hidden behind massive trees and sculpted gardens. Joel's townhouse block had originally been one large mansion, but it was renovated in the sixties and rezoned and sold off into three stately, compact homes. Joel had purchased it a decade ago, before housing really went through the roof. He'd be paying it off until he died, but owning a house was important to Joel. He'd been a foster child, and while he had no bad stories to tell about his childhood and only the fondest memories of the various families he had lived with, not having a permanent home remained a fear so engrained that purchasing a house had been his first priority.

They ran a long, twenty-kilometre circuit through the innards of the suburb before heading north, back up through the hills to Joel's. They were drenched in sweat, but relaxed. They hosed off in the front yard before going around the back to the laundry, fetching a towel and clean clothes from Joel to change before entering, aware of laughter drifting through the house from the lounge at the front.

Joel was in the kitchen and leaned in to kiss Clay as soon as he entered the kitchen. Joel was stirring something on the stove that smelt suspiciously like spaghetti.

"There's enough for everyone, if you'd like to stay," he said to Taylor. Taylor stuck his head around the corner to watch Sietta on the couch with Micah playing *Mario Kart*.

There was no mistaking them for anything other than brothers, sitting side by side. Same glossy black hair, bright blue eyes, caramel-tinted skin, long legs, lean build. Micah was shorter by at least a head, but he would grow, and then they would look uncannily alike. Micah wasn't as polished, not as graceful and practiced in his movements, but he also lacked the engrained caution to his actions and the hesitation before he spoke or reacted. Also, Micah didn't have those thick black Gucci glasses. Taylor hadn't seen those since the ferry.

"You lose again!" Micah howled his success, throwing the controller aside and fist bumping the air.

"Yes. It's a great victory to defeat someone who hasn't touched a video game in half the years you've been able to speak." Sietta rolled his eyes, getting up and moving immediately to the kitchen, straight to Taylor's side. He wrapped his arms around Taylor's waist and buried his face in Taylor's chest, inhaling deeply before relaxing.

Taylor was aware of Joel and Clay gaping at him, but he didn't care, wrapping his own arms around Sietta and kissing the side of his head, happy Sietta felt comfortable enough with him to do as he pleased.

"I missed you." Sietta's words were muffled in his shirt, and Taylor felt them rather than heard them, squeezing a little tighter before letting him go, then stepping back so he could tuck the hair behind Sietta's ear and get a better look at him.

"Those glasses...."

"Ah. Yeah. Micah got them for me. He got a few things, from the house, but I didn't want the other stuff. These are useful, though, takes me forever to read without them!"

"Micah went to the house?" Taylor turned to look at Joel for clarification.

"I went with him. Some ASIS agents took us. They were very nice about it."

"What does very nice mean?" Clay dipped his finger in the spaghetti sauce and licked it clean, but his attention was sharp and focussed on Joel.

"It means we had steaming hot agent sex in the bathroom," Joel announced, deadpan. "Stop being a jealous twat. I took Micah to get some of his stuff because he wanted it. That's what it means."

"Sorry." Clay leaned in to kiss Joel's cheek, but Joel still looked annoyed.

"Why didn't you say anything?" Taylor looked over at Sietta, thinking of all the legal documents Sietta had read since his emancipation. It must have been beyond irritating to do without glasses.

"It's not that bad, I just get a headache if I read too much without them. I'm not blind or anything. My prescription's only out by about point five." He shrugged as if it were nothing, and to him a headache probably was. Taylor sighed and ran his finger along the top edge of the left glass.

"You were wearing these when we met," he mumbled, equally as transfixed by them now as he was then. It put off that whole geek vibe, which Taylor had never liked until the moment he laid eyes on Sietta Salisbury.

"I was? Oh, right, on the ferry, I was studying downstairs.... You remembered!" He sounded so damn pleased, Taylor had to wonder if anyone had ever remembered anything about him.

"If you come in your pants in my kitchen groping a pair of glasses, you are not staying for dinner," Joel threatened, looking between them as if they'd defiled his kitchen in some way.

"That's super gross," Micah muttered where he was standing in the lounge, watching them. "The doing it in your pants thing, not the hugging thing. I'm gay. Obviously I don't care if you're hugging or whatever."

"Mind your own business," Sietta snapped, his tone harsh. Taylor jolted because it was the first time he'd heard Sietta be anything but kind, generous, and understanding with his brother. But he thought of what Sietta had said in the garage, and he wondered if Sietta was only now beginning to realise what he'd lost, and what had been given up.

"Okay, mister cranky pants." Micah rolled his eyes and went back to the couch, starting a new single-player game. Sietta didn't relax against Taylor until the music was starting to drive everyone half mad in the otherwise quiet room.

"I think we would rather go home, we'll grab some takeaway or something on the way," Taylor told Joel softly, and Joel didn't bother to say anything. Sietta took the hint and went to collect his things.

"I've got shift tonight. We're doing another round of arrests," Clay said softly while Sietta was in another room. "It'll be all over the news in the morning."

Annoyed he wasn't going to be part of it, Taylor nodded and clapped Clay on the shoulder, squeezing hard.

"Be careful. Make Mendel watch your back."

"Of course," Clay agreed, but he was looking at the bandage, and Taylor didn't bother saying anything else, wrapping an arm around Sietta when he came back in and leading him out front to the car. Taylor sighed in the driver's seat and stared at the townhouse with its out-of-control garden, its old terrace front, and Joel's mini coupe in the driveway, Clay's Hilux on the street.

"He'll be okay." Sietta laid his hand over Taylor's on the gearstick and stroked his fingers. It soothed in all the right ways, and Taylor started the car and got them moving back across the city.

"Are you...." Are you okay was a stupid question. Of course he wasn't okay, but Taylor wasn't sure how to ask.

"I'm okay. It's okay to ask. I don't mind. It's kinda nice." Taylor was left to wonder, not for the first time, if anyone had ever cared enough to ask.

They were quiet as he drove, but not awkward. Sietta seemed tired and watched the sun setting while Taylor focussed on the road and getting them home safely.

They were halfway there when Taylor deliberately turned down a series of streets, frowning as a SUV continued behind them on the obscure trip. Once he'd driven in a complete square, he knew the SUV was following them and swore under his breath. Sietta sat up and stared at him, following his gaze to the rear-view mirror and then turning to get a better look at the car behind them.

"You're kidding...." He looked again as if the vehicle might magically disappear, but it was still there. "They're following us...."

"They are." He didn't bother saying anything else because Sietta already had his belt on and he didn't know the answer to any of the other questions he might ask. Who were they? What did they want? What was going to happen?

Taylor voice-activated his phone and told it to dial headquarters, quickly informing them of the situation, and that he was heading to them in case it escalated.

He took a sudden left and sped up the ramp back onto the main road, hoping the traffic would slow them down, but peak hour had finished and the road was relatively clear. He put his foot down, trying to get some distance between them, but as soon as they hit the main road, their tail did the same, catching them quickly.

"Dammit.... You need to start thinking about who's trying to kill you."

"Excuse me?" Sietta gaped at him.

"Seriously. What's on the stick, what wasn't on it, what do you know that someone might want you dead over?" He swerved around another car and sped up, trying to outrun them.

"Now? You want to have this conversation right now?" Sietta jerked against the seat belt as Taylor dodged another car.

"Yes, I need the distraction. Think about it!"

"You need a distraction, in the middle of a fucking car chase? Are you fucking kidding me?"

"You swear when you're scared... good to know." He deliberately hit the brakes and watched their tail sail past, smirking as he slid behind another car and took the exit, amused when their tail tried to turn and go in the opposite direction up the highway to follow them.

"I don't know anything! Anything I knew is on that USB!"

"Then maybe it's got nothing to do with what's on the stick," Taylor pointed out. "What else do you know? What did you overhear, or see, or who do you know?" Taylor was starting to think it had nothing to do with the USB, that Sietta's face being all over the news was just a nice cover for what was really going on.

"I can't believe you want to talk about this in the middle of a car chase!" Sietta threw his hands up in the air. He was a spectacular distraction, which was good. The more distracted he was, the more Taylor drove simply on instinct, which was a good thing when you had sharp instincts. Clay often said he drove like a grandma, and would deliberately distract him so he would speed up and drive like he wanted to compete in NASCAR.

"What else do you know, Si?" He deliberately jerked the wheel to grab Sietta's attention, amused by the scowl Sietta sent his way.

"Wine? I was locked in a fucking wine cellar, so I guess I know wine?"

"I don't think anyone is trying to kill you over wine. Something else!" The tail was back, lights on high beam, probably in an attempt to blind them while driving. That was kind of clever; he'd have to remember that.

"Clearly you don't know wine. That shit's expensive!" Sietta snapped, but he was thinking. "I don't know! I know my family, the butler, the crazy fucking doctor?"

"The doctor's a good angle. You've ruined his career, he's going to prison… but I don't think he'd hire goons to run us off the road. I doubt he'd even know how to do that. Not to mention hiring people to shoot you. Tell me about the butler… seriously, who even has a butler these days?" He reached for his phone and hurriedly texted an SOS message to Hale. It was completely illegal, but he didn't have time to explain to Sietta what he needed done. Hale could get the rest of the details from Headquarters and would know what to do.

"Wankers, like my rich fucking parents, obviously." Sietta scowled while he sent the message. "You know it's illegal to text and drive, right?" But he was still thinking. If Taylor hadn't been attracted to him before, he would have been now. Sietta was angry but calm under pressure, able to follow orders, and had adjusted how he sat so he wasn't being thrown against the door anymore, braced against Taylor's seat and the window, and trying to do as Taylor wanted. Think. Maybe it was the adrenaline, but Taylor wanted to pull over and fuck him senseless. As soon as he got rid of the jerks following them.

"No, he's old, loyal to the point of obsession, but he lived in the house. He doesn't have those kinds of connections, I'm sure of it."

"Okay, that leaves your immediate family. Your dad's in a cell, as is Anders, but your mum and sister are out on bail. Do they have those sorts of connections?"

"Maybe?" Taylor hated the flicker of fear in Sietta's eyes, but he was proud of the way he took a deep breath and got back to thinking about it. "It's possible."

The SUV rammed the back of them, and Sietta swore as Taylor put the pedal flat, trying to keep his focus ahead, looking for anything that could hit them other than what was behind them. The last thing he needed was to collide at this speed.

"Mum... I don't know, she is just as involved in Dad's stuff as Dad is. She'd know everything. Viola, I honestly don't know much about. She swans around at all the socialite events, has a new guy on her arm every week, but she keeps to herself... It's hard to know what she's thinking, and she avoided me. Hates me, I think."

"Hates you how much?"

It made Sietta pause, looking out the window, for a moment entirely removed from the chase until they were rammed again and he closed his eyes, whispering something under his breath that Taylor didn't catch.

"What?"

"A lot, I guess. I told you, it's hard to say. She's never really talked to me much, always just did her own thing. I don't think I've seen her in years. Do I think she's capable of killing me? I guess? But I'd have no idea why."

"Why would she cut you out like that?" Taylor was really curious. If his own father hadn't been willing to kill him, why would his sister? Not that his father hadn't wanted to kill him. Johnathan Salisbury had simply assumed it was likely he'd get caught, which did tend to happen when there was a body. It had been smart to keep him in the basement instead, except he'd taken him out of the basement to show off. Sietta could definitely have caused a scene. That had been a stupid move, but they'd thought him cowed and under the thumb, so to speak. Fools.

"I don't know. She's homophobic sure, but she hated me way before that. She's... weird. She was never involved in a conversation, always thinking about something else, and she never had much empathy. I remember her horse broke its leg and had to be put down, and you'd think she'd never seen the animal, she cared so little." A shiver ran through Sietta.

Taylor grunted but was focussed on their tail, checking their location, judging the timing as best he could and suddenly slamming the brakes on and jerking the wheel. The SUV nicked the back of his tray and was knocked sideways without enough time to compensate. It careened off into the side of a warehouse building. Taylor slowed down and pulled over, watching in the rear-view mirror for movement.

Sietta was frozen, curled up in his seat, clutching his belt with white knuckled fingers, staring at nothing, wide-eyed. He exhaled suddenly and turned to scowl at Taylor.

"Why the hell didn't you do that in the first place?" Sietta huffed at him. It was ridiculously cute.

"Because *they* wouldn't have been here in the beginning," Taylor pointed out reasonably, watching the squad emerge from the shadows and surround the vehicle. The doors of the crashed SUV opened, and one of the perps got out, the other screaming for help in the front seat, trapped by the crushed metal. Served him right, but Taylor hated the idea of the lawsuit he would face for causing the crash. Still, that was what the department lawyers were for, if it came to that.

"Where were they... wow, they came out of nowhere...." Sietta watched through the window as an ambulance arrived and the crew cut the second man out of the SUV. The riot van emerged from an alley with a police car, and they drove off, escorting the ambulance. A third car pulled up behind the Hilux, and Taylor got out to speak to Hale.

He was at the rear, examining the damage, and Taylor crossed his arms as he stood beside him, taking it in.

"Coulda been worse." Hale shrugged. "Least it'll be covered by insurance."

"Coulda not happened," Taylor argued, wishing he could go follow the ambulance and beat the crap out of the idiots.

"Got any ideas on why it did happen?"

"Sietta thinks his sister could have something to do with it. I don't think it's to do with the USB. The AFP are focussing on that, but I think this is different. Something about it feels off."

"Alright, I'll look into it. Everyone else is out on the second round of arrests. I brought in a skeleton crew to back you up, but you got here right on time, so it was fine." The warehouse was a predetermined dump zone for chases. Close enough to the station that a team could mobilize into position in under ten minutes, but in a deserted area where no bystanders could be hurt. They were trained to draw in chases and knock out a tyre. There were enough old tyres lining the buildings to ensure that only the worst crashes would result in injury or death, but it was the best preventative, short of not having chases to begin with.

Sietta appeared on Hale's other side, standing back a little and looking Hale up and down, a slightly startled look on his face as he took in the black overalls, utility belt, armoured vest, boots, tactical gear, balaclava that he had rolled up around his forehead to show his face, helmet, goggles.... The riot squad always looked like the bad guys when you didn't know any better. It wasn't Sietta's first time seeing them, but it was his first time seeing them outside of his house raid. Taylor expected him to point out how badass the uniform was, not....

"You're really short."

Now that he mentioned it, Hale and Sietta were around the same height. Which wasn't short, really, unless you were standing near a Jameson. Taylor smirked at Hale's disgusted look.

"Be careful out there," Taylor ordered, moving back around to the front while Hale wandered back to his squad car. Hale waved and disappeared while Sietta climbed back in the Hilux and stared at Taylor's profile.

"Sorry about your car."

"Not your fault."

"Oh, I know. You could've shot that tyre out back before we even hit the highway and they never would've rammed you. That's totally on you." He put his seat belt on while Taylor frowned darkly at him, but Sietta ignored him. That he was able to ignore him was impressive in itself, that he did so was even better. Weariness suddenly swamped Taylor as he came down from the adrenaline high and started the car.

They were quiet on the drive home, quiet as they got into the apartment, but when Sietta went to put the kettle on, Taylor grabbed his hand and pulled him into the bathroom, leaving the light off, using the street light outside to see as he carefully stripped Sietta naked and pushed him into the shower. His own clothes were removed quickly, and he stepped in behind Sietta, then wrapped his arms tight around him, closing his eyes and letting the water run over them. Soothing away the vestiges of the chase and leaving them tired and shaken.

Someone wanted Sietta dead. They'd tried twice now. They didn't care that he was with a police officer, or they didn't know, but either way Taylor was the only thing between them and what they wanted, which was going to put a target on his back if he wasn't careful. That would put a target on Clay's, and that was not acceptable if Taylor could find a way to avoid it. He needed all of his attention on Sietta and couldn't afford distractions.

He would have to call Joel and tell him what happened and make sure an officer was still stationed to watch Micah. It would be an AFP officer, so he should call them as well and make sure they were aware of what had happened, and his suspicions that it was unrelated to their investigations into the ministers.

Sietta pulled back, his hands running over Taylor's abs, fingers teasing through each groove like a ladder, slipping lower and lower until his fingers trailed along the length of Taylor's cock as it slowly rose.

The way Sietta watched every shivering response made him harder, and Taylor carefully pushed Sietta up against the wall, giving him something to lean against. Taylor knelt, running his own hands down Sietta's sides, settling on his hips and holding him firmly in place, watching Sietta's face as he licked a long swipe along Sietta's length.

"Oh my God," Sietta gasped, eyes wide and unblinking as Taylor engulfed his cock in warm, wet heat, for the first time in his life. His head fell back hard against the wall, eyes hooded as he continued to stare down at the sight of Taylor on his knees sucking him off.

Sietta was beautiful. Taylor had never seen anything as perfect. Long dark hair stuck to soft caramel skin like wild strands of silk, moving in the rivulets caused by the running water as if it were a living thing. In the dark the blue of his eyes was shadowed, like the ocean at night, his lips red and swollen where he had bitten them. Taylor sucked harder, wanting him to give up control.

"Stop… I'm going to… oh… shit!"

Salty, creamy liquid spilled into his mouth, and Taylor swallowed, letting his tongue lave and swirl around Sietta's sensitive head, causing him to squirm and cry out, trying to push him away and hold him close at the same time.

Taylor finally released him as he was going soft, and rose to stand over Sietta, pulling him away from the wall and back into a tight embrace. Taylor ran his hands up Sietta's back and into the thick black hair, rubbing at his scalp, winning another loud moan.

"I'm going to assume you liked that."

"And that I want you to do it again," Sietta agreed breathlessly.

Feeling rather pleased with himself, Taylor cleaned them up and bundled Sietta in a towel before drying himself off and going to bed. He didn't bother with boxers and was delighted when Sietta hesitated only a moment before crawling in to bed beside him, gloriously naked. He pulled him in closer and rolled them over, spooning behind him, wrapping Sietta up in the safety of his arms, trusting him to be nowhere else.

He grabbed his phone in the dark and made the few calls he needed to Joel and Headquarters, then tossed it onto the bedside.

Sietta was warm and solid in his arms. Sleep came quickly and stole him away.

12
DRIVING PAM OFF-ROAD

"SOMEONE TRIED to ram you off the road?"

The sun was barely up, rays of light sneaking in under the curtains, crashing through the open bedroom door where Clay was silhouetted, still gripping the handle tight, his face fixed in a dark scowl.

Taylor lifted his head in confusion from where it had somehow ended up in Sietta's lap.

"Can you quit with the barging in on people?" Taylor snapped.

Clay paused, looked from Sietta, who was naked save for the sheet draped over his lap, then looked at Taylor, who was completely naked. He shrugged as if nothing at all were out of the ordinary.

"That's the second time, Tay! They've tried to kill him twice, and subsequently you! Third time's supposed to be lucky! What if they try a third time, huh? What are you gonna do then?"

"Die?" That would be the point in that scenario if the third time was lucky. But Sietta smacked him as if that were the wrong answer, and he sighed, grabbing a corner of the sheet and pulling it over himself, then sitting up beside Sietta against the headboard and taking a better look at Clay. He was still in his overalls from work. He was filthy, covered in dirt, dry sweat, and what looked like chalk. He had leaves in his short hair and a bandage on his arm. He looked rougher than Taylor had seen in a long time. He also looked worried, and for that Taylor felt the irrational need to apologise. He didn't, but he still felt like he should.

"We're fine. It was dealt with, easily."

"Easily? Have you seen your car? The back end is pancaked! It's gonna be in the shop for weeks! They hurt your Lux, man!"

"And it's repairable, and Si and I are fine. We're not even injured, which is more than I can say for you. What the hell happened?" He waved a hand in Clay's general direction, amused as he watched the scowl on his brother's face darken.

"I am never pairing with Mendel again! He almost killed me!" And with that, Clay stormed out of the bedroom, slamming the door, and a minute later they heard the shower in the main bathroom turn on.

Sietta looked Taylor in the eye, very serious. "We are putting a lock on the door."

"We are putting a lock on the door," Taylor agreed immediately, leaning in to kiss Sietta good morning, loving the way he melted back into the pillows and tried to pull him closer with a faint moan.

"Come on, I need to make sure he's okay. I'll make you a tea."

"Make sure he's okay?" Sietta mumbled as he followed him from the bed and started getting dressed. "I'm the one who had a Viking charge into their bedroom unannounced before the sun even came up. People must be so terrified when you guys do a raid. There you are just innocently dozing away—and *bam*! Door breaks down and Captain America-Hulk chimera comes barging in, screaming in your face. The poor sods who are innocent when you get the wrong intel...."

Taylor shut him up with another kiss, chuckling because it was cute when Sietta rambled. He left him to finish getting dressed and went to the kitchen, putting the kettle on and getting the coffee machine going. Clay looked like he could use a good sleep, but if he intended to stay up, he was going to need coffee.

While Clay was showering and Taylor was making coffee, he also rang Joel, putting him on speaker phone as he walked.

"Taylor?"

"Hey, Joel. Clay's here."

"Ah, cool. I wondered if he'd finished yet. He sent a message in the middle of the night saying he wouldn't be home until about seven."

"Yeah, he's had a rough night by the looks of it. He's pissed at me."

"I thought you were off duty for the rest of the week?"

Sietta emerged in his all-black ensemble and sat at the bench but stayed quiet, watching Taylor work.

"Yeah.... Our incident last night. It's freaked Clay out. Call the number they gave you and just check in, find out what they're doing, okay? It'll make him feel better. I'll call them too."

"Okay." Joel sounded concerned but didn't ask any questions, trusting him to deal with it. "Take care of yourself, yeah?"

"You too." He hung up and finished making the coffees before putting a cup of hot water in front of Sietta and watching him peruse the tea chest, selecting a bag of Russian caravan.

When the coffee was made, he sat beside Sietta on a stool at the bench and waited.

Clay emerged, looking cleaner but not necessarily any calmer. He had dressed in jeans and a plain black T-shirt, his hair still wet, dripping a little down his neck, feet bare as he walked out to stand opposite them, then grabbed his coffee and took a long sip before putting it down and staring at them. First one, then the other, then again and again, his eyes squinting the longer he kept it up.

"You deflowered the virgin," he accused suddenly, and Sietta choked on his tea, coughing hard. Taylor rubbed his back while rolling his eyes at his brother.

"I have not deflowered the virgin," he corrected, nonetheless amused that this was the discussion Clay was choosing to have.

"Well, you've done something to him. You were naked together, in bed."

"We can't sleep naked without doing naughty things to each other?" Taylor arched a brow, curious to see where his brother would go with the conversation.

"No, *you* can't."

"Well, we did," he pointed out, and Sietta nodded emphatically, looking like he'd rather be anywhere but right there. It was cute, but Taylor didn't let him get away. Sietta needed to get used to Clay, because Taylor refused to let go of either of them.

"You did something. I can tell!"

"Well, if you must know, I gave him a hand job yesterday, and last night I blew him in the shower," Taylor explained, as if talking about the weather. Sietta choked on his tea again, the blush Taylor loved so much infusing his cheeks, and even Clay looked startled, as if unable to believe he would confess that.

"I did not need to know that!"

"You practically demanded I tell you!"

Clay's mouth worked, but no words escaped. He took another huge gulp of coffee and then pointed between them. "So this is a thing? You two?"

"This is a thing," Taylor agreed, looking to Sietta to check, and holding his breath when he realised he wasn't the only one who got a say in it. But Sietta dubiously took a cautious sip of his tea and sighed heavily when no one said anything to make him choke on it.

"Huh. Shoulda seen that coming," Clay hissed under his breath. "I mean, I was hoping, but you're an asshole, so there was no guarantee he'd let you... you know."

"I know." Taylor rolled his eyes again, aware of Sietta chuckling beside him. It made him uncomfortably hard.

"Who's trying to kill you?" Clay demanded suddenly, this time staring at Sietta. Clay had spent the night executing warrants that in no way indicated any danger to Sietta. The attempts on his life weren't adding up, unless they had a different purpose.

"How do you just change topics like that?" Sietta spluttered.

"Practise. Our mother raised us," Clay grunted. "Someone tried to shoot you, and now they've tried to ram you off the damn road. Who?"

"He has no clue," Taylor intervened. "But we are looking into his sister. Also, we don't know they're trying to kill him. Maybe they just want to scare him. They've failed twice."

"Ah... that makes sense." Clay actually calmed down, grabbing a chair and dragging it over, sitting down with a heavy sigh and sipping his coffee while he thought about whatever was going through his head.

"I'm sorry, that makes sense how?" Sietta looked thoroughly confused. Taylor knew the feeling. "Viola hating my guts, or people trying to scare the shit out of me instead of kill me?"

"Oh, right. When they arrested Viola Salisbury, she was actually out in the western suburbs. Interestingly, she was in the company of Curtis Frey," Clay continued as if Sietta hadn't spoken at all.

"Who?" Sietta still looked lost, but Taylor swore and slumped forward, leaning his chin on his fist as he contemplated what that could mean.

"Seriously?"

Clay morosely drew patterns on his thigh and let Taylor think on it while Sietta glared between them, waiting for someone to explain.

"Frey's one of the biggest drug dealers in the city at the moment," Taylor tried to explain while he was still trying to work things out in his head. "We're still following down the leads, but we're almost certain he supplied the drugs on the ferry."

"Which makes even more sense if he's working with Viola. We always wondered how it worked, because Frey's not that smart, more a thug than anything, we couldn't see how he was running his ship. But if it's Viola behind him, that's a different thing," Clay mused. "Still doesn't explain why she's after you."

"I dunno...." Sietta seemed dazed but was forcing himself to work through it and think. "Kind of ironic, that he's free and she's been arrested, and not for the drugs but for being complicit in her parents locking up her fag brother."

They both frowned at him, but he didn't say anything else. He was right; it was ironic, if she was the mastermind behind the drugs. But it didn't explain why she'd decided he needed to die, and if she'd wanted him dead, there had to be easier ways to go about it. Ways that would actually succeed, because so far the attempts just ensured Sietta was better protected.

"How smart's your sister?" Clay asked.

"A little less Anders, a little more than Micah, but not me?" Sietta shrugged, as if comparing your siblings in such a competitive way were normal. To him it probably was.

"Oooh... what would that make us?" Clay latched on immediately. Taylor couldn't tell if it was because he was tired or the coffee high. He was honestly just happy they weren't talking about sex anymore.

"No Hay, way less Ash, a little Lei, but not quite Bray." Taylor drank his coffee in a few large gulps before it got too cold.

"No way, Ash is like the little cardboard cut-out version of you two," Sietta argued. "The older he gets, the worse it's gonna be. It'll be like there are three of you, or something."

They looked at him, horrified.

"I'm wounded." Clay shook his head as if Sietta had suggested he was going to cause the apocalypse.

"So she's smart, she's potentially a drug runner, and she hates your guts. Why is that again?" Taylor eyed Sietta dubiously. He said her hatred predated his familial incarceration, but that meant he'd barely been in his teens. What could he have possibly done to make her hate him like that?

"No clue. I told you, she's never really bothered to include me in her life. It's like we were never related." To him it was a fact of life. Viola hated him, case closed. He'd never needed a why. It just was.

Taylor couldn't imagine having that kind of toxic relationship with one of his siblings. His family was crazy, but at least they all knew they were loved.

"I rang Joel. Hale said he would arrange an officer to stalk him for you, and Joel said he'll keep a closer eye on Micah."

"Thanks." Clay sighed and fished his phone out of his pocket, quickly sending a text letting Joel know he was going to crash at home and then he'd be over after school for the afternoon and dinner before his shift.

"What happened to your arm?" Taylor pointed to the wet bandage, and Clay blinked at it, as if he'd forgotten it was there.

"Agh! I need you to clean it for me, or Bray's gonna bite my face off. We had this warrant for Joseph Summers...."

"Oh, he's a total dick! He did all these insider trading deals through his company with politicians and they used all the funds to top up election campaign funds...." Sietta trailed off at the looks he was receiving and sipped his tea, pretending he knew nothing. "The guy hates whales."

"So, Mendel and I were arresting Summers when the total dick decided to run out the back and get his Rottweiler to distract us while he tried to get away. Mendel jumped over the dog and tackled Summers, which left me to deal with Pam—the dog, who mistook me for a chew toy."

"Ouch." Taylor and Sietta winced.

"What was the white stuff?" Taylor distinctly remembered him looking like he'd rolled in chalk.

"Gypsum. I shoved a bag of it, sitting by the garden, in Pam's mouth to get my arm free, and she tore the bag wide open, flung it everywhere."

"Did it get in the wound?" Taylor got up and fetched the first aid kit from above the fridge.

"Yeah, but I went and saw Bray, and he cleaned it all out. I needed a few stitches, but he said I should clean it again when I got home and make sure it wasn't getting infected. He wouldn't let me leave until I swore I would let you look at it this morning."

"Good," Taylor grunted. Clay was terrible at getting first aid, which was hilarious considering he was the first one to demand someone else go get it.

Taylor peeled the bandage off, wincing at the jagged line of tidy stitches and the assortment of punctures and grazes. The dog had done a good job, but so had Brayden. The wound looked clean, but Taylor rinsed it in antiseptic to be sure, placed a fresh gauze over it, and wrapped it in a new bandage. The whole while Clay sipped his coffee, watching Sietta, who sipped his tea and tried to ignore him.

"Stop staring at him," Taylor grumbled as he tucked the corner of the bandage into place.

"Why? He's pretty, I like looking at him."

While it was fun to watch Sietta blush, Taylor didn't like sharing, even with Clay, even for fun. "He's mine."

Taylor was very aware of the eyes staring at him, but he refused to look at either of them, and neither dared to say a thing. He cleaned up the coffee machine and finished his cup.

"Well, I am going to crash for a few hours. Please try not to get killed before this afternoon." Clay headed for his bedroom.

"Sure." Sietta watched him go before putting his cup in the sink and grabbing Taylor's arm, tugging him around to look at him. He was smiling. Taylor thought that was probably a good thing.

"You're mine," Sietta mumbled, pulling him down for several long, toe-curling kisses that left Taylor warm in ways he'd never been warm.

Taylor's phone buzzed on the counter, and he picked it up quickly when he saw Brayden's name. "I just finished bandaging it and sent him to bed."

"How bad's your car?"

Taylor groaned, cursing Clay for telling Brayden and praying Brayden had the sense not to tell anyone else what had happened. If he was lucky, he'd get it into the panel beaters in the next few days and it would be back in one piece before the family ever knew something had happened.

"It's fine, I got rear-ended a few times. Not a hard fix."

"And you?"

"Not a scratch on us."

"Us, hey?"

Taylor inwardly cursed again. Stupid mouth. Stupid brain. "Us," he agreed, eyeing Sietta as he put his shoes on. They were going somewhere? He started searching for his boots.

"Emma wants to see your car. Send me a photo."

"Sure she does." Taylor sighed. "I'll send one when I go to the car," he promised. "Honestly, it wasn't a problem. It was more a nuisance than anything."

"Only you would think getting rammed by fools trying to kill you was a nuisance."

"We don't know they were trying to kill us," he reasoned, even if he 100 percent knew they were trying to kill them. He didn't need to worry everyone else with that idea, even if they already thought it as well.

"Please, I was a soldier. They are trying to kill him, and you're with him, so they're trying to kill you. I wasn't born yesterday."

"You were a medic," Taylor corrected. "Besides, they could be trying to scare him."

"Still counts. To what end?"

"It's fine. I know what I'm doing. Let me do my job and you do yours."

"You're still my little brother, I'm still going to worry, and I'm still going to tell you to be careful."

"Yes, sir." Taylor chuckled and hung up, turning to see Sietta on the couch, watching him.

"Wanna make out for a while?"

Hell yes he did.

"Why do we need shoes on to make out?"

"What…? My feet were cold, idiot."

HIS PHONE rang again and Taylor fumbled over the side of the couch to pick it up off the floor where it had fallen from his pocket at some point while he was trying to crawl inside Sietta's mouth.

"Hello?"

"Come let me in. I don't want to wake your brother by knocking on the door," his father demanded, and Taylor sighed, forced himself from the couch and his comfortable position curled up around Sietta, then went to open the front door.

"Hi." He stepped aside, and Daniel stalked in, far more energetically than usual. Which meant he was pissed. Great. Taylor wondered what he'd done this time, but he didn't have to wait long. His father fixed him with a glare from the middle of the living room, arms crossed over his chest, standing at his full formidable height. They'd inherited it from one of their parents, after all, but it rarely looked like Daniel since he was always lazing in a chair somewhere.

"What happened to your car?"

"It got rear-ended," he mumbled, really not wanting to have this conversation.

"You let someone rear-end you?" Daniel believed it less than most.

"Well, I wouldn't go so far as to say I let them," Taylor grumbled, crossing his own arms and echoing his father's pose subconsciously.

"Though he did extend the car chase long enough that they had time to rear-end us, so in a way, he did?" Sietta came up behind Taylor and put a gentle hand on the small of Taylor's back. Taylor couldn't believe Sietta had thrown him under the bus like that.

"Car chase?" Daniel peered down at Sietta. He had the sense to wander back to the couch and sink into the cushions.

"Someone followed us home from Joel's last night. I called the squad in and we took care of it."

"Has Joel been told this? Is he under protection?"

"Dad, this is my job! I know what I'm doing! Of course he's been told!"

A dishevelled Clay entered the kitchen, heading for the coffee machine, and his dad's silence surrounding both of their traumas said more in that moment.

"I forgot." He didn't sound happy. "I came here on business," Daniel pulled a collection of papers from his briefcase, handing them to Sietta. "These are...."

"I don't need to know, just tell me where to sign," Sietta assured him, and Daniel pointed to the coloured tabs he'd put everywhere. He still explained each document as Sietta signed. More statements, a few contracts, what he wanted to do with his belongings, few as they were, what he wanted to do about different charges, who he wanted to nominate for legal proceedings, who he wanted marked as next of kin... the list went on, but Taylor's heart warmed when he put both Micah and himself as next of kin, and Daniel jerked but otherwise didn't say anything, professional as ever.

"Done." Sietta handed the pile back, and Daniel packed it away in his briefcase.

"Thank God. Now leave spawn of Satan," Clay moaned from the kitchen. "I can't believe you woke me up an hour before my alarm! That's not cool, old man!"

"Excuse me?"

Clay seemed to realise a moment too late what he'd said, his mouth opening as if to say more, but Daniel stopped him with a silent hand.

"You can help Taylor teach Leila to drive."

"You agreed to do what now?" Clay froze, horrified.

"It's punishment for the both of you getting hurt and worrying your parents!" Daniel did not seem in the mood to argue, so they wisely didn't.

"Like he had a choice." Sietta looked at all three men, and his expression suggested he was wondering how any of them had survived this long. Clay seemed to realise he had no choice either and slumped over the coffee machine.

"Fine, fine, Leila will be the death of me. So be it. Least I'll have time to make sure my will's all good for Joel and Micah."

Taylor didn't bother to point out he'd included Micah in that familial decision.

"Good, it's settled." Daniel collected his things and headed to the door. "I expect to see all of you on Saturday for lunch!"

The door closed to the sound of their collective groaning.

"Why did you put him in a bad mood, huh?" Clay shook his head as he made two coffees and reached over to put the kettle on.

"I did not tell someone to follow me home last night and ram my car repeatedly," Taylor pointed out reasonably. He wondered why he still expected reasonable to work on any member of his family. It never did.

"Well, I didn't ask a dog to chew my arm off, but I still got blamed for it!"

"Why didn't you shoot the dog?" Sietta asked casually, and they both gaped at him.

"So glad you're sleeping with the sociopath." Clay shook his head. "Why didn't I shoot the dog," he imitated, clearly put out by the question. "I don't hate dogs, that's why! Poor animal was just defending its rotten owner."

"Well, then it's your fault you got bit." Sietta shrugged. "You weren't willing to shoot the dog; instead it bit you."

"This is about me waiting until the warehouse to shoot the tyre, isn't it?" Taylor put his mug in the sink.

"Yup."

Clay looked at him, lost, and Taylor shook his head, pretty sure there was no pleasing anyone.

"I'm gonna go for a run before I head to Joel's. You keen?"

"Yeah...." Taylor looked at Sietta.

"Hell no! Do I look like a guy who runs? No, I don't. Wanna know why? Coz the last time I ran, I got, like, two steps and remembered I was still chained to a wall, and the only reason I wanted to run was to get away from someone beating me with a wine bottle. No one is currently trying to beat me with a bottle, so nope, not feeling the overwhelming need to overexert myself doing something as stupid as running!"

Clay and Taylor blinked, decided neither was willing to say anything to that, and went to change into some shorts. Sietta followed Taylor into the bedroom, closed the door behind him and sat on the edge of the bed, watching.

"What's that look for?"

"Just waiting for the show." Sietta smirked, leaning back on his elbows and patiently waiting.

Taylor obediently began to remove his clothing. He drew his shirt over his head and tossed it at Sietta before letting his jeans drop to the floor, where he left them in a pile, then walked in his briefs to the tallboy. He fished out a pair of shorts and languidly pulled them on before grabbing a singlet and tucking it into the front of his shorts. He made his way back over to the bed, aware of Sietta's gaze on him at all times.

"Thank you." Sietta grinned, reaching up to loop his arms around Taylor's neck and pulling him in for a languid kiss that left Taylor's knees weak and his heart wanting to beat its way out of his chest.

"I'll give you another show when I get back."

"I'll hold you to that."

He wouldn't need to, but Taylor didn't bother pointing that out. He stole another kiss and left Sietta to some likely much-needed alone time. Clay was already waiting at the door, shaking his head as if he thought they'd been up to something.

"We weren't doing anything," he grumbled, a little annoyed after the years Clay had spent fooling around with Joel at every free moment.

"Wouldn't have mattered if you were." Clay held the door open for him. "It's nice, seeing you with someone. It's just going to take some getting used to. You usually would've gone full asshole by now and pushed him away."

"Yeah, well, there's still plenty of time for me to fuck it up. It's not like I know when I'm being an asshole." But Taylor hoped to hell that didn't happen. He couldn't imagine anything that would make him want to push Sietta away, but he couldn't tell the future either. All he knew was he wanted more of what he'd been getting, for as long as he could get it.

"Nah, he's different. You're different with him. He likes you, even when you're being a dick. Hell, I think he likes you because you're a dick." Clay looked up and down the street. Taylor followed his line of sight and spotted the unmarked AFP vehicle easily, mostly because the officers were in uniform in the front seats. Clay waved to them to make sure they saw them leave and hurried to catch up to where Taylor was waiting by the fence. Taylor bumped into him before falling into an easy jog.

Being a twin wasn't as easy as people imagined. There was a social construct people believed in, that twins had some crazy mind-meld thing going on, and could read each other's thoughts and that they preferred each other's company, or something like that. But they missed the point. Being a twin meant never being alone; it meant sharing not only a space but a face, and that every time someone saw your face, you could never be sure if they were seeing you, or the other. It meant representing the other simply by breathing, by living. Over time, you grow together, you watch the other more than you watch anything else. You listen and hear them more than your own parents. Every achievement is shared, every birthday a duel affair. Yes, it's an incredible thing; a good thing. But it's heartbreaking in equal measure. Crushing, to only be half of an identity, never whole on your own. To share is to give, but twins give more than anyone else, and that sharing had cost Taylor over the years. Clay was a more giving person by nature, and he didn't mind the things he gave up. Taylor minded. Always had, always would.

It had been hard to let Joel into their small unit. People had expected him to fight it more than he had, and he could see their reasoning. It had always been "the twins." Joel forced them to be apart and to be individuals, but Clay had struggled more with that. For Taylor it was like having someone finally take a bird out of its cage and let it free, knowing it would come home every night for dinner. Taylor couldn't imagine breathing without Clay, but he relished time alone, apart. He'd felt guilty as hell the first time he realised he enjoyed it, when Clay went on one of his first dates with Joel. Clay had rung every half hour until Taylor turned off his phone. Then they'd turned up at the apartment in a panic, thinking something had happened. They'd both needed time to change, to grow used to Joel being a part of them.

Taylor knew part of that was Clay feeling guilty that he was leaving Taylor alone. He'd tried to make Clay understand that he didn't mind, but he'd only hurt Clay more making him think he'd wanted to be alone all along. They'd hurt each other, over and over, learning to share outside of themselves. Ironic, when they'd had to share everything between them.

He listened to the way their feet dropped at exactly the same time, and no matter how much he tried, he couldn't break out of it. If he sped up, Clay instinctively did as well. If he slowed, they slowed together. It was as natural as the way their breaths moved in and out of their bodies in perfect synch. He never wanted that to change.

He didn't want to hurt Clay again. He looked at Clay's profile, and he stared longer than intended because suddenly they were slowing down into a jog again and Clay turned to glare at him.

"What are you staring at me for?"

"I'm not...."

"Seriously?" Clay was still tired. He never did well tired, adopted more of Taylor's attitude. It made him smile, liking that there were signs of each of them in the other. That their alikeness wasn't only external.

"Just. I don't want things to change with Sietta. I know it was hard with Joel, stuff had to change. Just... don't think you have to change anything because I'm—"

"Seeing someone? At last? So I can leave you at home to make out with your own boyfriend when I'm going off to have sex with mine? Are you kidding me? I've been waiting for you to meet someone for four years! Nothing will change, I promise. I'll just feel less fucking guilty all the time."

"I thought I told you—"

"Oh, shut up! Seriously, I'm me, you're you. You can enjoy being alone in your sad, lonely little tower all you want, and I can feel guilty while I go out and party it up with my sexy professor. We're allowed to be who we are, that's what you're always harping on about, right?"

Taylor bumped into Clay's shoulder, picking up the speed again, because yes, that was it exactly. As long as they remembered they were the same, and separate, at the same time. Everything would be fine.

They made their way along their favourite route, down around the football oval at the bottom of the hills, and back up through the local shopping district, mostly to inhale the scent of coffee for that last kick up to the apartment zone, weaving through several side alleys to their complex.

They jumped in the pool to rinse off before heading for the stairs, jogging up them so quickly Taylor almost barrelled into Clay when he froze on the top step near their door. Then Clay was up against the wall, in work mode, and Taylor felt his pulse roar to life in his ears as he stared at the open front door. The broken lock.

Taylor glanced down at the street and saw the police car was still there, but the figures in the front seat were hard to see through the fogged windscreen, slumped on the dash. Someone had blocked the exhaust.

A pedestrian was walking past with their dog, and Clay called out to them, pointing to the unmarked car.

"The exhaust is blocked! Break the window, right now! And call an ambulance!"

Confusion passed over the stranger's face, but then he was looking for something to break the window. They trusted him to succeed and continued into the apartment, moving quickly because they needed to check on the officers as soon as possible.

Neither of them were armed, but they acted as if they were, moving in formation as they would for any entry, checking rooms as they carefully worked their way through the apartment.

The empty apartment. With the smashed coffee cup on the living room floor, the couch pushed off the wall, the cushions askew. The small signs of struggle.

Clay was already on the phone, calling in the break-in, the likely kidnapping, and the injured officers downstairs. All Taylor could do was stare at the pieces of broken mug. He should never have left him alone. The police had been right there on the street, and no one had known where he was staying. It should have been safe.

Or they were being followed the whole time. That wasn't a nice thought.

They'd been able to follow his car. They'd known he was at Joel's. They knew where they all were. How?

His phone was in his hand before he'd given it more thought, dialling Joel.

"Twice in one day! I'm honoured."

"Is Micah okay?" He'd never heard that waver in his voice.

"Yes," Joel replied immediately. "He's here in my office at work with me, there's an officer at the door. Why…. Taylor, what's wrong?"

Taylor closed his eyes, grateful Micah was safe but feeling anger growing in him he'd never felt before. He'd never had something taken from him, not like this.

"Taylor? Is Clay okay?"

"He's fine. They… they took him."

"Uh…." Joel sounded confused. "Who took him? How could he be fine if…. Taylor?"

It was so hard to breathe, to think straight.

"No, they… they took Sietta."

They stole him. He was going to steal him back.

13
POMCORN AIR B'N'B

"YOU NEED to calm down!" Clay took a moment to glare as if that might make Taylor understand the seriousness of the situation, before his eyes were back on the road, pushing the silver Hilux hard in the direction of the office. An ambulance had taken the gassed officers to the hospital, and they looked set to make a fast recovery. The local police had been and gone from the apartment, taking what evidence they needed, but Taylor remained unsatisfied.

"How exactly would you like me to calm down? How about I go take Joel and see if you can calm the fuck down!" Taylor wasn't feeling cooperative. He was aware he was going to have to at least act like he didn't care if he wanted to be on the task force that went in to find Sietta, but he had no idea how to do that. He'd never actually cared enough about something that he had to hide the fact he cared about it. The boss would not put him in the field if he was unable to compartmentalize his emotions from his job and prove he wasn't a liability.

"Losing your temper is not going to help get him back."

"Not losing my temper isn't going to help either," Taylor pointed out. They had no idea who had taken him, or where. Someone was already investigating, sure, but that didn't mean they would have any answers, and the more time that passed, the less likely it became that they would find him. Australia was a huge country with a small population. People went missing all the time, and the fact was not a whole lot of them were ever found. There was that poor guy a few years back, his family put signs everywhere asking if anyone had seen him. They found his body a year later, a few hundred metres off a main highway, not far from his car. He'd gotten out to piss, got bitten by a snake, and died. Simple story, almost impossible to find him. That was just how big the country was. If you wanted to hide a body, there was nowhere better.

He had to hope no one wanted to hide Sietta's body.

"Whatever the hell you're thinking that put that creepy-ass look on your face, stop it," Clay ordered. "Sometimes I don't know how we're related."

"Excuse me?"

"You're being ridiculous. Call Dad and tell him what's happened."

"Why the hell would I do that?" The last thing they needed was the family being their usual weird selves while they were trying to do their jobs.

"Because Dad is Sietta's lawyer, and the firm is going to need to know what's going on. Also, because he's probably the only person who might be able to make you calm down and act like your usual asshole self instead of the asshole on adrenaline I'm stuck with at the moment. Now call."

That actually made sense. Taylor pulled his phone from his pocket and wondered why he hadn't thought of it. Maybe he really was as unhinged as Clay was hinting at. He needed to get his shit together; Sietta needed him to get his shit together.

He dialled. Daniel picked up.

"Dad? Sietta's been kidnapped."

"Wow, way to ease into it, buddy," Clay muttered, but Taylor ignored him, listening to his father calling for Ben, and then he was on speaker phone.

"How long ago?" Ben demanded.

"Unknown. We found the apartment broken into twenty minutes ago."

"Alright, keep us informed."

Click. That was definitely a click.

"Did he hang up?" Clay kept the wheel steady and gaped at the phone in Taylor's hands while Taylor stared at it.

"He hung up." Taylor shook the phone as if it might magically reconnect from the force of his frustration. "Why would they hang up?" So much for calming him down, Taylor wanted to march over to their law firm and deck everyone who worked there.

"I guess they had stuff to do and they didn't think we had any more important information." Clay got off the highway and followed the few turns left down to the station.

"I can't believe they hung up on me!"

"Really?" Clay eyed him, parking.

Taylor got out before Clay had even turned the car off.

"Dammit, wait for me!" Clay hurried to catch up, the beep of the autolock behind them.

They had barely opened the main doors when the boss's voice boomed at them. "Get dressed! Full tactical, now! We're a go in ten!"

Clay ran for the lockers immediately, but Parata came over to stand in front of Taylor, eye to eye, face unreadable. "I'm assuming you can keep your head on straight for this."

"Yes, sir."

Parata studied him dubiously, brow twitching. "You're part of the raids only. You don't give any orders, you don't ask any questions, you just break doors. Mendel is in charge. Anything he says, goes. Got it?"

"Yes, sir."

"You're on shift. Even if you find him, you put him in an ambulance, and you return to the office and give me a full report. I expect it to be entirely unimpeachable."

"Yes, sir." Taylor would agree to the demand.

"Don't make me regret it." It was abundantly clear that if he had anything to regret, Taylor would no longer be on the squad. He understood that.

"Hurry up. We're leaving without you if you're not ready." Parata waved him toward the lockers.

Taylor ran for the locker room, almost running into Mendel, where he was dropping his vest over his shoulders.

"How'd you lose the kid?"

"Not now, Mendel," Clay snapped, aware Taylor wanted to kill him immediately.

"We're moving in on Frey." Hale stepped out from behind his locker and strapped his helmet into place. "Boss had planned to bring him in tonight at a drop off we've got a lead on, but... we're moving now."

Taylor was absorbed in the task of prepping, falling into old reflexes and going through the motions. He could get ready for a raid in his sleep; he'd done it so many times. Which was good, because his thoughts were on who might have taken Sietta, and what they might do to him. Not that Sietta was small or weak or anything like that; he'd been mistreated, worse than most. But being locked in a cellar by uncaring relatives was not the same as being kidnapped by people who wouldn't hesitate to test a new narcotic on you just to watch how much pain you perished in. It was like comparing Harry Potter living under the stairs to growing up with Hannibal Lecter as your dad and watching him peel strips of your skin off to eat with his morning bacon. Not the same at all.

"Seriously, whatever you are thinking, you gotta stop. You look like you're about to murder someone, and everyone here is friendly, yeah?" Clay checked Taylor's clasps, and he checked Clay's, still on autopilot.

"I want him back."

"No shit," Clay muttered, shaking his head. "I want a pet unicorn, least your dream is achievable."

"Hmm… you could do the *Star Trek* thing and stick a horn on a dog and call it an exotic unicorn?" Taylor forced himself to participate in the stupid conversation. It helped. He managed a few deep calming breaths, reminded himself this was what they did for a living and that they were good at it. They would get Sietta back. It was going to be fine.

"Labracorn?" Hale smirked.

"Terricorn!" Mendel shouted as he stalked out of the locker room, looking more like a tank than a person.

"Boxecorn!" Clay snickered, shaking his head as he bumped shoulders, and they headed out.

"Too bad there's no pop dog breed…. Pomcorn? I'm gonna watch a movie and pet my pomcorn?"

"I don't want to know about you and your pomcorn," Taylor snapped, pretending to sound scandalized, succeeding well enough that Jones looked between them, horrified, and moved to the other end of the truck.

"What the hell's a pomcorn?" they heard Jones whisper to Hale.

"Pomeranian unicorn." Hale was distracted, loading his gun, entirely missing the confused glare Jones was giving him, but not needing to see it. "Don't ask. Jameson's just trying to distract Jameson."

"Which one?"

"It matters?" Hale shoved the last bullet home and closed it up right as Harris hit a particularly large pothole.

"Harris!" was the collective shout from the team.

"Sorry, that wasn't there yesterday."

"Yeah, coz potholes magically appear overnight." Mendel scowled.

"Pomcorns, man." Clay smirked at him. "Pomcorns."

The drive was quiet save for Mendel defining the operation, its parameters, and what was permitted. It was always the same: entry with a split team, Jamesons on the door from the front with backup, a second team from the rear. Avoid shooting if possible, disarm as quickly as possible, find the target, neutralise threats. Taylor barely heard anything. Frey had been under surveillance, and the comings and goings from his house were suspicious. There was sufficient evidence to believe Viola Salisbury could be hiding on the premises. There was definitive evidence there were drugs in the garage; an undercover officer had successfully purchased some the day before. Frey was blasé about his business and seemed to believe himself immune to the law. A suspicious man had arrived at the house last night, and they were being sent in to see what was going on.

The house they pulled up to was nice. It didn't look like a dealer's house, but then that was the point. Also, Frey wasn't a dealer, he was their master. The importer, the distributor, and the brains behind the hundreds of other houses that looked ready to fall down from neglect while their owners wandered the streets handing out the merchandise. Those were the dealers.

This house was a neat brick two-story suburban typical of the housing boom of the early nineties. The lawn was mowed, the gardens well-kept, and the windows sparkly clean. Frey obviously had a housekeeper, or someone lived there who really cared about appearances.

They approached on foot from a park several houses away, not wanting the van to give them away. Taylor hefted the ram on his shoulder and wished he was behind, but Mendel only let him on the ram on the condition Taylor was in front this time. It would stay that way until his skull fracture was completely healed.

There was always a moment before a breach when there was nothing to do. Everything was in position, ready to go, but it was as if the world paused, giving you that brief moment of respite to take a breath and contemplate your life choices. Taylor usually loved that moment, as the adrenaline pumped high in his system and he imagined what was about to go down.

Today he wanted to punch that moment and whoever was responsible for it in the face. Today he knew exactly what he wanted to happen, and he didn't need a few extra breaths to think about it. He gripped the ram so hard his fingers were aching from the pressure, and he had to force himself to relax or he'd hurt himself on impact. Again.

Mendel's call came through his earpiece, and Taylor swung in unison with Clay, the ram seeming suddenly to weigh nothing at all before they slammed it into the lock, and the door crashed inward, splintering around the smashed lock and falling away. They let the momentum of the ram carry them forward, falling low with it and putting it in the small foyer they found themselves in, before drawing weapons and turning, Clay left and Taylor right, scanning the room as the others piled in and moved ahead of them.

Clay followed Mendel, Taylor was behind Hale. He caught a glimpse of Jones coming in through the back, and then Mendel was shouting in one of the rooms. *Police, get on the floor, hands...* the drill was so familiar, he didn't bother to listen. They kept looking.

"Police!" Hale managed to get out and nothing more before the woman had already screeched and thrown herself onto the carpet face-first, arms and legs spread-eagled. She looked like one of those animal rugs, what with the leopard-print dress clinging to all the wrong places.

"Leopacorn!" Hale whispered, and Taylor chuckled, checking her for weapons and cuffing her when he was certain she was clean.

"Clear!" The shout came from each team, and Mendel pronounced the house clear. They had three people, none of them Frey. One was the housekeeper, another was a friend crashing on the couch, and the Leopacorn, who revealed herself to be Frey's mother.

"Where's your son?" Taylor demanded.

"Like I'd fucking tell you," she spat at them without getting up from the floor. It was quite the achievement, and if he wasn't so angry, Taylor would have sort of been impressed. She'd spat it like a snake or an archerfish. It landed near his boot, which was at least a metre from where she lay prone.

"I'd rethink that strategy if I were you," Taylor snarled.

"Or what? You can't hurt me, I haven't done anything wrong!"

"Oh, you think so, do you?" Hale crouched down in front of her, making sure she was aware his gun was pointed directly at her face. "If we were on a drug raid, you'd likely be correct, but since we're on a search and rescue, our warrant gives us permission to detain anyone on the premises who might be withholding information on our victim's whereabouts." He stood up again and looked at Taylor. "She seems to be very uncooperative, doesn't she?"

"Definitely would seem to be withholding information," Taylor agreed, hauling her to her feet while she screeched that it was a violation of her rights. It wasn't.

Sirens sounded outside the house: their backup. Mendel was in the lead, and he handed over the three witnesses for debriefing and or arrest if the local police deemed it necessary. They were signalled back to the van, and while Taylor wanted to beat the witnesses until they told him something, he reined in his anger and forced himself to follow orders.

They were walking too briskly back to the van, the only sign that they weren't done. Mendel was in the lead, but he waited until everyone was belted in and Harris was driving before giving directions that Taylor realised he recognised.

Point Piper? If they passed through the city that way, they were definitely heading to Point Piper.

"The guy on the couch knew nothing of Frey's business. He flew in last night... he was from airbnb, can you believe it? Unknowingly booked himself into a drug house."

"Poor bastard," Jones muttered.

"How does that work, anyway?" Harris asked from the front.

"You just go on the website and book like a hotel, then the owner contacts you to say yes or no to letting you stay and gives you directions or instructions or whatever for your stay," Hale called over.

"Huh. Sounds good." Harris got them on the main highway.

"Sure, it's great, until you wake up to the riot squad demanding you tell them about a kidnapping victim and anything you know about the whereabouts of the house owner," Hale reminded him. "Then I'd say spending five bucks extra on a hotel's the better deal."

"I dunno, what if someone's died in the hotel room? They never tell you that stuff. It's way creepy." Harris shook his head, and they all stared at his reflection in the rear-view mirror. "What?"

No one bothered to point out Harris had some creepy hang-ups about a lot of creepy stuff.

"He said Frey was there at breakfast with a woman," Mendel cut in, shaking his head at the direction of the conversation. "He said they mentioned meeting at her place. A team was dispatched to Viola Salisbury's house at the same time we entered Frey's, but it was found empty. We are going to the home of Johnathan Salisbury. It's empty at the moment: a good place to hold a hostage."

A good place to dump Sietta back into his worst nightmare. Clay shared a knowing look with Taylor and placed a heavy hand on his shoulder.

"Stay calm. You can't help him if you lose it."

Like he didn't know that. It was the only reason Frey's mother was in one piece. That, and Taylor liked his job and couldn't help Sietta if he was behind bars himself.

They rechecked their gear as Harris drove them through the city, down toward the ocean, and into the harbourside eastern suburbs, the houses growing in size and extravagance the closer they got until they entered Point Piper and the houses became palatial mansions dotting the coastline against a backdrop of royal blue sea. The Bridge was visible in the distance behind them, the iron arch so familiar, shining in the sun, too bright for Taylor's dark mood.

"It's so pretty," Hale mumbled.

"Pretentious bastards," Clay echoed Taylor's thoughts. He hated Point Piper. He knew he was biased and that the place wasn't responsible for what happened there, but he associated it with what had been done to Sietta and doubted anything would ever change that.

"Jamesons, on ram," Mendel ordered before Harris had even reached the gates. They grabbed hold in preparation anyway, and Harris rammed the gates with the car, the heavy steel breaking off the sandstone pillar and crashing into the white pebbles beneath. He drove straight up to the front of the house, not bothering to hide. It was a hard call: they could approach on foot from the street, but it was a long way, and it was late afternoon. They'd be easily seen long before they ever got near the house. Harris drove fast and pulled up at the front door, a faster approach but anyone inside would know they were there as soon as they hit the gate.

Clay and Taylor jumped out, aware of the team moving into position behind them.

They rammed the door. It was still broken from the last time they broke it, and it crumbled into several pieces this time, falling around them as they slid in, dropped the ram, and drew weapons.

This time there were guns. Lots of guns. That was fine by Taylor.

He dived to the left with Clay, rolling behind a wall as two bullets slammed into the foyer wall, shattering a vase. Mendel returned fire and someone screamed before Jones breached behind them and started shouting. There was no returning fire from that end of the house, so Taylor concentrated on the shooters at the front.

"Police!" was all Mendel managed to say before more bullets came flying, but he finished his spiel anyway, mostly so that they could fire back if force was required.

A shadow briefly passed over the doorway on the opposite side of the foyer. Scanning the empty space, Taylor saw a statue in the hallway and decided it was definitely ugly. He picked it up and threw it across the foyer into the opposite room, satisfied when it hit something solid and a cry of pain followed its shattering demise.

Hale followed it, weapon up, and Taylor ran in after him, stepping hard on the man's hand where he lay beside the statue, trying to grab his gun. Another lay on the ground nearby, clutching his arm, which was bleeding profusely where he'd been shot.

"We've got two," Mendel shouted.

"Two more in here," Jones replied.

"Not who we're looking for," Clay muttered, gun up and already heading for the cellar. Taylor followed, leaving the rest of the team to do the arrests.

They opened the hidden door off the kitchen and stepped onto the landing with the two doors, the left off to the back veranda. They opened the right, hurrying down the corridor to the stairs for the cellar.

"Police!" Clay shouted into the darkness. They strained to listen, but there was nothing for several minutes before a light came on and a figure came striding down the hallway to the stairs. The figure conscientiously placed his gun on the step before moving back with his hands in the air.

"Oh. You got me." Curtis Frey smirked at them. He was an attractive man, for a criminal, tall and lean with a thick Maori tattoo over one shoulder despite the fact he'd never even been to New Zealand. His sandy hair was longer than the last arrest photo of him, hiding a heavy scar by his left ear. His brown eyes were small and squinty but somehow fit the rat-like look of his face. He was dressed in loose jeans and a Bintang singlet. Not exactly normal criminal attire, more like Sunday barbeque.

"I don't like this," Clay hissed, but he kept his gun on Frey and took a step back.

"Keep your hands up, and come up here," Taylor ordered, watching as Frey strolled up the stairs as if he were not in any trouble, and stopped in front of them. They marched him out to where the others were, and Mendel cuffed him and sat him on the floor with the others.

"Where's Viola?"

"Who?"

"Your girlfriend?" Mendel demanded. "Pretty, black hair, blue eyes, tall, long legs? Used to live here? Ringing any bells?"

"Nah. This is just some rich guy's house!" It was obvious he knew exactly whose house it was, and who Viola Salisbury was, and what was going on. It was as if it were all going to plan, for him. The squad were all uneasy, watching the group sitting on the floor and waiting, but nothing happened other than the man who was shot rolling around and begging someone to help him. They stared at them while more police cars pulled into the drive and came in to start processing.

Clay and Taylor went back to the cellar door and peered down at the hallway. A slither of light lit the usual black hole. The near-blackness cried danger, but they followed procedure and worked their way down. It helped that they had been there before.

As cellars went, it was beautiful. Polished wood with stonewall accents, kept at exactly thirteen degrees, two whole walls of aging bottles of wine from floor to ceiling, a small bar and a shelf of glasses, and a beautiful carved stone bench.

But Taylor hated it. Worse, huddled in the corner with his arms wrapped tight around his knees was Sietta, feet bare and foot once again shackled to the floor. He didn't seem to have heard them, head down, hair loose and hiding his face.

"Shit," Clay cursed but stayed by the door on guard while Taylor strode over and knelt in front of him, not bothering with words, pulling him into his arms and holding on while his heart tried to remain contained in the confines of his chest.

Sietta jerked but realised who it was almost immediately and wrapped himself around Taylor as if he could merge them into one being. Shivers racked his body, skin icy to the touch, his fingertips pale, nails purple, and lips tinted blue. He was only in a thin T-shirt and jeans, and there were bruises already forming on his arms where he had been grabbed, and a dark streak of purple coloured one side of his face.

"Is there a key?" Taylor looked for one but lacked the patience to give it his full attention.

"I dunno," Sietta whispered, the shaking getting worse. Shock, Taylor knew, as well as the cold.

"I'll see," Clay called and then was gone. If there wasn't, he'd find something to cut him out with.

"It's okay." Taylor stroked a hand over Sietta's head soothingly, as much for himself if he was honest. "Everything's going to be okay."

"I know… I just… I never thought I'd be back here. It's…." His breath shuddered as he struggled to stay calm. "I can't be back here. I need to get out of here."

"Shhh, in a minute, I promise. Clay'll be back in a minute. I'm so sorry. I shouldn't have left you alone, I didn't think—"

"No, it's…." Sietta swallowed. It sounded painful, as if he'd been crying and was dehydrated. Taylor didn't mention it and held him tighter. "You must've been worried. I'm sorry. You're sorry. Everyone's sorry, so let's not do sorry, okay? Get me out of here. I need to—"

"I know," Taylor soothed. "You're right, no sorry. We'll get you out of here…."

"Right now," Clay agreed, coming over with a small pair of bolt cutters and severing the chain, leaving the shackle on for now, prioritising. They would need bigger tools to get through the cuff.

Taylor didn't bother to ask Sietta what he wanted as he wrapped him in the blanket and picked him up easily, then, holding him close, stormed up from the cellar and out the front door, not wanting him to have to see the men who took him or speak to them.

There was an ambulance outside and five cop cars. Taylor went straight to the ambulance and climbed inside with Sietta, closing the door so Sietta wouldn't see the house.

Sietta was silent as he sat trembling while they looked him over. They frowned at the shackle and stuffed some bandages between it and the skin to stop it rubbing. They gave him water, checked his vitals, and asked questions they only got grunts and whispers in response to. It was a long process, but they declared him okay to go, as long as someone removed the shackle.

Taylor took him out of the ambulance as they lifted in the man who had been shot, and Taylor drew Sietta over to the squad van, sitting him on the back and holding him again, disturbed by how pale he was and how badly he was still shaking.

"What do you need, Si?"

"I want to go home," he pleaded, pulling back far enough to look up into his eyes. Taylor swallowed, his throat dry and painful as it seized around his pain. He wanted to go with him, but he was on shift, and it wasn't finished yet. He wanted to take them in, watch them be charged. He needed to see it through, to trust the job was done, especially since it was so close to home.

"Is it okay if Brayden takes you?"

Sietta jerked as if slapped, but Taylor watched his thoughts flickering in a myriad of expressions over his face before he nodded, understanding without needing to be told, and Taylor realised that was it. Sietta was the first person who understood him intrinsically. That was what drew him in, what snared him, why he was so stuck. And he realised in that same moment that he would never be unstuck, because that understanding would never falter, or even waver. But he couldn't say it, the words struck dumb by the weariness in every line of Sietta's body. Later, when he could shower him in kisses and warm him to the bone. That would be the time to talk.

He pulled his phone out and waited, his breath feeling too loud in his ears now his pulse was settling as the adrenaline waned.

"Hey."

"No, it's Tay, not Hay."

"Oh, now you want to be funny," Brayden fairly growled down the phone. "Tell me you've found him."

"He's safe," Taylor breathed in agreement, looking down to check for himself. "I need you to come get him."

"Geez, that's fucked," Brayden muttered, but Taylor heard him getting up, collecting keys that jangled over the line. "Where are you?"

"Point Piper house."

"You cannot be serious?" Brayden swore, long and profusely, going on quite the rant about criminals, war, wankers…. It was impressive really, and audible to Sietta whose eyes grew increasingly wide until something Brayden said had him laughing, falling into Taylor's side and wrapping his arms around him as if finally realising things were going to be okay.

"See you soon," Taylor managed to say in between something about Kelly and dishes. He hung up and lifted Sietta into the back of the van, leaning in to kiss him hard. He was relieved when Sietta had no hesitation in kissing him back.

"I'm…." He'd been going to say sorry, but they weren't doing that. "I'll be home as soon as my shift ends."

"Aren't you supposed to be off duty until the end of the week?" Sietta arched a curious brow. "I don't think participating in raids counts as off duty."

"Yeah, well, the boss said I could work as long as I proved I could behave and stop ordering people around… I guess I'll just get bellowed at when he finds out, at which point it'll be too late for him to do anything about it. Actually, he'll probably give me indefinite nightshifts or something…" There would be a punishment, but he also knew the boss would understand. He'd done his job, and he hadn't broken any laws. But he was focussed on Sietta when he should have been completely focussed on the job, and he knew the boss would see to it that he was reprimanded for it.

"Don't you need to go help?"

"No, right now I'm protecting the victim," he pointed out smugly. He felt sorry for Jones, who was being sent with the perpetrator to the hospital to guard him while he got the bullet taken out of his arm. Never a fun gig. They usually swore at you, a lot.

"A victim again, huh…."

"Not who you are," Taylor pointed out softly. "Just something that happened to you." Sietta stared at him a long time, his expression stuck somewhere between stunned and amused.

"Look at you being all philosophical."

"Don't get used to it. Was Viola here?"

"Oh, no, I wouldn't dream of it." Sietta studied his face, looking for some sort of sign, but to what Taylor did not know. "I heard them talk to her on the phone, but they didn't talk about me. They were talking about you. Well, not you specifically, but the riot squad." That didn't sound good. It was another thing that linked events to Taylor, rather than Sietta, but he couldn't figure out what the goal was.

"Get used to me being around, okay?" Taylor changed the subject again.

"How often?" Sietta looked sceptical.

"Always. Like, annoyingly in your face at all hours of the day. Up in all your business, wanting to know your favourite colour, the whole works, yeah?"

Sietta was gaping at him and trying to laugh at the same time. Sietta pulled him in for another kiss. Taylor figured that was a good sign.

"Blue."

"Huh?" He was distracted by kisses.

"My favourite colour, asshole. It's blue."

"HEY." BRAYDEN appeared at the vehicle's back door, startling them where they were curled up on the edge in the sun, watching the arrests going on around them. "This place is a madhouse."

"No kidding," Sietta grumbled, but he slipped free of Taylor's hold and stood, stretching and groaning as his muscles protested. His bruises were getting darker, a vivid reminder to Taylor of what had been done because he decided to go for a run. Idiot.

"Are you okay?" Brayden was looking Sietta over and taking in the bruises with a dark scowl.

"Sure. I got kidnapped and beat up. Nothing out of the ordinary."

Taylor and Brayden both glared at that, but Sietta didn't seem to care. He had a dark sense of humour, and they were just going to have to live with it. Hopefully for a very long time.

"Are you sure? Because there's a shackle on your ankle." Brayden pointed to it, as if Sietta might have somehow missed that it was there.

"Oh!" Sietta stared down at it. "Right. I'm still fine."

Brayden glared at Taylor, and Taylor stared back because it wasn't his fault they had nothing to cut it off with. Brayden hung his head and shook it, as he did when Jay and Emma did something that defied all reason and left him baffled. He studied the shackle for a moment before waving a hand as if it might magically disappear. It didn't and he huffed.

"I'll figure something out on the way home. I'm not letting you walk around with that thing on."

"Awesome. Coz it's heavy." Sietta grinned. Brayden swore. Taylor waved as they walked to Brayden's car and left.

"He okay?" Clay appeared at his side, and Taylor nodded because he suspected Sietta was doing far better than he should have been, but that was because he was weird, and weirdly accustomed to being held against his will. That wasn't anything to be pleased about, but it was also a fact of life that Taylor was going to have to accept.

"I think I'm in love with him."

"Uh…." Clay stared at him, then burst out laughing. He slung an arm around Taylor's shoulders and hugged him tight, laughing harder when Taylor swore at him.

"Dude, you've been in love with him from the moment you laid eyes on him. If you only figured that out now, you're more repressed than I thought! Fuck, you took him home to meet Mum! Everyone knows you're in love with him."

Well, that was weird. "Define everyone."

"Uh…. Mendel knows." Good definition.

"Fuck!" That really was everyone.

As Taylor looked around, it became obvious they were finishing up. Everyone was being loaded into paddy wagons, and the squad was doing a final sweep while the forensics team took over the scene. They waited by the truck as the team ambled over, locked weapons into the cage on the inner truck wall, and climbed in. They slumped against the seats, the adrenaline finally leaving them worn and ready to go home. Unfortunately the sun was only starting to set, and they had six hours of shift left.

It took ninety minutes to get back through the city and out to the west where the station was. They spent it mostly in silence, Mendel and Hale slept on the benches, leaning against one another and snoring. Taylor and Clay sat side by side, whispering so as not to wake anyone. Harris drove.

"It just doesn't make sense. They barely put up a fight, just enough to ensure they were arrested," Clay pondered, his frown lines deep.

"Nah, the kidnapping would ensure they were arrested. The force ensured we'd take them in with us…." Taylor frowned at that. "Frey was way too calm, like we were playing into his hands. He barely even blinked at Si when we brought him out, couldn't care less that we had him."

"And Viola was nowhere to be seen. If they'd taken Sietta to kill him, he'd be dead, and if she wanted to torture him, she would have been there. As it is, there's no motive for taking him. No one got a ransom or anything."

"Something's not right."

"What if Sietta was merely a guarantee we would be the ones to arrest them?" Taylor mused, not liking where his thoughts were headed, but feeling like he was on the right track.

Frey was the master, not the dealer. That was important. He needed to figure out why. What was the plan?

"Why would they want to be arrested?" Taylor asked Clay, an idea starting to take shape.

That was the million dollar question. Millions of dollars....

"Sietta was able to get all that information on people because he understands what motivates them." Clay picked up on where Taylor's thoughts were going. "He said Viola's like him. She knows people."

"Knows what makes them tick," Taylor agreed. "She would have no qualms using the brother she hates as bait for us to come pick up Frey's men. If the crime's bad enough, we'll take them in."

"Again, why would they want to be arrested?" Mendel woke up and asked blearily. He was missing the point.

There was a loud screech, and the world turned to pain.

14
HOME INVADERS

THE VAN was almost home to the riot squad office when it hit something hard, throwing them into the sides, seat belts snapping raw against their shoulders. Mendel kicked Clay in the shin by accident, Hale slapped Taylor in the shoulder where he'd been shot. Pain licked at them where they collided with hard metal, and there was the distinctive sound of the tyre blowing. The undercarriage ground against asphalt and the van slid, ploughing into the road before it slammed into the side of the car garage, and they were thrown around again on impact.

"Fuck me, Harris!" Mendel spat, then hit the release on his belt and hurriedly checked everyone over, but their body armour had protected them for the most part. Just bruises, not that they didn't hurt.

"I'm okay," Harris called out from the front seat. "Think I might have broken my leg."

"How is that okay?" Hale muttered, rubbing his elbow where it had hit the weapons rack hard.

"Well, I'm not dead. I consider that a positive," Harris griped, and Hale climbed through from the back to help him. "That pothole… it's kinda big now."

"Wha…." Mendel shoved the rear door open and looked down at the massive hole they'd hit.

"That didn't happen naturally." Clay peered over Mendel's shoulder at the gaping wound in the bitumen. "Looks like acid."

Taylor looked from the hole to their crashed van and the paddy wagons lined up out the front, empty, then swore loudly.

"Keys, Mendel!" Taylor grabbed the keys before Mendel could even react, snatching them from Mendel's belt before unlocking the weapons cage as a bullet was fired from their office windows at the back of the van, barely missing Mendel's leg. He pulled it in, and Clay slammed the door shut, another bullet hitting the side of the van. It was bulletproof, and they didn't worry about it, focussing on arming instead.

"What the hell is going on?" Mendel demanded.

"It's a setup. They wanted us to arrest them to get in the building."

"Why?" Hale asked, as he tied off the makeshift splint he'd done on Harris's leg then climbed back over to grab his gun.

"Because we have the largest haul of ice in Australia's history sitting in our basement," Clay realised, then swore under his breath as he grabbed some extra ammo and shoved it in his pocket.

"And all the cocaine from the ferry," Taylor added. "There's 1.5 billion dollars' worth of drugs in there." Several recent sizable drug raids meant none of it had been destroyed yet, the backlog sitting in the basement, waiting for the paperwork to come through before it could be dealt with.

"They can't have taken everyone in the office! How'd they get out of their cuffs?" Mendel grabbed a second weapon and shoved it in his ankle holster.

"The Custody Manager would have removed them during processing," Taylor reminded them, cursing procedure and the reviews that would likely follow.

"How'd they get the guns?" Mendel picked up a knife and hid it behind his belt.

"We brought the guns in," Taylor watched Mendel's armouring in fascination, wondering how many weapons the man had hidden.

"The rocket launcher raid," Clay grabbed two Tasers and clipped them on a loop of cord on the front of his vest.

"Seriously?" Taylor had fond memories of the gun raid, but he wasn't sure Tasers would help them this time.

"You never know when you're gonna want to electrocute someone in the balls." Clay checked they didn't interfere with movement and then happily put a can of capsicum spray in his pocket.

"I could use a rocket launcher about now," Hale lamented, clearly unimpressed with Clay's choice of arsenal. He grabbed the sniper's rifle instead and crawled back to the front of the van, opening the passenger-side door, which was hidden from the office view by the angle they'd crashed.

"I'm going next door, there's a good roof shot at the windows and a good line of sight for front and rear."

"Report as soon as you've found a position," Mendel instructed, and Hale disappeared without another word. "Harris, stay here and mind the van." Harris chuckled and agreed, sounding pained. The break must be bad. "Call an ambulance. And some backup."

"On it."

"How do we want to do this? There's three of us, at least four of them."

"They've been planning this for a while, if the attacks on Sietta were to lure us out," Taylor pointed out. "They'd have let more men in by now. There's no way they could hold the building with four guys. Hell, they probably had others arrested today by the other teams. Or some of the warrants we executed last night."

"Agreed," Mendel grunted. "The garage is the best entry, we know where the cameras are and we can move unseen. Go straight to level three, and move down through the building from there, clear as we go and try to catch them from behind. Our backup should arrive before we get to the ground and we can sandwich them."

Mendel took point, Clay went in the middle, and Taylor brought up the rear. The sun was setting, offering them the cover of darkness to work in. Unfortunately it gave Frey and his men the same cover.

The entry to the garage was easy, and there was no sign of getaway cars, which made sense. If anyone triggered the alarm, the carpark would seal, locking everything in. The logical choice would be the rear loading bay, which had a dumbwaiter down to the basement for loading and unloading of large hauls. It was how they'd gotten the drugs in to begin with.

The stairs were harder. There was a guard on the first floor, but they Tasered him and Mendel punched him hard enough to knock him out. They gagged him and cuffed him to the stairwell to be sure he stayed put and didn't make any noise, then kept moving. They had to jump from one barrier to another to avoid the cameras, which was hard when you were carrying a good thirty kilos of extra weight in gear, but it was what they trained for.

The third floor was abandoned, save for a lone armed man stalking the walls who was easily taken care of, and a sniper in one of the windows. Unfortunately for him, he was too busy looking outside to worry about what was inside, and Clay and Taylor crept up from either side and hogtied him before he could put his finger on the trigger.

Mendel picked up the rifle and looked down the scope, checked the opposite building, but saw nothing.

"Hale?"

"I see you. I have a visual. You've got multiple gunmen on the second floor. They've corralled everyone in the main office. I see at least eight guards, all armed. There's another group by the rear and five men on the ground floor near the dumbwaiter."

"If it looks like they're going to take the drugs, shoot."

"Acknowledged."

They moved on, stopping in a classroom to replace the cartridges in their Tasers from a stockpile used to train new recruits. Mendel shoved a few extra cartridges in his breast pocket, just in case.

Mendel led them to the side wall not visible from Hale's vantage point or the loading bay, and they silently set up rappelling equipment.

"Taylor, you're going down. Clay and I will take one of the end stairwells each. Wait for my signal, and we'll move in from four sides."

Taylor reached out to haul Clay in and bumped their helmets together but didn't bother saying anything, just let him go and watched as he slipped back out into the hallway and disappeared in the dark. Mendel left through the other door, and Taylor hurriedly checked his gear before opening the window and climbing out.

The sun had finished setting and the breeze was cooler, but Taylor barely felt it through his fire-resistant overalls, the balaclava on his face, and the gloves on his hands. He walked cautiously down the side of the building to the floor below, not hearing much coming from the offices where they had corralled everyone. It was a good sign; it meant everyone was playing along, no one was trying to be a hero, following procedure so no one on the outside had to worry about getting anyone inside killed when they did come in.

Taylor settled by a window and pulled out a small mirror, using it to get a look at what was going on. They had the blinds pulled down, but there was enough of a sliver to see in. There weren't many hostages, only ten to Taylor's count. Most must have been called out. No doubt somewhere far out and obscure in the suburbs that didn't actually have a problem.

There were nine gunmen, one of them in the hallway. The ninth man would be invisible to Hale.

"Nine," Taylor spoke softly into his radio. No one replied.

He had one of those moments, and this time he was grateful for it. The pause, as if the world had frozen for a moment, and all he had to do was hang there and breathe, checking his weapon and getting into a position where he could break the window easily with his boot and shoot immediately.

"Three, two, one, breach."

Taylor slammed his foot into the glass, keeping his other foot stable against the brick and shoving his gun into the raining glass, firing two shots at the shooter not visible to Hale, aware of Clay crashing through a door to his left and another window shattering opposite as Hale picked off two men before anyone knew what had happened. Officers rolled under desks and started opening drawers, each arming themselves in quick efficiency with whatever was available.

It was textbook. Ten seconds and the room was in their control. Taylor sat against the sill and wondered why anyone bothered anymore. There was no way to succeed in taking hostages. You were definitely going to get caught, and more than likely you were going to die. It made no sense. But then, he wasn't a criminal, so maybe he just didn't understand. Everyone was unique, and different, and entitled to their own opinion, and all that new-age jazz. He only had to be there when that opinion differed a great deal from the opinion of the law, which thankfully usually matched his own opinion nicely.

Mendel strode in and issued orders while Taylor waited patiently at the window, checking below to make sure no one had heard the breaking glass and come to check, but they were distracted by the broken windows at the front and luckily no one came looking.

"Jameson, rappel to the next level, be prepared to provide backup if required."

Taylor did one quick visual check of Clay before stepping farther down the wall.

The building was eerily quiet, considering what was going on inside. Taylor scanned the streets around them and spotted several police cars with no headlights on sneaking through nearby streets, creeping up on them, making a barricade. No one was leaving tonight, and Taylor relaxed. Frey was screwed; he just didn't know it yet.

Taylor reached the window on the first level and then wondered what the hell he was doing there. He could literally drop a metre to the ground, but he hadn't been ordered to do so. It would depend on what needed doing, how necessary his position was. At the moment it wasn't.

"Harris?" Taylor switched his radio to the digital channel for the van, curious how he was doing around the corner.

"I'm good. Your sister's here taking care of me."

"You poor bastard," he chuckled.

"Nah, it's good… your sister is hot! How did I not know this?"

"Married! My sister is married!"

"Divorce statistics are huge these days," Harris contemplated.

"Murder's on the rise," Taylor heard Hayley grumble, and he left them to it, falling back into silence and switching back to the closed communication channel for raids.

He contemplated the ground, but he was in a better position to break the window and get in fast from the rope, so he waited, using his mirror to check inside.

The room was empty, everyone no doubt gathered by the loading dock. "The wall's clear, I'm dropping from the wall and moving around the back to approach."

"Affirmative," Mendel agreed, and Taylor dropped out of his harness, taking a steadying breath and heading around the back. There was a lone gunman, and Taylor got him from behind and gassed him into unconsciousness before he could shout and alert anyone to Taylor's presence.

"One subdued." Someone would be sent in to collect.

"Acknowledged." The voice was new, from whoever was in charge of the vehicles forming the barricade. Taylor spotted dark shadows closing in on the building, and smirked. The cavalry had arrived.

He reached the corner of the building and used his mirror to check what was happening on the other side of the wall. They were moving fast, aware they were in trouble, ducking and weaving behind trucks and doors to hide from Hale, making it clear they were aware of the sniper.

Hopefully Hale was also aware and watching his back. It was likely they would send someone up to try to deal with him. It was equally likely Hale was already in communication with their backup, who would send a second sniper to help if Hale thought it necessary.

"Three, two, one, breach." Mendel's voice came cold over the comms.

Taylor wasn't even sure where everyone else was, but he watched a man go down with one of Hale's bullets and didn't hesitate further, firing two shots into a gunman's chest, watching him fall into another who became an easy shot for Hale as they stumbled into the open.

Taylor moved in, trusting Hale to cover him as much as possible, deliberately aiming for those in hiding, trying to at least shift them into the open for Hale.

More shadows emerged around him, and the cavalry took over, so Taylor left them to it, heading into the loading bay and clearing the area, meeting Mendel at the door. He knew it was Mendel because he was massive, in head-to-toe black, and even Taylor felt a little intimidated.

"Frey's not here. He must be in the basement," Mendel explained. "Jamesons, on the dumbwaiter."

That was new. Taylor didn't hesitate, hurrying to the chute doors for the dumbwaiter and stepping up beside Clay as Mendel drove the handle hard, bringing it back up. They had their guns drawn, aiming as the doors opened, but there was just a pallet of ice on it. They pulled it out, putting it in front of Mendel as a shield if it was needed, and stepped on.

"Think Mendel can hold us both?" Clay asked.

"Please. It's like taking my daughters to school."

"You have kids?" Taylor was stunned. He couldn't imagine anyone putting up with Mendel long enough to have kids with the man. Or surviving the sex.

"Do you seriously pay attention to nothing?" Clay hissed. "Mendel's got three girls. The oldest goes to Jay's school!"

"Why would I know that?"

"Because you're supposed to give a shit about the people you work with!" Clay seemed disturbed but not surprised.

"Why?"

"Just because, you socially inept dweeb!"

Taylor wanted to reply, but Mendel started lowering them into the basement and they fell immediately silent. The doors opened, and Frey was standing there, gun in hand. Well, *gun* was an understatement.

"You've got to be fucking kidding me!" Clay dove out and rolled, and Taylor did the same as Frey tossed a grenade into the dumbwaiter, showering them in debris, fiery heat washing over them and up the funnel of the waiter to the upper floor. Flames rippled across the walls and the ceiling rained dust and mortar, smoke quickly filling the room.

Taylor rushed forward on hands and knees and ducked behind one of the burning pallets of drugs, hitting his shoe to try to put out the flames melting the soft rubber sole. Thankfully, their overalls were fire retardant and the material smouldered.

There wasn't enough cover. The basement was a long corridor with cages on either side for storing paraphernalia they accumulated on raids. Drugs, guns, illegal goods, cigarettes, anything they needed to keep somewhere until the government told them what to do with it. But the cages were locked, save for the door cut off halfway down where the ice had been stored before they had dragged it into the corridor.

There was nowhere for Clay to run, and Taylor watched, horrified as Frey drew a handgun from his belt and fired at Clay. Realising he had nowhere to hide, Clay had rushed forward, hoping to reach Frey before he reached his weapon, but he was too slow.

The bullet slammed into his vest, throwing him back hard into the cages. It wouldn't kill him, but it likely broke a few ribs and would hurt like hell. Frey charged forward and, to Taylor's horror, kept firing.

"Clay!" He forced himself to react, grabbing his gun from where he'd dropped it when he rolled.

Taylor steadied his hand and fired once. He didn't need a second chance; it was a clean shot. But he couldn't think about it. Turning instead, he hurried down the corridor, checking for anyone else. He found a second man in the open cage, and he Tasered him rather deliberately in the nuts before cuffing him to the cage and leaving him sobbing for someone else to deal with.

"I'm okay," Clay shouted, but he didn't sound okay. Taylor rushed back down the corridor to his side and knelt down, hauled him into a sitting position, and checked him over. Clay clutched his leg and blood pooled over his fingers, soaking his clothes and splashing the floor.

"You got shot!" Taylor bellowed.

"Obviously!"

"Shot is not okay! Fuck!" Taylor pushed his balaclava up over his goggles so he could see what he was doing, and pulled Clay's up to get a good look at his face. He was pale and in a lot of pain.

"You said you were fine when you got shot." Clay covered the wound while Taylor fished out first aid supplies from his vest. They started bandaging, shoving padding on the wound before tying it up tight to try to stop the bleeding.

"Mine was a scratch."

"No, yours was in your fucking shoulder! Mine is in my damn leg! Same-same!"

"No, not same-same! Yours is bleeding all over the fucking place. Look, you're sitting in a pool of blood! It looks like you got your damned period!"

"Excuse me?" Hayley shoved him out of the way. "That is disgusting!" She was accompanied by a team of dark-clad officers being lowered through the gaping hole where the dumbwaiter had been to secure the scene. Her partner pronounced Frey dead and came to help with Clay, leaving the body for the next ambulance to arrive at the scene.

"You try and explain to him that he's been shot, then!" Taylor snapped, furious mostly at himself for not having stopped Frey before he could get to Clay.

"Clay," Hayley advised while they hurriedly set up a stretcher. "You've been shot."

"No shit! You know there's like three more bullets in my vest, right? I'm very much aware that I've been shot! Now can you get me the fuck to the hospital?"

"Shhh." Taylor reached out to pet his cheek since he couldn't pat his head with the helmet on. "I'll call Mum and tell her what happened."

"Fuck!" Clay screamed in frustration, letting Hayley and her partner get him strapped to the stretcher. Her partner's name tag put him as Ford, not her usual partner whose name Taylor was pretty sure was Greg.

"Pretty sure you're all high," Ford chortled, waving a hand at the smouldering drug pallets. "Can we please get him lifted out of here?" He called up to Mendel who tossed some more ropes down to attach to Clay's stretcher.

Taylor wanted to go with him, but he'd just shot a man in the head. He would be required to do a lot of statements and reports, and he would need to help clean up. The boss was going to be pissed. Joel might actually kill him, which would be easier than having to face Brayden. Worse, it would be on the news, and his mother would find out he'd killed a man. She was going to lecture him to death about the sanctity of life while, in the same breath, berate him for not killing Frey sooner before his brother got shot. He was never going to hear the end of it. Emma was going to cry.

He went with Hayley as far as the loading bay, standing with Mendel as the ambulance drove off. At least Clay would have Harris to keep him company.

"Motherfucker," Mendel swore, and Taylor turned to look up at him as he took his helmet off. "Parata's never letting me run an op again."

"Wasn't your fault," Taylor attempted to soothe.

"There's a hole in the basement, Jameson," Mendel growled and they both stared down into it.

Taylor put a hand on the man's massive shoulder and squeezed. Mendel was right, he was going to be punished. He'd be sent to train new recruits, guaranteed. "Have fun teaching at Goulburn."

"Oh, screw you."

15
YUP, BROKEN

THE HOSPITAL stank. Not bad or anything, Taylor just didn't like the smell of sickness and antiseptic. He stood there in his black overalls, open at the collar to reveal what had been a white T-shirt but was now covered in dirt, explosives, and blood, and stared at his own sleeping face.

Clay had bruising over most of his body, peeking out from under all the bandages and the hideous hospital gown he was in. He had nine fractured ribs and a bullet hole in his thigh. It had taken an hour in surgery to dig the bullet out and get him stitched up. By the time he was settled in a room, Taylor had been released from the endless tirade of retelling the events that had taken place and was allowed to go home. Taylor had rung Hayley and come straight to the hospital.

Mum had beaten him there, sitting by Clay's bed, clutching his hand. She looked like she had been crying. It took her a while to realise he was there, and when she looked up at him, she burst into tears again. The guilt was incredible, but Taylor shoved it aside and folded over her, wrapping her up in arms that didn't feel strong enough but would have to do. She never seemed so small to him as whenever they were really hurt.

"What, it wasn't enough that you got shot? He had to get shot too? You do know you can do things separately, right?" She was struggling to make light of the situation, her pain laced with anger and frustration at her inability to do anything.

"He's fine, Mum." Weirdly, he believed it.

"I'm fine." Clay sounded groggy.

"What, you couldn't stay under another hour?" He reached out and brushed Clay's hair back, trailed his fingers down his neck to his shoulder, and squeezed. "You scared the shit out of me."

"Well, now you know how it feels," Clay mumbled. "But I'm fine. Really, Mum. Just bruises."

"And a bullet hole!" Chloe scolded him.

"And a bullet hole," they agreed, well aware there would be lectures and reminders to not get shot again for the foreseeable future.

"Clay?" Joel ran into the room and barely pulled himself up before slamming into the side of the bed, then leaned over and planted a frenzied kiss on Clay's lips that had Chloe laughing through her tears and Taylor skipping out of the way before he got run over. Micah hovered in the doorway, and Taylor ushered him in, bemused when the kid ran to his side and wrapped his arms around his waist.

"Hey, he's fine. Just some bruises. Everyone's fine, I promise. Sietta's on his way."

"And a bullet hole!" Chloe snapped at him, and he could tell she was working up to yelling at him for letting Clay get shot. He wasn't sure how that worked. When he got shot, it was his fault. When Clay got shot, it was still Taylor's fault. There was something seriously askew in that logic, but it was Chloe, so he wasn't game to argue.

"And a bullet hole," he agreed quietly instead.

"Notice how she doesn't screech about the broken bones?" Hayley pointed out as she came in, making the room feel a little crowded in a good way. She also had a point.

"Oh please, if I harped about broken bones, I'd never have had time to write while you were growing up. Besides, a little pain teaches you a lesson, and broken bones heal."

And that was more like it. She sniffed and the tears dried up, and Taylor silently high fived Hayley behind Chloe's back. No one bothered to point out that if it didn't kill you, a bullet hole also healed.

A soft knock came at the door, and Daniel appeared, Brayden and Sietta behind him. The hospital room was now feeling miniscule, but they shifted to let Daniel in to sit with Chloe at Clay's side, pushing Taylor to the back of the room with Micah, where they pulled Sietta into a tight hug, Taylor kissing the top of his head.

"He's okay?" Sietta toyed with the ends of his hair, idly rubbing it on his chin.

"Are you okay?" Micah looked up at him, staring at the now very dark bruise on the left side of Sietta's face that ran down his neck and across his collarbone. Sietta blinked before he realised what Micah was staring at, and then he waved it off.

"Yeah, I'm fine. Just bruises."

The glare Chloe gave Sietta could have stripped the skin from an elephant. "Is that a shackle on your foot?" She pointed deliberately to it so that everyone in the hospital room ended up turning to stare.

"Ah, yeah...." Sietta looked for help.

"Sorry, I haven't figured out a way to get it off yet without a blowtorch or something." Brayden scratched his head, unperturbed by the annoyed look Taylor gave him.

"Seriously, you had one job!" Taylor crouched down to get a better look at it. The rust was bad, and the keyhole had had something poured into it, so even if they'd had the key, they wouldn't have got it open. He had to admit, a blowtorch would work, but the metal was brittle and he thought he might be able to cut it with some large bolt cutters.

"I think I've got something at the office that'll work. I'll ask someone to bring it over." He sent off a quick text to Jones, trusting him to get it sorted. Mendel had been in a foul mood when Taylor left, still stuck doing reports. They were going to be doing paperwork for weeks. Months. Hell, it could take years.

"So, it's a shackle." Chloe sounded incredibly unimpressed with all of them. Her gaze turned back up to Taylor, and the anger was back. "You let that boy get kidnapped again?"

Was it even worth arguing? She needed a target, and he had to admit he was a pretty big one. "I did."

Her mouth was moving, but no words were coming out.

"Her mouth is moving, but no words are coming out," Sietta observed, copying his thoughts exactly. Taylor nodded in agreement and carefully extricated them from the room. Brayden followed them out, closing the door behind him and taking a deep breath.

"Clay really is gonna be fine. The bullet didn't do much damage, his ribs will heal fine." Taylor sighed in relief. It wasn't actually his fault he hadn't been able to get to Frey in time, and he was glad no permanent damage had been done. He was also pleased the injuries would at least keep Clay behind a desk for the foreseeable future. Not that they all weren't going to be desk-ridden until the paperwork was finished.

"Hey." Jones came jogging up the hall, bolt cutters in hand. "I was still here with the guy we shot, figured they'd have a pair of these in the shed downstairs, and what do you know?"

"Thanks." Taylor went to grab them, and Jones shook his head.

"You look about ready to drop. I got this. Sit down, Salisbury." He pushed Sietta over to a bench against the wall and knelt down, carefully looking the shackle over for its weakest point and sliding the cutters in underneath it. It took four tries, but the metal gave and fell away.

"Ta-da!"

"Thank you," Sietta smiled brightly, carefully rolling his ankle and then lifting it to rub at the abraded skin.

"Anytime. I'm off shift, so I'll return these and be on my way. Get some sleep, Jameson, you look like shit."

Taylor's gaze didn't leave Sietta, focussed on how ridiculously pleased he looked to be free of the unwanted jewellery.

Brayden knelt down and checked the ankle over, frowning before he looked seriously at Sietta. "I want to bandage this. The skin's quite damaged, but it's swollen and you're favouring the leg?"

"I think they might have fractured it again," Sietta agreed. "I was hoping it was just a bruise, but...."

"Are you shitting me?" Taylor snapped at him. "Why didn't you say anything?"

"Because I wasn't sure, and because I wanted to go home not to the hospital!" Sietta snapped back immediately, startling Taylor, who understood the desire all too well. He looked to Brayden for help, not sure what to say.

"We'll go do a quick X-ray to check, and take care of it." Brayden got up and wrapped an arm around Sietta's waist to help him down the hallway. "You stay here, we'll be back in about an hour, I think."

Taylor watched them go, left in the hallway feeling suddenly cold and deserted. His boyfriend was in the hospital. His brother was in the hospital. He hadn't kept them safe. Worse.

He'd killed a man, yet felt no remorse.

EVENTUALLY HE'D sat down. He had no idea when, but he must have because he was sitting down, staring at the white wall opposite him when the white morphed into a small familiar face, and Emma crawled up into his lap, wrapped her tiny arms around his neck, and hugged him. His arms came up on reflex, wrapping around her and cradling her tight against his chest as the tears finally came. He was too tired to fight them any longer.

"Don't cry, Uncle Tay. Uncle Clay's gonna be fine, Daddy said so. It's just bruises."

He hiccupped and clenched his eyes shut for a minute before nodding in agreement and pulling back to smile at her.

"Yeah, princess, he's gonna be fine." He looked up at Kelly standing there with Jay at her side, his small hand held tight in hers. She looked uncertain, shocked to see him such a mess. She'd never seen him outside of the cocky, arrogant, and often rude attitude-ridden mess he was around the family. He didn't care, and neither did she, leaning forward to kiss his cheek and smile reassuringly.

"You need sleep, Taylor."

"I need my boyfriend, but your husband took him."

Her eyes went wide, and then her smile went wider and she tried to cover it with her hand too late. "Your boyfriend?"

He glared at her, daring her to say any different.

"Wait." Emma frowned at him, squirming in his lap. "Is Sietta your boyfriend now?"

"Yeah, babycake."

"That makes him my uncle, right?"

"Uh-huh."

"Awesome! More Christmas presents!" she exclaimed excitedly to Jay, who agreed with her immediately. She hopped off his lap but leaned in to give him a wet, sloppy kiss on the cheek.

"I love you, Uncle Tay."

"Love you too, sweet pea."

"But you look like shit. You should get some sleep."

"Emma!" Kelly snapped, horrified. "Language! Gosh, I don't know where she keeps getting this stuff from!"

Taylor arched a brow at her, and she sighed. They both knew exactly where she was getting it from: Saturday barbeques and phones on speaker. Actually, probably more the phones, since people tended to at least attempt to watch their mouths in person.

"Sorry. Least it'll make parent-teacher interviews super interesting!"

"Oh, don't remind me. I had to go to Jay's last week. The teacher was telling me all about how the class was asked to draw a picture of what they did on the weekend, and she was very concerned that Jay drew Emma in the refrigerator."

"Ah...."

"I lied and said he had an overactive imagination. Then she reminded both of us about it being bad to tell lies...."

"I let Mum's fib slide," Jay put in proudly, and Taylor gave him an obligatory fist bump. He was a smart kid. A little too smart, perhaps.

"It's bad to lie, Mum." Emma grabbed Kelly's free hand and tugged. They all sighed.

"Let's go in and see Uncle Clay, okay?"

"Yay!" they said in unison, and Kelly opened the door quickly and disappeared. Emma came running back out and gave him a final hug before running in again, the door closing behind her. It wasn't thick enough to muffle her indignant bellow.

"Uncle Clay, what sort of crap cop gets shot?"

Taylor covered his mouth, startled by the loud laugh that erupted in front of him. He looked up at Sietta and Brayden, then stood and replaced Brayden's arm around Sietta's waist with his own. There was a thick, heavy plastic-padded boot from Sietta's knee to his ankle.

"Broken," Sietta acknowledged, but he was still chuckling. "God, Emma's my hero."

"Try living with her," Brayden muttered. "She lectured me about margarine this morning. Apparently it's made from plastic and it's not allowed in the house anymore."

He left them in the hallway, bracing himself before he went into Clay's room and disappeared.

"Home?" Sietta asked hopefully.

"Home," Taylor agreed, shifting his arm and leaning down to loop his other under Sietta's knees. He swung him up and hugged him close to his chest, kissing his forehead. Sietta cried out in surprise and hurriedly wrapped his arms around Taylor's neck to keep from falling, chuckling softly when he settled in his arms.

"Seriously?"

"Seriously." He didn't care what anyone thought. He wasn't letting Sietta out of his arms.

"Could be an awkward drive," Sietta mused, but he appeared to be enjoying the ride and that was all that mattered.

"You can steer."

His laughter still did the strangest things to him.

TAYLOR HAD no idea what time it was. The sun was up, bleeding through under the blinds of his bedroom window, and gentle fingers were tracing the lines of his chest.

"Hey," he mumbled, tilting his head to find he was lying against Sietta, head on his shoulder, Sietta's broken leg propped up on a pillow in front of him while Sietta's hands wandered.

"Hey. You look better." Sietta smiled, leaning in to kiss him, slow and languid. He tasted like he'd brushed his teeth recently, but Taylor must have slept through it. He had no memory after coming home, showering, and literally falling into bed.

"You look... the same as always," Taylor studied Sietta's face. "I've never seen you sleep."

"I don't really sleep." Sietta shrugged, as if that were an entirely reasonable explanation. Taylor struggled to sit up against the pillows until they were eye to eye and fixed a steely glare on him.

"You're going to have to explain that to me." Because that wasn't possible, was it?

"I micronap. Apparently. That's what Bray called it. Tiny little lapses through the day when your brain shuts down for a few seconds—"

"I know what a micronap is. That's all you do? You don't sleep at all?"

"Occasionally I get so tired that everything just turns off, but not for long and only every couple of days. Usually only if there's no one around and I feel...."

Safe. It was something that had clearly developed over time. Over years, in captivity of being terrified someone would hurt him while he slept, or he'd miss something important. Taylor wanted to punch something. Instead he pulled Sietta into his arms and rolled him on top of him, careful of the cast on his leg.

"Brayden gave me some drugs he think will help, but he said it will take time. I'm not used to sleeping, so I have to train myself to do it."

"You were sleeping when they took you," Taylor realised. He and Clay had gone for their run, and with the house locked and quiet, an armed police escort outside, Sietta had actually slept.

"Yeah." He'd let his guard down and been taken again. No wonder he'd been so freaked out when they reached him. First time he slept in years and he ends up right back where the problem started.

"You felt safe enough to sleep here?" He felt lighter suddenly.

"Well, yeah." And Taylor started to realise what Sietta had been saying all day.

"You think of this as home."

"Uh… yeah."

"Good." Taylor drew him in for more kisses, rewarding him for such good thinking. "That's very good."

"So…."

"This is home," Taylor agreed. "Me, you, here. That's what I want. Us."

"Good." Sietta relaxed and let his full weight fall on Taylor. "So… I was just part of a big plan, huh?"

"This time, yeah," Taylor didn't like that at all.

"And Viola's still out there?"

"We have no proof she had anything to do with this, but I think you're right and she's behind it. And yeah, she's still out there. We'll have to wait and see if she shows for her hearing for the original accessory to crime charges from your kidnapping before we can question her."

"Not likely." Sietta stalled his touch over Taylor's throat. If he was afraid, he didn't show it, but Taylor didn't think it was fear stilling his fingers. More like frustration that he could once again do nothing but wait and see what happened.

"Can I distract you?" Taylor pushed a hand to Sietta's chest and stroked upward, over his Adam's apple to his jaw and held him steady, feeling his breaths as he inhaled and exhaled, his eyes hooded and watching him. He licked his lips, and Taylor could feel his hardness pushing against his own.

"Good," Taylor whispered, drawing Sietta down and kissing him, taking his time, letting his tongue explore inside his mouth. He stroked the roof of his mouth in an attempt to learn the pattern of bumps and valleys by heart. When Sietta pulled back to breathe, Taylor didn't stop, moving along the smooth ridge of Sietta's jaw and down his throat, finding the vein and nibbling on it, delighted by the way Sietta shivered and moaned in response.

He rolled them, pinning Sietta beneath him and kissing him again while his hands found the edge of the T-shirt Sietta was wearing and pulled it off, amused to see it was one of his with PORS written in big white letters across the front. He tossed it aside and ran a hand down Sietta's side to grip his hip tight, then pushed him into the mattress to prevent him from moving away while he licked at his nipple until it was hard beneath his soft lips.

"Shit... oh, that feels good!" The stunned look on Sietta's face was a harsh reminder of how innocent Sietta still was. It struck Taylor that this was Sietta's first time, and he had to take a few deep breaths and remind himself to slow down. It wasn't hard; he wanted to take his time, to explore and enjoy, and Sietta seemed happy with whatever he wanted to do.

It was a good thing Clay wasn't home, as the more of Sietta's body that Taylor touched his tongue to, the louder and more confident Sietta's small outcries became.

"There! Oh, Tay... there!"

He'd found a small spot below Sietta's hip bone that made Sietta thrust his hips up at his face, demanding more, and made Taylor chuckle and happily give in to kissing it again, sucking the sensitive skin into his mouth until it bruised, leaving a dark red mark that contrasted against the actual bruises against Sietta's skin.

Drawing Sietta's underwear off and tossing it aside was more exciting than Taylor could ever remember it being. He took in a deep breath and stared at the beautiful man spread beneath him, cast and all. Taylor wondered suddenly what he'd ever done to deserve so much as looking at him. But he didn't question it, stroking sure hands up the inside of Sietta's thighs and smiling when Sietta dropped them open in invitation.

Taylor slid down his body and deliberately licked at the head of Sietta's hard cock, chuckling when Sietta's hips bucked and he clutched at the sheet to keep from grabbing anything inappropriate. As if Taylor would mind him grabbing him as hard as he wanted.

He took the full length into his mouth and sucked hard, loving the strained groan he won from Sietta. He wasn't particularly fond of sucking cock, preferring hand jobs or sex, but he suspected that had a lot to do with the fact he'd never been big on foreplay. It had always seemed such a waste of time, but it was different. With Sietta, he was different.

He enjoyed it. He felt a small thrill every time Sietta gasped or moaned, and his own cock hardened with each stuttered plea for more.

"Stop. Oh... God, stop!" Sietta finally reached down and pulled hard on his hair, winning a laugh from Taylor as he pulled away and blew on Sietta's dick instead, making him laugh as well. "Stop! I don't wanna come yet!"

"Fine, fine," Taylor was still chuckling as he reached over and grabbed a condom and some lube from the bedside. Sietta stopped him, looking at the supplies and meeting his eyes.

"I've never...."

"I know." But Sietta didn't seem nervous about it, at all.

"No, I mean. I trust you, and I'm clean so...." He grabbed the condom and tossed it aside, thoroughly startling Taylor, who watched its small journey through the sky like a shooting star, until it smacked into the wall and dropped like a stone. He stared at it on the floor until Sietta's long fingers grabbed his jaw and turned his head to look at him. "Okay?"

"Yeeeeah...." He had one final glance at the condom, and then Sietta had all of his attention once more. He couldn't believe Sietta trusted him like that. He almost wanted to say no, that they would use it, that Sietta couldn't possibly know what he was doing, but that was insulting to both of them. It wasn't hard to trust Sietta, and he had to trust that Sietta felt the same about him. This was Sietta's way of telling him in no uncertain terms how completely he was in this. In Us.

His hands moved on autopilot, spreading lube on his fingers and teasing, stroking the small hole he found between Sietta's cheeks. He slipped inside so slowly it almost felt like one of those moments, and they just breathed. Sietta's wide blue eyes locked on his own until Taylor momentarily forgot where he was, drowning.

"I love you."

"I know," Sietta gasped. "I love you, too, but so help me if you don't hurry up and fuck me, I am going to murder you!"

Stunned, Taylor froze, then laughed, slipping a second finger in and stroking until he found Sietta's prostate, deliberately stroking it while Sietta moaned until he almost cried and demanded he hurry up.

"Now, now, now!"

"So spoilt," Taylor muttered, sliding a third finger in, wondering if Sietta had stopped to consider that he was not a small man and things were definitely in proportion, and Taylor was just trying to be a nice guy and not hurt the love of his life.

Oh shit, was he the love of his life? Taylor froze again, stuck in another moment. Sietta was the only thing he'd loved as much as his brother. Shit.

"Taylor...."

He silenced Sietta and his own mind by sealing his mouth over Sietta's, sucking the air from both of their lungs, then pushed one of those deliciously long legs up, hooking it over his elbow while he lined his cock up with Sietta's hole. He didn't give Sietta a chance to think or breathe, sliding in as gently as he could, aware of Sietta biting his lip but not feeling the pain.

He stopped only when he was fully in, marvelling at the tight heat, the way Sietta clutched his shoulders and pulled him closer, wrapping him completely in heat at the same time he let Taylor smother him and shelter him from the world. He'd never felt so complete.

"Move," Sietta insisted, breathless and panting, shifting his hips impatiently, and Taylor listened. He pulled back and built a rhythm that almost broke him with his need to concentrate on the loitering push and glide, building it so slowly he wanted to scream in frustration but able to hold it because Sietta was crying out for him, begging for more, pleading for him to go faster.

He made it last, made sure Sietta enjoyed every moment. He waited until Sietta lost control of his words and gripped him so tightly his knuckles were white as he shouted his release and spilled across Taylor's stomach and hip. Then Taylor filled him, aware there was nothing catching his release but skin and bone. He was marking Sietta in ways he'd never thought he would, and his brain was struck dumb, whiting out with the force of his pleasure.

"Breathe," Sietta panted at him, and he forced air into his lungs, collapsing over him, pressing them together so Sietta was as covered in his cum as he was.

"Let me stay...." He wasn't ready to pull out yet, still softening and enjoying the feel of Sietta's muscles shifting around his cock.

"Can't move," Sietta murmured. "Feel so good."

Taylor chuckled breathlessly, held him tight, and kissed his closed eyelids, his temple, his nose, his cheeks... every piece of him he could reach without having to move. He prayed Sietta had liked it and would let him do it again.

"Thank you," Sietta whispered against his skin.

"Oh, anytime. Believe me. Anytime."

"Like… in an hour?" Sietta opened his eyes and smirked at him, winning the laugh he obviously wanted from Taylor.

"Sure." He didn't think Sietta would be ready, but that was okay. An hour, a day, a week, Taylor would wait as long as he wanted. He'd never been so happy in his life. He slid out reluctantly and moved off the bed, then reached down to hoist Sietta into his arms and kissed his temple again as he carried him into the shower. He took off Sietta's cast and left it on the closed toilet lid before turning the water on.

It was hot and cleansing, and he soaped them up before rinsing away the evidence of what they had done, paying careful attention to every part of Sietta's long limbs. He deliberately teased the new ticklish places he had found, thrilled that no one else had ever found them, that he was the first, and determined to be the last.

He dried them off and put the cast back on Sietta's leg before curling up around him on the bed.

"You know I love you, hmm," Taylor mused, grinning at the memory now he thought about it.

"Mmm," Sietta hummed in agreement. Taylor loved the way his chest vibrated against his. "I knew when you body slammed me into the footpath outside your mum's house."

"We were being shot at," Taylor grumbled at the description.

"Body slam," Sietta whispered, then laughed.

"Brat."

He lay there, wrapped tight around Sietta, until he fell asleep. When he woke again, it was to the gentle hum of Sietta's steady breathing, and he realised with a swell of intense heat in his chest that Sietta was asleep.

THE BEDROOM door slammed open.

Taylor woke to the patter of small feet and had just enough sense to pull the sheet up over their waists before Emma dived on the bed and landed on Sietta. Luckily, Sietta was awake and caught her easily.

Emma, however, froze. She stared wide-eyed at Sietta, her bright smile turning to confusion.

"You're not Uncle Tay."

"No."

"You're Uncle Sietta."

"Yes."

Everything froze for a minute before Emma quickly crawled over Sietta and flopped down between them. Taylor saw Sietta cover his reaction with his hand and cough.

"Good morning, princess."

"Morning, Uncle Tay." She beamed at him, squirming a little until she was comfortable and then sighing happily. "Your bed is comfy."

"Uh-huh." He looked at the open doorway and saw Brayden carrying a bag of groceries into the kitchen. That explained Emma's presence, not Bray's.

"You do know your daughter is in bed with two naked men, right?" Clay's voice came from somewhere else in the apartment, and Taylor sighed. That explained Bray's presence.

"She's not *in* the bed!" Sietta corrected. "She's *on* it!" Apparently this distinction was important.

"I don't think that makes it any better." Joel's voice chimed in.

There was movement, and then Clay appeared in the doorway, a crutch under one arm, wincing as he hobbled his way into the bedroom and flopped down on Sietta's other side, curling up around him and sighing.

"The hell?" Sietta and Taylor said in unison.

"What? He's warm. And pretty. And naked."

"And not Joel," Joel said from where he was leaning on the doorframe, but he was clearly amused by his partner's antics.

"Uncle Joel has to go to work, so we're gonna babysit Uncle Clay," Emma informed them.

"We are?" Sietta sounded unconvinced, looking from Joel to Taylor and then trying to look past Joel to Brayden, who was being suspiciously quiet on the subject.

"Not you," Emma corrected. "You're as bad as he is." She waved an imperious hand at Clay, who smirked and threw his bandaged leg over beside Sietta's cast to prove her point. Apparently they were both on the babysitting list.

"Sorry," Joel apologised. "I have a lecture today and there's no one available to cover for me."

"It's fine," Taylor assured him, amused that he was apparently being dumped with all three of them for the day. "What's your excuse, Bray?"

"I'm on shift, Kel has to take Jay to some show thing for school, Emma desperately wanted to take care of Uncle Clay instead of going to day care, and it saves me a hundred bucks?"

"Good excuse," Taylor and Clay muttered together. Ironclad, really.

"Can I get paid?" Sietta asked suddenly, and they all stared at him. "I mean, he was gonna pay a hundred for day care, right? So...."

"How did I never think of that?" Clay frowned at Emma, no doubt thinking of how much money they could have earned by now.

"I'm going to say because the type of family he grew up in likes to chain children to walls, while the kind of family we are likes to babysit for free because we love each other." Brayden rolled his eyes, ignoring their horrified looks.

Emma's eyes were wide as she turned to Sietta, her small face far too serious for any good to happen.

"They chain you to walls?"

"Uh...." Sietta searched for help, but found none. "Yes."

When in doubt, go with the truth. That was the saying, wasn't it?

Emma crawled closer, and then closer still until they were nose to nose and Sietta could no doubt feel her breathing on him as she searched his face for something.

"Are you a dragon?"

They all remained perfectly still and silent, and turned to Brayden for advice on that one.

"Honey, no, Uncle Sietta isn't a dragon, and he didn't lick the walls for water, to survive. He just got kept like one. *Merlin*, guys, come on... you watch TV! Emma, honey, Uncle Sietta's a normal guy, okay?"

She did not look convinced. At all.

"Don't lick the walls. I'm not cleaning that up," she whispered to him, then flopped back into Taylor's lap and curled up, apparently content.

"Welcome to the family, dude," Clay whispered to Sietta. "When Emma's giving you orders, it means you're one of us."

Sietta studied the small child, then smiled and leaned his head on Clay's shoulder, giving in. He no doubt thought the Jamesons were weird, sure, but they loved each other. They knew what family was, and they didn't have to try to make it work. It happened naturally. For Sietta, it had to be like falling into an alternate reality and realising the way family worked on TV or in books wasn't a fairy tale after all. His parents had simply been more interested in money and appearances than their children, and that was just another sad fact he was going to have to accept and move away from. Taylor hoped that was easier to do, when you were ensconced in a warm bed surrounded by people who accepted you.

"I have to go." Joel came in and gave Clay a soft kiss. "Be good. Emma. Call me if he's naughty!"

She saluted him.

"I'm off too," Brayden said, giving Emma a kiss and a hug. "Take good care of your uncles, and don't eat all the marshmallows!"

"What if Uncle Tay eats them all?"

"He won't. I will know it was you, and you will not get marshmallows again."

"What, ever?" She was horrified, and Brayden nodded sternly. They watched her wilt in his stern glare. "Okay. But can I have ten?"

"Just ten!" Brayden agreed and then abandoned them.

There was a moment, but it wasn't one of the calming ones where everything stopped and gave you a time out. It was poignant and full of terror as they wondered what was about to come out of Emma's mouth.

16
No Secret Desires and Boom.

"Leila, Micah, out of the pool! Lunch is almost ready!" Ash called from the barbeque where he stood, in board shorts and thongs, flipping sausages and steaks.

"Almost ready is not ready, Ashley!" Leila refused to move from where she and Micah were sprawled over the back of a giant inflatable swan, sunglasses on and empty plastic cups in hand, sprigs of mint sticking out. It was almost the identical shot Micah had put in his Instagram two hours ago, the pair not having moved except to check the ridiculous number of likes they had received since and laughing over the comments asking who the model was Micah was spending the weekend with. They'd passed the twenty thousand mark some time ago, much to Chloe's amusement.

"When you drip all over your bread and it gets soggy and your sanga falls to pieces, blame yourself!" Kelly struggled to pull the floaties off Emma's arms so she could eat without hitting herself in the head.

"Ew! No one eats bread anymore!" Leila called back, still not moving.

"I give it a day," Chloe drawled from where she was lounging, eyes closed at the edge of the patio where the sun was still bright.

"I give it till dinner." Hayley snickered. "No way is that girl saying no to garlic bread with her spaghetti."

Taylor ignored them, his gaze fixed on Sietta, in the living room with Daniel, Ben, and Joel, signing off the last of the paperwork that would leave Micah fostered with Joel indefinitely. They'd already spent the morning wading through the charges that the rest of Sietta's family had faced. Johnathan Salisbury had been given twenty years for the various crimes committed. Louisa had been given twelve, with a chance for parole after eight, much to Sietta's chagrin. Anders had been given ten years, Viola five—only Viola was nowhere to be found. There were permanent restraining orders for the family, to protect Micah and Sietta.

The paperwork had been obnoxious, but Ben had led them through it with ease, explaining everything in almost painful detail. Sietta had simply put his name to everything, page after page until they sat back and Daniel poured them all a drink.

Sietta hobbled out the screen door, still unwieldy with his cast, and sat down heavily in Taylor's lap, relaxing completely against him and sighing in relief. Joel followed him out but sat beside Clay rather than on him, much to Clay's chagrin.

"All done?"

"Mostly," Sietta agreed. "There's a publisher interested in picking up my book. I have to send them a copy, but I'm gonna let Taylor read it first."

Taylor was going to hate it. He would be in a foul mood for however long it took to read it, but he wanted to read every page before anyone else got their hands on it. He refused to let anyone have a part of Sietta that wasn't his first.

"Thank you."

"So… this grenade they shot you with." Ben emerged from inside, still in his suit, but he'd taken off his tie and undone the top three buttons, the coat sitting inside on a lounger. He'd even rolled up the sleeves and let his hair down. It was a dramatically different look from the court proceedings he'd been involved in that morning.

"I didn't get shot with the grenade!" Clay let his head fall back and groaned. "They threw the grenade at both of us, in the dumbwaiter! Then I got shot with a handgun!"

"It just doesn't make sense that the handgun did more damage than the grenade," Hayley muttered, waving at his bandaged leg.

"Tell that to the dumbwaiter. That thing's like a giant hole in the basement. They can't remove anything from the storage lockers until the repairs are done, but the structural damage to the building is pretty bad, so it'll be months yet." Taylor had had to help move the drugs to a different facility, and without the dumbwaiter that had proved a complex task.

"So it killed your building and barely scratched you?" Hayley stared at him dubiously.

"Uncle Tay is in-struc-ble." Emma was finally freed of her floaties and moved straight to Taylor's side, glaring at Sietta until he obediently moved into an empty chair and gave up Taylor's lap to the midget.

"Uh-huh…." They were all entirely unimpressed and did not agree with her assessment at all, which was understandable, since while his black eye had healed, he still had a bright pink scar healing from his own bullet wound, though the bandage was long gone.

"Where did they get a grenade?" Ben asked.

"From this raid we did on this illegal import." Clay waved his hand, indifferent, clearly trying to end the conversation before it got out of hand.

"Yes, but how did they import them?" The conversation had awakened Chloe's writer's curiosity. "I mean, this is Australia. We have laws for that sort of thing."

"Illegally?" Brayden pointed out, clearly dumbfounded that no one seemed to be catching on to that part of the story.

"Yes, but did they bring them in on a boat, a plane, did they build them at home… there's a lot of ways to do something illegal, you know!"

"We know," Clay and Taylor said in unison, Clay rolling his eyes.

"It's pretty easy to smuggle stuff in on a boat," Ashley pointed out. "We've got a lot of coast and not a lot of coastguards."

"Speculation is not fact." Ben frowned at them all. "If you don't know how the guns got here, how are you going to stop it from happening again?"

"Well gee, if that was my job, I suppose I'd have to give it a bit more thought. Fortunately, my job is just to go in when they fail to stop the import, and seize it." Taylor rolled his eyes. He was so done with the conversation and deliberately turned to Ash.

"So, you got a new car." A nice shiny, new ute as a matter of fact.

"Isn't it sweet?" Ash put a massive tray of meat in the middle of the table amongst the salads Kelly had already laid out.

"It's awesome, Uncle Ash!" Jay came running out of the house, abandoning his movie in the lounge room to investigate the scent of food.

"It's expensive," Daniel countered. "What happens when you decide to park it at the fire again?"

"That was one time!" Ashley protested. "And you'll be pleased to know I got reprimanded for taking my own vehicle to a fire, so shut up about it already!"

"Language!" Chloe scolded. "Do not speak to your father like that."

"Taylor speaks like that all the time!"

"Taylor's an asshole," Clay reminded him, and Ashley sighed and started making a sausage sandwich instead of arguing. Smart boy.

Micah and Leila appeared by the table, dripping a small lake of pool water as they tossed steak and salad on plates and hurried off to bake on the lawn in the sun, trying to find the perfect position to lie in for another Instagram-worthy shot.

"I want to be young again and have nothing more to worry about than whether that filter makes me look fat," Hayley moaned. "I should never have gotten married."

"You're married?" Sietta choked on the cheese square he'd just popped in his mouth, coughing to get it to go down. "To who?"

"Joe," everyone said in stumped unison, as if this were common knowledge.

"Okay." Sietta looked around the table, but no one elaborated so he looked to Taylor for answers. "Where is Joe?"

"Joe's smart," Taylor replied, nodding as if this was sage information. "Joe works for an engineering firm where everyone is happily married, with kids, and no one wants to work Saturday and miss family barbeques...."

"Joe works Saturdays," Sietta acknowledged, then laughed at the disgusted look on Hayley's face. "Joe is wise."

His phone buzzed, and Sietta fished it out of the pocket of his black jeans, staring at the small Nokia screen, which wasn't backlit and so was hard to read in the sun's glare.

"You need a new phone," Clay muttered.

"Never. This one will never die. It will outlive all of you," Sietta distractedly disagreed, still trying to read the text.

"Good news?" Taylor asked.

"Yeah, that cellist I mentioned is keen to start playing together."

Sietta had been panicking about even contacting the mysterious student he apparently liked to stalk in his free time. He'd not been able to go to the guy's concerts while locked in the basement, but he'd heard about him and sent Micah with a video camera to record him. It had been simple curiosity at first, but eventually Micah had been sent to every single show the poor guy did, and Sietta would sit and watch the footage and ask a hundred questions that Micah didn't know the answers to. Taylor had heard all about it in an hour-long bemoaning session when they had Micah over for dinner, and Sietta had asked where the guy was playing next.

Taylor had got tickets, and while it was not his kind of music, he'd sat through a two-hour recital of Bach cello solos, and even he had to admit the sound of the instrument was haunting. That did not explain the epic crush Sietta apparently had on the way the man played.

Had it been the man himself Sietta was interested in, Taylor would have been furiously jealous. But when he'd managed to get Sietta backstage to talk, and he'd watched and listened to the conversation that took place, it became painfully obvious that Sietta was socially ridiculously inept and interested only in what the man would do with his instrument, much to the poor cellist's dismay. He'd been interested.

They'd exchanged numbers, and Taylor had put up with Sietta prowling the apartment incessantly day and night until Taylor had messaged the guy and asked if he'd be interested in putting a group together to play around the city.

And he was interested. Thank God.

"Wait, you're gonna play?" Micah sat up excitedly. "For real?"

"Is this a thing?" Leila asked around a massive spinach leaf.

"It's totally a thing! Si hasn't played in public for years! And he's so good! Like, seriously, the best!" It was cute, watching him fanboy his brother. Almost as cute as the scarlet blush that swept over Sietta's face and the way he sank into his chair.

"We're gonna try and see how it goes," he muttered.

"It'll be fine." Taylor brushed his fingers through Sietta's hair where it hung around his shoulders. It was cute how worried he was. Taylor had been going every night to the university where Joel kept booking a practise studio, so he knew Micah wasn't exaggerating. Taylor wasn't an expert, but you didn't need to be to know Sietta was something special. He'd never heard anything like the sounds that came out of that practise room.

"Tell us when you're playing, we'd love to come." Daniel smiled brightly.

"If the venue's child-friendly and not a school night, we'll be there," Kelly added, and Brayden agreed.

"Count me in," Ben agreed, and Sietta looked stunned for a moment before he remembered where he was and who he was with.

Taylor loved those moments when Sietta remembered he had a family who cared. It was taking some getting used to, but there was less confusion about the whole thing now.

"Are any of you actually going to eat? I slaved over this!" Ash waved a hand at the food sitting forgotten on the table.

That was all it took. They dug in, plates being passed around and food piled onto plates. Taylor let Emma drop half her lunch all over him and finished off what she didn't eat while she sprawled in his lap, Sietta at his side. Complete and satisfied.

CLAY SAT on the pool edge with Taylor, sipping his beer. Taylor sat sweating at his side with a stubby cooler in hand, bare feet chilling in the water. Clay had a hideous pair of board shorts on because most of his clothes didn't fit over the bandages.

"You okay?" Taylor asked him. His bruises were fading, but he still walked with a crutch and cradled his ribs when he laughed.

"Yeah, I'm fine. Even get to go back on shift next week, though I'll be on desk for another month at least."

"Yeah, I'm on desk until I pass a psych eval."

"Ew." Clay scrunched up his nose, and Taylor couldn't agree more. He wasn't looking forward to the evaluation; he wasn't even sure what to say this time. He'd never killed a guy before, and he suspected he was supposed to feel remorse, but he didn't. He felt good, and that worried him. You weren't supposed to enjoy killing a person, and while he wouldn't really classify it as enjoyment, he was glad Frey was dead. He hadn't suffered; it had been a quick and relatively painless execution. He'd been going to kill Clay; the decision had been so very easy. Worse, he'd hurt Sietta—had hurt the two people closest to Taylor. The guy got what he deserved.

He doubted that was what the shrink wanted to hear, but he'd always figured the truth was the best option, so it was likely what the guy was going to hear.

"Thank you, for protecting me."

"Seriously?" Taylor squinted at Clay, wondering if he'd hit his head. As if he wasn't going to protect him. He was his brother, in all things.

"Yeah, I know, but still… thanks. It's different when you've got to kill someone. I think."

"Yeah, it is," Taylor agreed. "But not harder. It was easy."

Clay studied him for a long time before sighing and taking another long sip of beer. "I'm not moving out."

"I don't want you to." Taylor laughed at him. "But you practically live at Joel's anyway. You've just still got a room at our place when you want to crash there."

"Okay," Clay agreed. "No having sex in my bed."

"Ew! Tell me you have not had sex in my bed!"

"When? You're always in it," Clay countered.

"Well, I have no intention of having sex in your bed, that's creepy as!"

"What if Sietta wants to?" Clay waggled his brows.

"Sietta has no secret desires to sleep with you," Sietta assured him, stepping up behind them and draping himself over Taylor's back as best he could when he couldn't kneel on his cast.

"Are you sure?" Clay pulled a decidedly unsexy face.

"Positive." Sietta laughed at him and relaxed, letting his full weight fall on Taylor. "I have everything I want."

Joel appeared with fresh beer, handing them out before taking a seat beside Clay, dropping his bare feet into the water with a pleased sigh.

"This is nice." Joel smiled. "Quiet."

They glared. Right on cue, there was a loud explosion, a startled scream, crying. Brayden bellowed at Jay, and Ash ran past with a hose. Smoke billowed out of the house. Chloe remained in her sun chair while Leila and Micah dived in the pool to escape. Daniel and Ben were shouting in the kitchen, hidden from view by the dark smoke cloud that had engulfed the room.

"Microwave?" Clay mused.

"Oven," Taylor corrected.

"Deodorant can, I think." Joel sighed.

Kelly came out of the house, dragging Jay by the back of his shirt and yelling at the top of her lungs.

"You could have killed us! What possessed you to put it in the oven? It says explosive right there on the canister!"

"Exactly," Taylor mumbled, sipping his beer, enjoying the show. Ash was drowning the kitchen through the window and someone must have fetched an extinguisher from his car because white snow suddenly squirted out of the house, covering Ashley in a filmy coating.

"You're grounded, you hear? No dessert for a month! And no TV! You've obviously seen too many movies! I'm going to send you to Uncle Joel for tutoring so you understand what chemicals are!"

"Oh, hey now, what did I do?" Joel protested while Clay snickered and Kelly glared at him. "And why is my tutoring a punishment? My classes are fun, Kelly!"

"On what planet does any kid enjoy chemistry when they could be writing, Joel?" Chloe called out from her sun chair, from which she still hadn't moved.

"They're called boys, Chloe!"

"Well, that boy just tried to blow up my house, so now you can teach him better."

"Give up, man, there's no arguing." Clay shook his head forlornly. "We just became Jay's babysitters for the foreseeable future."

"Have Micah tutor him," Sietta suggested. "He's a complete science nerd. It's half the reason he likes living with you so much."

The fire was out, and Ben and Daniel emerged, looking worse than Ash, covered in black grime and white powder, clothes and hair singed and smoking.

Brayden appeared with Emma, who did a full circle, taking in the whole yard before planting her hands on her hips. "Uncle Ash, you are not a very good fireman."

Taylor choked on his beer. Clay laughed so hard tears sprung to his eyes. Ash looked stunned as he stared her down. But he had the sense to turn to Brayden instead, fixing him with a glare.

"Stop letting your kid be a psychopath!"

"Letting him?" Brayden gaped, waving an arm around at the smoking mess.

"Oh please, you were worse. Remember when you were little and you built a rocket and decided you were going to launch Hayley into space? You shot her a good ten metres into the air, and then she landed on the roof and broke her arm," Chloe chided.

"You did what now?" Hayley stood, aghast. "You told me I broke it because I climbed up there!" she accused her mother.

"You were too stupid to remember what really happened," Chloe countered.

Brayden sat beside Taylor, staring at the disaster and sighed heavily, cracking open a cold one.

Ashley entered the pool yard, but bombed into the water to rinse off. A dark cloud erupted where he landed before he stood up and shook the dirty water out of his hair, then reached out to pinch Sietta's beer, drinking the whole thing in a few long swallows.

They stared at the smoking house.

Sietta started laughing. "I fucking love Saturday barbeques!"

LINDSEY BLACK lives in Darwin, Australia, where the weather report permanently reads 'humidity at 100%, only going to get worse' for ten months of the year and 'monsoon at 4:00 p.m. for exactly fifteen minutes' for the remaining two. Between teaching and studying full-time, she escapes this oppressive environment to bushwalk for weeks on end wherever the mobile phone reception has zero bars for as long as possible and the weather report reads something along the lines of 'blizzard likely.' She enjoys martial arts, music, and mayhem, which explains the untidy state of her home where she attempts to write while splitting her minimal amounts of spare time between her incredulous husband, lazy Chinchilla cat, and crazed Siberian husky. If you expect her to sit and have a chat, it's best to have a matcha green tea latte with almond milk on hand and your hiking boots within reach. Oh, and be sure to bring a guitar for impromptu jam sessions.

You can find Lindsey on Facebook: www.facebook.com/LindseyBlackAuthor

BLACK BEAR GUEST RANCH

Do You Trust Me?

B.G. Thomas

A CARLISLES novel

SHIFTING
VIEWS

MEG HARDING

FOR
MORE
OF THE
BEST
GAY
ROMANCE